Chanita

CASH MONEY CONTENT

MURDERVILLE

FIRST OF A TRILOGY

FROM THE MINDS OF

ASHLEY & JAQUAVIS

ACKNOWLEDGMENTS

JAQUAVIS COLEMAN

First, I would like to thank the most high for blessing me with the gift to paint pictures with words. It's something I don't take for granted and realize the opportunity that you placed in front of me. To do what I love every day and earn an honest living from it is a blessing.

Second, I want to thank my beautiful wife and best friend for holding me down and being my foundation. Thank you for giving me unconditional love, which is only found rarely. You also gave me the best gift a woman could ever give and that was my child. I love you, Ashley.

To my boy: I love you with all of my heart, son. I will always be there for you, and you make me go hard every day. I see myself in you, and you make me a better man.

To Baby and Slim of Cash Money: Thanks for standing behind our product and giving us a platform to display our passion to the world. Great minds think alike, and I'm glad to be part of the Cash Money family. From the first conversation, we knew that we were a part of something major. Thanks to all of the Cash Money Content staff for making this machine run. To many more years!

Carl Weber: for giving much more than my first publishing deal. You showed me how to become a better businessman one conversation at a time. You broke down business dealings in such a way a kid from the streets could understand, and now I have a burning desire to expand my horizons. Natalie Weber and Denard "G": love you guys like family. It's an honor to know and be affiliated with you. Shout out to my girl Davida Baldwin: you are amazing.

Marc Gerald: What can I say? Within the first sixty days of meeting, you made things happen in a manner that I couldn't forsee. You are truly amazing, and after the dust settles I know I can call you a friend much rather than an agent. You are the best in the business and that's documented. Let's triple up this year. A special thanks to Molly Derse and Sasha Raskin. You two ladies are amazing and I wouldn't rather work with any other agency.

To Silk White: We connect on many levels and you my man outside of this book shit. Keep doing what you are doing and the sky is the limit.

Love you, Aunt Kamela and Shay.

Thank you to my best friends and brothers Jon Love, Pooh Bear, Shelton, and Lil Recco for keeping me grounded. To my cousins Shawna, Loretta, Ebonie (love all of you). Naldo Bonner and Julius Rutherford… Y'all my brothers until they put dirt on me. Special thanks to Black and Nobel for being real and authentic. I consider you guys family. What up Hakim! I appreciate the love. Shout out to Johnnie Coleman Jr (Pop). R.I.P M.T and Lovie Price (Mama).

And to my Jersey Plug. . . . I would never mention ya' name.

JaQuavis Coleman

ASHLEY ANTOINETTE COLEMAN

Of course I want to thank GOD for my many blessings. HE has showered me with so much happiness in my life and has allotted me with HIS favor. I am always appreciative and acknowledging of HIM because without his love I would not be the woman that I am today. I have shouldered many burdens and encountered many roadblocks in my life, but I know that HE walks beside me and helps me to remain strong and focused. For that I am eternally grateful. I will continue to use this gift of writing to share with the world.

To my husband: I love you. Since meeting you I have been on a natural high and nine years later we are still going strong. My heart belongs to you, and I am so honored to be able to spend forever with you. I appreciate you for loving me and for taking care of me. You are the pillar of strength when I am weak and my inspiration when I lose sight of our destiny. Our fate is intertwined and our bond is unbreakable. Our connection is so strong and pure that I am sure our love was written in GOD's original plan. HE made me to fit you. You are my best friend. I believe that you will take over the world one day, and when you do, I will be right there as your number one supporter, holding you down, standing beside you like I always have. We have a love made for the history books.

To my heart, my joy, my reason for everything that I do . . . my son, Quaye Jovan Coleman: I love you. I love you. I love you. I don't know any other way to say it. You are the seed of true lovers and the most perfect baby for whom anyone could ask. I am looking forward to seeing you grow and learn. Your mommy would do anything for you and I cherish you. Since the day I found out I was pregnant, you have brought me so much joy. Your love is untainted...the purest thing I have ever felt. You teach me to be better every single moment of your life. You inspire me, and you are the fuel that sparks my ambition. On the worst of days you brighten my world. I will forever be indebted to you for the serenity you give me. You are the legacy of two great people and you were made from true love. I know that the mark you leave on this world will be remarkable. Greatness is in your bloodline so always live up to your potential. If you never believe anything else in your life, believe this. I love you from the depths of my heart.

To Carl Weber: there are not enough words to express the amount of respect and gratitude that I have for you. We are family and you have truly helped me build a reputable brand in this business. After so many acknowledgements, I'm running out of things to tell you, lol. Thanks for all of your wisdom and for believing in my talent. You are a great mentor, dear friend, and GODfather to my son. We have so many feats to conquer ahead of us in this business.

To Baby, Slim, and Vernon of Cash Money Content: Thank you for the wonderful opportunity. I appreciate you for recognizing my talent and for elevating A&J to the next level of street fiction.

To our super agent, Mr. Marc Gerald: You are the best at what you do, and I think this new relationship is a perfect fit. Can't wait to see what the future has in store. Thanks for everything that you do and for having our best interests at heart.

To Molly, Sasha, Natalie, Brenda, and Denard: Thanks for all of your hard work. I appreciate each of you.

To Davida Baldwin: your creations are unmatchable and so remarkable. You are so talented and I thank you for the wonderful cover designs. You're the best at what you do.

To all of the readers: I value you more than you will ever know. Thank you for riding with A&J. I hope to never disappoint you. I love what I do, and I put every piece of me into these stories. I appreciate your loyalty and support. Without the fans, we would be irrelevant. I hope you enjoy our new classic.

Ashley Antoinette Coleman

MURDERVILLE

ONE

"BLOW HIS MUTHA'FUCKIN BRAINS OUT, A'SHAI!" THE man ordered. His heavy accent laced every word as he stared at the young rebel that stood before him. The boy was inexperienced when it came to murder and was intimidated by the chaotic madness that he was amidst. The older rebel looked at his protégé while slyly grinning in sick satisfaction, as he anticipated the fatal gunshot. A'shai's hands shook as he held the rifle firmly and looked into the terrified eyes of the man who lay on the ground. A'shai was only twelve years old and was about to kill for the first time. The man who was about to become a victim was three times A'shai's age; tears filled his eyes as he begged A'shai for mercy.

"Do it!" the older rebel instructed A'shai as he smiled in amusement. A'shai's mind urged him to pull the trigger, but his index finger wouldn't budge. The look in the man's eyes was a reflection of his own emotions: in them A'shai saw fear. The sight of the grown man's submission did not make

A'shai feel powerful . . . instead he felt powerless because there was nothing he could do to save him. A'shai gripped the rifle even tighter and grit his teeth, trying to muster up enough courage to do it. His adrenaline pumped furiously and despite the guilt growing on his conscience he knew that he had to pull the trigger. His manhood depended on it. Once he made his first kill, he would be respected as a man and his childhood would be over. Just as A'shai found his nerve, his heart dropped in sympathy as he saw the dark stain spread through the fabric of the man's pants. He had shamefully pissed on himself. A'shai was just as afraid as the man he was ordered to kill and his shaky aim gave him away. A'shai urinated too as his eyes grew big as golf balls and his breathing became heavier.

"Shoot!" the man yelled at the top of his lungs. A'shai let out a roar while pulling the trigger and closing his eyes, sending a bullet right through the man's chest. A dark red circle appeared on the man's shirt and spread as he hit the ground and his blood seeped out into the dirt. The recoil from the blast sent A'shai flying onto his back, sweeping him clean off his feet. A'shai's hands shook violently as he took in what he had done. He looked over at the man that he had just shot and noticed that his chest was rapidly moving up and down, signaling that he was still alive.

"Look at you . . . pissed your damn pants," the older man said mockingly as he shook his head out of disappointment. He had hoped that A'shai was ready, but from his hesitation it was obvious that he was still a child. "You didn't even finish!" he added as he stepped over the wounded victim. He then reached into his waist and pulled out a revolver. He put two bullets in his head, rocking him to sleep forever. A'shai flinched at the sound of both shots. He knew that he was expected to be just as callous as his mentor but A'shai couldn't conform to the ways of bad men. He didn't have it in him to kill recklessly as the other rebels around him did. A'shai looked into the eyes of the ruthless killer. Ezekiel was the head of the Rebellion, a radical group of hoodlums who terrorized villages and took a violent and lethal stance against their government, but also against humanity. The tyranny that they caused wreaked havoc and spread hysteria throughout many areas of West Africa beginning in Sierra Leone. The mob of men went from town to town killing the men, raping the women, and recruiting the children to work the diamond mines. The young girls were usually kept for sex slaves or servants.

Aside from being the leader of the violent clan, Ezekiel was also A'shai's father and a strong disciplinarian. "Now get up boy!" Ezekiel yelled as he snatched his son by the arm and yanked him to his feet. "Look!" Ezekiel grabbed A'shai's chin and made him look at the dead man beneath them. Tears streamed down A'shai's face as he looked at the corpse. Ezekiel struck A'shai across the face, delivering a hard slap. A'shai's neck felt as if it would break as his head went flying to the right. Ezekiel knew nothing about how to be affectionate towards his child, and he thought he was showing tough love. He gripped A'shai's chin tightly . . . painfully once more.

"Look at him, son! No tears. Rebels do not cry!" Ezekiel yelled. "Say it! Rebels do not cry!"

"Rebels do not cry!" A'shai repeated as he wiped his tears away and stuck out his small chest. Ezekiel nodded in approval as he watched his son assume a soldier's stance. He rubbed A'shai's head and smiled.

"Come on!" his father ordered as they left the tent and entered the bloodbath that was taking place at the hands of his group. The village was being annihilated. A'shai gripped his gun in terror and watched helplessly as a surreal pandemonium unfolded.

Tat! Tat! Tat! Tat!

The sounds of automatic assault rifles exploded in A'shai's ear and angst overwhelmed him causing his heart to race frantically. The people of the village ran for their lives, causing dirt to fly up in the air from the mini stampede. A'shai couldn't believe his eyes. He was horrified as he witnessed Ezekiel shoot a round into a fleeing man's back. It was a complete massacre unfolding, and the blood of innocents stained the earth.

The roaring laughter of Ezekiel echoed through the air as the man dropped. Ezekiel acted as if he was hunting game instead of slaughtering humans. Seconds later a little girl came running out of a hut and went to the slain man's side. "Papa! Papa!" she cried as she flung herself over the man's body, becoming soaked in his blood. The ten-year-old girl had just witnessed her father be brutally murdered in cold blood. The girl kneeled next to her father as he lay there motionless. She began to shake him, hoping that he would get up but there was no use . . . he was silenced forever.

A'shai looked on in anguish as he saw the young girl cry

while hugging the dead body. He was frozen in terror and plagued by guilt. When he noticed the other rebels run to the girl and snatch her up, he snapped out of his trance. A'shai didn't think about what he was about to do, he just reacted. He immediately sprinted over to the men as they taunted the girl, groping her backside and private area as she cringed at every touch.

"No, leave her alone! Let me have her," A'shai yelled as he grabbed her butt and then pulled her into an empty hut nearby. As she kicked and screamed, A'shai's heart ached because he realized that she was terrified of him. He didn't know why he was drawn to the girl, but it was something about the way she looked. Her features resembled his dead mother's and had instantly piqued A'shai's interest. She was the most beautiful girl he had ever seen.

"Little A'shai is about to get his first piece of poo nanny," one of the rebels yelled as they watched A'shai force the girl into the hut. The rebels cheered as the two disappeared from sight, believing they had just witnessed what was to be A'shai's rite of passage. In their eyes, he had just been initiated into the Rebellion officially.

"Nooo! Help me!" the young girl screamed as she kicked and punched wildly. She fell onto her back as A'shai tried to grab her hands and calm her down.

He placed a firm hand over her mouth to stifle her panicked cries. "Shhh! Please stop hitting me. I am not going to hurt you. Just pretend like I'm hurting you ok?" A'shai said as tears began to form in his eyes. He did not want to harm her in any way, he only wanted to save her from the other violent rebels. He grabbed her tightly and put his hand over her mouth. "Listen. I am not going to hurt you. Trust me. Now, I'm going to take my hand off your mouth and I want you to scream like I'm hurting you, okay? I promise I will not touch you. You have to stay in here with me for a while and don't run out. The rebels out there will rape you," he said as he looked into her eyes, showing his sincerity. She nodded her head in agreement and A'shai slowly stood up and took two steps back, letting her know that he didn't have any bad intentions.

The girl screamed at the top of her lungs and A'shai could hear the rebels outside of the tent laughing while cheering him on. A'shai was ashamed to be a part of such a mob and as he looked at the girl, he wished he could save her . . . but inside he knew that he couldn't.

Fifteen minutes had passed and A'shai watched as the girl cried in the corner as she shivered violently. He didn't know what to say to comfort her so he said nothing at all as he awkwardly watched over her. Just then, Ezekiel entered the hut.

"A'shai! Time to go!" he said as he glanced at his son and then over to the young girl.

"She's beautiful," Ezekiel said as he looked at the frail, fair-skinned girl who sat balled up in the corner. A'shai remained quiet as he looked at his father's lustful eyes and wondered what would happen next.

"Come on! Take her with us!" his father ordered as he waved his gun in her direction. A'shai wanted to protest, but held his tongue knowing that disobedience would not be tolerated. A camouflaged jeep full of rebels was waiting outside of the tent and A'shai reluctantly did as his father said. He ran over to the girl and picked her up and then forced her into the back of the Jeep. That single event would change both of their lives forever.

A'shai awoke suddenly in alarm and instinctively reached for the pistol that lay concealed in his waistband. With sweat glistening on his brow, his heart raced, and his tense body was on full alert. It wasn't until he heard the steady beep of the heart monitor and saw the silhouette of Liberty's body that he realized where he was. He had experienced another nightmare . . . another reminder of the world he had left behind so long ago. Peace was foreign to him. In his twenty-five years he had never known serenity. His childhood had been filled with mass murders and brutality. Make money, not friends: it was the mentality that had been drilled into his head. He had learned how to shoot a pistol long before he had learned to shoot a jump shot. Growing up in Sierra Leone he had no childhood; all he knew was money and destruction. It was that same thought pattern that had allowed him to survive and make a name for himself in the States. He was the epitome of the American dream. If he was white, he would have been a businessman, but with skin as dark as mahogany he felt that his rightful place was on the throne as the king of the streets. As he rubbed his goatee he leaned forward in the uncomfortable wooden chair, resting his elbows on his knees as he looked at the love of his life. Liberty was beautiful—even with her chapped lips, sunken eyes, and unruly hair he had never seen a woman as exquisite as she. She was the perfect example of the female specimen. She was his lady, his everything . . . she was the better part of him. The world was too corrupt for an angel like Liberty. The world didn't deserve to feel Liberty's footsteps upon it. She was too pure, too good, too beautiful to be a part of such an ugly place. That is what A'shai told himself when he thought of her condition. That's the logic he used to justify her situation. GOD had better things intended for Liberty. HE could show her a greater love than A'shai . . . at least that's what he convinced himself of to stop his heart from breaking. He had seen many tragedies and survived much devastation, but no loss had ever felt as great as the one he was facing. Just thinking about it put a damper on his spirit. Liberty was one of the very few people who could ever make him feel. He prided himself on being as sturdy as a brick wall. He was unbreakable, like the Great Wall of China. He was impenetrable, like the mighty gates of Rome. Untouchable, like the infamous Nicky Barnes. Despite all of these things, Liberty had broken through his cold facade. She penetrated his guarded heart and touched him in a way that was so intimate only the two of them understood. Now she was sick . . . dying the doctors said, and there was nothing that he could do but sit back and watch as destiny slowly took over.

The dark hospital room was illuminated as the door opened and the light from the hallway spilled inside. A'shai sat upright as Dr. Simmons, a man that he had come to know well, entered the room.

"Hello A'shai," Dr. Simmons greeted.

"Dr. Simmons," A'shai replied in acknowledgment. "Did you get the test results back yet?"

Dr. Simmons nodded and held up the large white folder. "I did. I'd like to discuss them with the both of you," the doctor replied. The doctor's pessimistic tone gave away the dismal results, but A'shai remained hopeful. He looked at Liberty. She was sleeping too peacefully to awaken and he didn't want her to hear the news first. He wanted to be her filter . . . to receive any bad news to come and give it to her in his own way.

"Can we talk privately doctor? I would like to tell her the results myself . . . good or bad," A'shai stated.

Dr. Simmons nodded and led A'shai to the hallway. A'shai stared at Liberty through the room's window.

"Liberty has a heart condition called cardiomyopathy. The swelling in her abdomen, ankles, and feet are all signs of impending heart failure," Dr. Simmons stated.

A'shai's throat went desert dry and his stomach turned sour as he lowered his head and leaned against the windowsill outside of Liberty's room. "Don't say that to me, Doc. Tell me what I can do to make her better."

"I'm sorry, but there isn't much that you can do," Dr. Simmons replied. "She needs a new heart."

"Then let's get her a new heart. Money isn't an object. Whose palms gotta get greased to make this happen?" A'shai asked as he looked up, pinching the bridge of his nose to stop the tears from forming in his eyes.

"This isn't a problem that money can fix," Dr. Simmons said.

"Money can fix everything," A'shai replied assertively.

"Unfortunately it cannot fix this. These things are conducted under a specific set of guidelines, A'shai. There is a list that all heart patients are placed on. Liberty is next on the list for her blood type, but there isn't a heart available right now," Dr. Simmons explained.

A'shai's mind instantly went to the gutter as he thought of what he would have to do to give Liberty a new heart. He would kill the next man to save this one woman. He was desperate for a resolution, but he knew that in reality there was none. He didn't want to taint Liberty by committing murder on her behalf. She didn't believe in it, and he knew that she would never accept a heart obtained in such a way.

"So we'll wait for a heart," A'shai whispered.

"I'm afraid that Liberty doesn't have enough time to wait. She needs a heart now. Unless her organ notification pager goes off soon, you have no choice but to prepare for the inevitable," the doctor said sadly. He had lost many patients and although death was around him daily, Liberty was a special case. He was truly broken up about seeing her life come to an end.

"How long do we have?" A'shai asked.

"She doesn't have long to live. A few days, a week, a month at the most. Liberty is dying," Dr. Simmons said sadly.

"No, no, no," A'shai whispered as his fists hit the wall in frustration. He couldn't stop his emotions from spilling down his face. He couldn't breathe and he saw red as he looked through the hospital window. He saw Liberty stirring from her sleep and he put his head down so that she couldn't see his distress.

"Can I take her home?" A'shai asked. "I don't want her to die here. I want her to be home with me . . . in her own bed."

He wiped his face and pulled himself together as best he could.

"I think that's best," the doctor replied. "Make her happy. Think of the good times. You don't have much time to spend with her. Make it count. You will know when her final moments are nearing. The pain will start to fade."

A'shai nodded and then looked up to see Liberty watching him through the window. She smiled and a warm feeling instantly spread through him. Everything inside of him loved her. He could feel her spirit pulsing through him. Just the mere sight of her made the little good he possessed shine through. He smiled back and then turned to the doctor.

"Thanks, Doc, for all of your help," he said as he extended his hand. The men shook hands and then A'shai re-entered the room. He tried to mask his turmoil, but Liberty knew him too well. No one else would have picked up on the sadness within him, but Liberty could see it in his eyes. It was in the way he blinked: slowly, methodically, to stop the tears from falling.

"You look like he just told you your dog died," she joked, trying to make light of the situation.

He smirked and replied, "Very funny."

Liberty grew serious and reached out her hand. "How long?" she asked. She already knew that her life was on a countdown. She could feel in her bones that her time was coming to an end on this Earth. She was so weak and sometimes she had a hard time remembering things. All she could see was the shining light in front of her . . . she could no longer recall the darkness of her past. She was actually looking forward to death. The only thing about life that she would miss was the love of a man . . . her man . . . A'shai. In her eyes, he was the only positive. Life hadn't been all that good to her so she didn't fear death. Instead she embraced it, thinking unconventionally as she wondered what her afterlife entailed.

"Not long at all, but I'mma be with you every second, ma. I'm in this with you forever . . . believe that," he said.

He reached down and kissed her lips gently as she wrapped her arms around his neck. He scooped her up into his arms as she rested her head on his chest.

"I'm taking you home," he whispered.

A'shai carried Liberty into their luxury home. He had hustled hard for everything they had. The travertine stone floors, the Brazilian hardwood cabinets, the imported Parisian furnishing . . . it was all sheer opulence—the epitome of the American dream—but as he carried a dying Liberty in his arms he realized how foolish it all seemed. What was it all for? He had spent countless hours in the street, grinding, hustling night after night to give her material things. Wanting to provide for her and give her the world, he had saved every dollar, never spending anything without first sharing it with her. He had wasted time hustling and as he thought of what he could have done with all those hours, he was filled with regret. Time was something that he thought he would always have. Never had he ever thought it would slip away from them so quickly.

"Stop, Shai," Liberty whispered as she stared up at him. Their connection was so tangible that she knew what he was thinking. "Don't babe."

A lone tear betrayed him, rolling down his cheek as he nuzzled his face against hers. "I love you, Libby."

"I know you do," she replied. "Now I believe you owe me a warm bubble bath."

Through it all she was able to muster a smile, reminding A'shai why she was the most beautiful person he had ever known.

"I can do that," he said. He placed her down on the couch and propped a pillow beneath her head before going to draw her a bath. He would cater to her, he would love her, and he would do whatever she needed him to in order to make her transition easier.

As he placed her body into the steaming water she sighed in relief as it soothed her ailing bones. Everything seemed to hurt. Her entire body was weak and the water was like a vacation from her everyday torture. Candles filled the air with a French vanilla scent, and she inhaled deeply as she sat back and watched A'shai remove his clothes. His body was marred with wounds . . . some had been attained in war, some in the streets, some she had put there herself from her fingernails digging into his back as he filled her with intimate strokes. All of them told a story and as he joined her she reached for him, pulling him between her thighs as she kissed his scars.

"I'm too heavy, ma," he protested.

"Shhh. Let mama take care of her man," she whispered as she grabbed a sponge and washed his back. Even though the sponge was light as a feather it felt as if she was holding a fifty-pound brick. It took all of her strength to bathe him, but nevertheless she washed her man's back. Their love was one unmatched by any other. They were so many things to one another: lovers, friends, adversaries at times . . . but they loved each other so deeply, so unapologetically, that it was parental in a sense. Liberty may as well have been A'shai's mother and he her father, because they had made one another. Their love had been birthed . . . their union blessed . . . their lives' paths intertwined.

A'shai kissed her kneecaps as she washed his back. He cried so silently that even he forgot that he was weeping.

"I just want you to be happy, Shai. After this is over I want you to live. You've been dying right along with me for too long," Liberty said as he started to turn towards her, wetting his face to wash away his anguish before finally facing her.

"I can't believe this is it, ma. I've got all the money in the world, and it can't do shit for me. I'm just sitting back watching you leave me . . . watching you hurt," A'shai said in frustration. "You don't deserve this. GOD chose the wrong one."

"He chooses everyone babe," she whispered. "Everyone has to face death one day. That's what makes life worth living."

A'shai had not yet come to terms with the inevitable, but Liberty had a way of poetically putting things into perspective. They washed one another silently until the water ran cold, then A'shai carried her into their room.

He laid her in the bed and sat in the cozy, leather La-Z-Boy that was positioned beside it.

"Let's talk," Liberty said.

"You should rest, baby girl," A'shai asserted.

"I don't want to sleep. I want to keep my eyes open and hear your voice for as long as I possibly can. Tell me the story," she insisted.

"You know the story, Lib. You lived it with me, ma. Besides that story ain't always happy," A'shai replied.

"But it's ours, Shai. The good, the bad, the ugly . . . it doesn't matter because it's our story, and I want to hear it again. That story is the only legacy I'm leaving behind. Please, babe. You know you're going to end up giving me my way so you might as well just say yes and start talking," she shot back with a weak smile.

There weren't many requests of hers that A'shai wouldn't oblige. He had spared her of nothing, and he couldn't remember a time when he had told her no. Spoiled and well-kept whenever she was in A'shai's presence, Liberty was his rib. He never wanted to hurt her because it would be like hurting himself.

He sighed because he knew that the tale he was about to spin would bring about a lot of emotions . . . stirring old ghosts. He stood and went to retrieve a box of Kleenex, knowing that Liberty would need it for the tears to come. He was about to unlock an old closet that had been stuffed with memories, mostly bad, but the sporadic occasion of good times that hid inside were so joyful that they outweighed all of the horrendous times that came along with them. He went into his custom wine cellar and looked around at all the bottles of aged wine that were neatly arranged inside. He scoured the shelves until he found exactly what he was looking for and pulled the old bottle down. It wasn't the most expensive one of the bunch for sure, but at that moment it was exactly what he needed. When he returned he sat down, put the Kleenex on the nightstand, and gave her a knowing look.

"I'm not gon' cry," she defended with a laugh, trying to be tough.

"You always cry," he replied as he kissed her forehead and took a seat. He took a sip from the drink he had prepared for himself and then said, "You ready?"

She nodded, the muscles in her neck so weak that her head bobbled back and forth loosely. She was trying to muster as much strength as she could because she didn't want A'shai to worry, but everything was so hard. It took everything in her to get into a comfortable position on the stack of pillows behind her.

"Relax, Liberty. You don't have to do anything but listen," A'shai said as he helped her adjust.

He took a sip of his drink and began to tell her the last bedtime story that she would ever hear.

TWO

2001

LIBERTY'S DESPERATE EYES PEEKED OUT FROM THE back of the tarp-covered Jeep as she watched her old village burn to the ground. Her entire body shuddered as fear took over her. Gunshots rang out as the rebels whooped and hollered in victory, their testosterone-driven adrenaline justifying their immoral actions.

Liberty didn't understand why she was being taken. Her home had been ransacked. Most of the women and children had been raped, tortured, then eventually killed, including her mother and siblings. Her young eyes had been a witness to the mass murders of her father and the other men in the village. Tyranny had erupted without warning and now as she was whisked away to a destination unknown she cried uncontrollably. She felt as if she had been spared, but what she didn't know was that what the rebels intended for her would be worse than death itself. The men that surrounded her held automatic machine guns. Some of them could hardly be called men, their young faces revealed no more years than Liberty's. She could not understand how someone her age could be so threatening . . . their faces showed no remorse, no signs of childhood antics . . . only malicious, cold-hearted eyes that stared back at her.

Liberty cried a river as she tried to stifle herself, her chest heaving up and down violently as tears cascaded down her face. The five-hour drive back to Sierra Leone was excruciating for Liberty. Too afraid to close her eyes she cowered in the bottom of the vehicle, her nerves attentive as the men bragged of their conquests around her. Other captives huddled together but none dared to speak, silenced by fear. The blood of her loved ones dried on her ashy skin, torturing her as she watched it crust on her arms and legs. When the jeep finally stopped moving Liberty was forced out, dragged through the muddy village by her hair.

Terror gripped her stomach as she was forced into a thatched hut house. She fell to her knees, scraping them on the cement floor, and as the door slammed closed the entire hut went dark.

A'shai peeked through the hole in the side of the hut trying to peer inside at the beauty he had captured. Something inside of him was glad that he didn't have to kill her. Her light skin seemed to glow in the dark as his heart beat out of his chest. He didn't know why Ezekiel had saved the girl, but he knew one thing for sure: he wanted to know her. He had never seen a girl so pretty.

A hand clasped around the back of his neck causing A'shai to drop the weapon he was carrying.

"You've got to learn the art of the kill son," Ezekiel said as he removed the gun from A'shai's hand and guided his son away from his spying spot. "You like her?"

A'shai shook his head and replied, "I was just looking. What are you keeping her for?"

Ezekiel entered his home with A'shai following curiously behind him.

"We need someone to cook and clean around here," Ezekiel replied. "Need a woman here. Eventually she will make a fine wife."

A'shai was too young to see the lustful look in his father's eyes. Ezekiel needed a woman around all right, but Liberty was still a child. A ten-year-old little girl to be exact and Ezekiel's cruel intentions for her were purely pedophilic.

Ezekiel approached Liberty, causing her to back into the corner and cover her eyes. He stopped abruptly, realizing that she was afraid. Knowing that she wouldn't be easy to manipulate if she feared him, he gave her space. He walked over to A'shai and whispered in his ear. "Make her comfortable. Tell her she doesn't have to be afraid here."

Young A'shai's eyes sparkled at the chance to interact with the girl. He nodded his head and watched his father leave.

A'shai ran to the rickety wooden table and grabbed a piece of bread before approaching the girl.

"It's okay," A'shai said as he kneeled beside her. "You don't got to hide. I'm not going to hurt you. You hungry?"

He held out the bread for her, but she didn't take it. She wouldn't even look at him. She kept her eyes on the floor. A'shai placed his hand on her arm causing her to tense up.

"I'm not going to do anything bad to you," he said. "I'm Shai. What's your name?"

Again she was unresponsive.

"Okay. Well I'll leave this food for you just in case you get hungry," he said. He stood and left her alone, hoping that she would eventually warm up to him.

Ezekiel made it clear that she was to tend to the duties of his house and to avoid the brutal punishments she saw other women and kids endure, she obliged. A week had passed, and Liberty still had not spoken a word. Untrusting of everyone and too afraid to open up, she did what was expected and nothing more.

A'shai watched her from the side of the house as she washed clothes in the wooden basin out back. He couldn't figure her out and the more he tried to get her to interact, the more she withdrew. He felt badly about her family and knew that she was hurting, but his youthful ego took a blow each time that she snubbed him. A youngin' with a schoolboy crush, he was determined to make her pay attention to him. As she washed diligently under the blazing sun, A'shai snuck up behind her. The clothes that hung on the makeshift clothesline hid his approach.

"Arghhhh!" he screamed obnoxiously, startling Liberty. Her first reaction was to flee but as she stepped backwards she tripped over a metal bucket, causing her to fall into the large washing basin and soaking her to the bone.

Enraged she screamed at the top of her lungs as she lunged for A'shai and pulled him into the water.

He fell face first into the basin and came up spitting out sudsy water. The two wrestled and grunted as they fought one another, pushing and shoving and cursing. They tipped over the basin causing clean clothes along with themselves to spill out into the dirt.

"Look what you made me do!" Liberty shouted in frustration, knowing that if Ezekiel saw the dirtied laundry there would be serious repercussions. Soaking wet, she fell to her knees and picked up the clothes.

A'shai could see the terror fill her as she scrambled nervously. As much as he hated chores he knew that he owed her one. He wouldn't be reprimanded if Ezekiel found out but she would, and the last thing he wanted to do was get her into trouble. He bent down and helped her out.

"Just go away," she mumbled as she put the clothes into the basin and grabbed water buckets to go retrieve more water from the river.

"Sorry!" he screamed after her. "I was only playing. Hey, wait up!" A'shai said as he ran after Liberty. "Where are you going? Hey! I want to help."

"You've helped plenty!" she shot back as she stomped away.

A'shai knew that if she tried to bring the water to the well it would take all day. A'shai scooped up the dirty clothes and ran after her. He was a thinker and would rather let his brain do the hard work than his body.

"What are you doing?" she asked in annoyance.

"You can wash and dry the clothes by the river. Trust me. It'll be done before my dad even knows we're missing," A'shai stated. He ran past her. "Come on!"

Reluctantly Liberty ran after him until she was out of breath. By the time she caught up to him, A'shai had the clothes in a fishing net that he threw into the flowing water. She stopped and looked at him in amazement while thinking, *Why didn't I think of that?*

He sat on the shore and then patted the space beside him. "So what's your name anyway?" he asked.

She sat down a few spaces down from him and replied, "Liberty."

It was all they said to one another the entire day but the ice had finally been broken, and Liberty appreciated A'shai's offer to help. Hours later as the sun began to set, A'shai helped her remove the clothes from the tree branches they had dried on and then they raced one another back to the village. Ezekiel hadn't arrived home yet causing Liberty to breathe a sigh of relief. As Liberty prepared for bed, A'shai approached the makeshift cot that she slept on. Without warning he leaned forward and kissed her on the lips. The peck was so quick that Liberty wasn't even sure that it even happened and without saying anything, A'shai nervously retreated to his own room. His confident swagger hid the nervous butterflies that danced in his stomach. A small smile spread across Liberty's young face as she touched her lips gently. She had never kissed a boy before, and it made her blush in flattery. It was the first time that Liberty hadn't been afraid in her new surroundings. Although she did not let him know, A'shai made her feel comfortable. She didn't think about the rebels, the war, her family, the blood-stained hands of his father. In his presence, Liberty felt safe . . . as if the little boy could protect her from the big bad world.

THREE

LIBERTY AND A'SHAI BECAME INSEPARABLE. SHE DISTRACTED him from his duties as an up-and-coming rebel because he wanted to spend all of his days with her. They never spoke about the raid of her village, but just looking Liberty in the eyes made A'shai realize how wrong the rebel campaign truly was. If girls like Liberty were hurt in the process then A'shai wanted no part of it. He was smitten by her infectious laugh. Taken aback by her flawless skin. Enthralled by her remarkably kind heart. They were best friends, and as each day passed she opened up to him more and more.

Ezekiel was pleased with the way his son had cracked Liberty's hard exterior and as he watched the two playing behind his home he cleared his throat, announcing his presence.

Liberty stopped dead in her tracks as her eyes grew large. She was terrified of Ezekiel, and she avoided him whenever she could. She had seen him carry out the most lethal of threats and although they had not interacted much, he intimidated her.

"Shai, we need wood. Stop all this playing and go retrieve a few bundles," Ezekiel stated sternly.

A'shai nodded and tapped Liberty's arm. "Come on, let's go!" he shouted.

"Go alone. She has chores to do," Ezekiel said.

"But I'm going to need help carrying . . ."

Before A'shai could get the sentence out of his mouth Ezekiel shot him a cold stare that silenced him instantly.

"Go get the wood," Ezekiel demanded. He walked over to Liberty and placed a heavy hand on her shoulder and then led her back into the hut.

Liberty craned her neck as she watched A'shai kick a rock in frustration as he headed out to the woods. She wanted to call out to him or to even run after him, but the hold Ezekiel had on her fragile neck was so strong that she was afraid he might snap it if she disobeyed.

Ezekiel had waited long enough for Liberty to become accustomed to her new life. He hadn't needed her to cook or to clean or to wash or to sweep. She was one of the spoils of war, a sexual conquest. She was too beautiful to kill like the others of her village. He wanted her, and as he closed the door, he unbuckled his army fatigue pants as his manhood grew in sickening anticipation. Ezekiel approached Liberty. Shirtless, his hairy chest trapped the scent of his funk as he grabbed her wrists and pulled her down onto the floor forcefully.

His hands roamed her body, and she pushed them off

repeatedly. "No, stop," she cried as his fingers penetrated her, hurting the space between her legs. "Stop!" she screamed.

A'shai got halfway into the woods when he realized that he had forgotten to take an axe. Knowing that this was going to set him back and keep him away from Liberty even longer he took off as his youthful speed brought him back to the village in less than ten minutes. A'shai trudged to the back of the hut to retrieve his axe when Liberty's shrill screams cut through the air and pierced his young heart. A'shai ran into the house and when he saw his father struggling to subdue Liberty on the ground he snapped. He had seen his father do horrendous acts, but the sight before him made his stomach hollow in utter disappointment.

"Get off her!" A'shai barked as he lunged at his father's back, swinging with all the might that he could muster. His fists did not faze Ezekiel, they only incited his anger. Ezekiel stood, sweating and heaving like a crazed bull.

Liberty's eyes met A'shai's as she wiped the blood from her nose. Like a deer in headlights, A'shai froze as Ezekiel approached him menacingly. A'shai stood his ground as he looked his father in the eyes. Inside he was fearful because he knew that the conflict to come was an unmatched and unfair bout, but he still stood tall, firm, his fists balled as he prepared to defend Liberty.

Ezekiel didn't say one word as he loomed over A'shai. Without warning he issued a blow to A'shai's chest that sent him flying backwards into the door. His twelve-year-old chest caved in, making it hard for him to breathe and causing stinging tears of shock to accumulate in his eyes.

"Shai!" Liberty called out.

"You want to be a man?! You want to barge in here like you are a man?!" Ezekiel shouted as he looked down on his son. "She is a whore! A Liberian whore! That is what she is here for!"

Ezekiel was enraged that his son had the gumption to go against the grain, and he was determined to beat him into submission. If A'shai was willing to buck against him over Liberty, he would eventually buck against the rebels in an attempt to have his own mind. Ezekiel was determined to teach A'shai a lesson he wouldn't soon forget.

"Stand up!" Ezekiel demanded with fiery anger burning in his menacing eyes.

A'shai staggered to his feet while Liberty looked on fearfully. As soon as A'shai planted both feet on the ground, Ezekiel leveled him once again . . . hitting his son so hard that it felt as if A'shai's chest cavity had been broken. Tears threatened to spill, but A'shai refused to cry, especially in front of Liberty.

"Stand up!" Ezekiel yelled.

Panting on the floor, A'shai knew that he could not take much more of this. He glanced at Liberty who was crying and staring at him with worry in her eyes. He couldn't let his father hurt Liberty. It was in that moment that he knew he had to make a choice between his father, a man who he had admired all his life, or Liberty, a girl he barely knew.

"I'm sorry," A'shai whispered. Ezekiel smiled wickedly as he watched his son concede defeat. He turned to finish what he had started with Liberty but he didn't take two steps in her direction before he felt the sharp blade of the axe split his back wide open. A'shai wasn't apologizing for defending Liberty. He was apologizing for stabbing his own father in the back—literally. Ezekiel fell to his knees as he tried to reach behind him to remove the blade, but his arms were too short.

"Come on!" A'shai yelled as he grabbed Liberty's hand before running out of the hut. They could hear Ezekiel's screams as they darted through the village. A'shai knew that his father wasn't dead and if he caught them there would be hell to pay. The beating would be so severe that it would be worse than death. They both understood this and it was that fear that caused their legs to keep flying as their hearts pumped furiously. They didn't stop until they were on the outskirts of the village and Liberty could no longer keep up with A'shai's pace. Out of breath, she called out, "Shai wait!"

His momentum slowed as he looked back. He stopped completely when he saw her panting from exhaustion.

"Are you okay?" he asked. "Did he hurt you?"

She shook her head. "No, no . . . you came in before he could. Where are we going?" she asked. They had no food, no money, and no direction but the one thing that they did have was each other and for A'shai that was enough. He had no idea where they were headed but he wanted to seem like a man . . . like he knew exactly where to lead her. He wanted her to feel as if she could depend on him. So even though he had no plan and felt just as lost as Liberty, he grabbed her hand and asked, "Do you trust me?"

She hesitated before answering, but she knew that A'shai was all she had left and after what he had done for her today she couldn't say no. Nodding her head yes she replied, "I trust you."

They interlocked pinkies, sealing their faith in one another and took off in the opposite direction of what was once home.

They ran for hours, until the soles of their feet were so tender that they ached. As the leader of the rebels, Ezekiel was too powerful not to fear. His reach was long and if they stopped moving, undoubtedly they would be caught.

"Shai, I cannot run anymore. I'm tired and I'm hungry," Liberty said as she nursed the cramp that had been building in her stomach.

Breathing heavily, A'shai looked at her. He could see her distress. They had traveled two towns over but were not far enough to feel safe. Traveling by foot would only be delaying their inevitable capture. They needed a ride and as A'shai looked around he formulated a plan in his head. The busy capital of Freetown was bustling with traffic, allowing A'shai and Liberty to go unnoticed. Noticing a man leave his car unattended, A'shai grabbed Liberty's hand and ran to the back of the vehicle. Lifting the tarp he ushered her quickly inside before climbing in behind her.

"Where are we going?" she whispered.

"Wherever he takes us," A'shai replied as he wrapped one arm around her shoulder while holding onto the side of the Jeep. They heard the car start and the relief that filled them made them optimistic, feeling as though they were home free.

As soon as the car stopped moving A'shai and Liberty hopped from the back and took off. They didn't know where they were, but as long as they were far from Ezekiel they no longer cared. The smell of salt water filled the air as Liberty stared out at the single ship that was docked in the port. She was amazed at the sight. She had never seen so much water in her life. As she held onto A'shai's hand she wondered how so much water could be in one place when it was so scarce in her old village.

"I'm going to get you some food," A'shai said. "Stay here."

"No I want to come with you," Liberty said. A'shai was all she had left and despite how they had been brought together, she never wanted to be torn apart from him. He was the only friend she had and the only person who had ever made her heart's pace pick up. The puppy love she had for him was one of loyalty and protection. He made her feel safe, and she trusted him without limits. They noticed a metal crate that sat open on the port that contained imported vegetables. Knowing that he didn't have much time, A'shai ran over to the shipping crate to steal a snack. He lifted his foot and kicked through one of the wooden containers, causing tomatoes to spill out onto the crate floor.

"Hurry, Shai," Liberty whispered as she shuffled her feet nervously.

"Here, wrap these in the bottom of your dress," he instructed. He handed her five large tomatoes and then stuffed as many as he could into his own loose pockets. They were both running on empty and just the sight of the ripened fruit made their mouths water. Something as simple as a tomato was like a luxury dish for them. It was what the wealthy people in Sierra Leone had access to.

It looks so good, Liberty thought. She could hardly wait to bite into it.

She was jarred from her thoughts when a firm hand grasped her shoulder.

"What are you two doing in here? You little port thieves!" a man yelled as he turned Liberty around forcefully, causing the tomatoes to fall out of the folds of her thin fabric dress.

A'shai immediately sprang into action. "Let her go," he yelled, trying to force bass into his voice.

"You're not supposed to be here. You're . . ." before the man could finish his sentence A'shai had kicked the man square between his legs, causing him to double over in pain. Without needing instruction, A'shai and Liberty took off, running to the other side of the port.

"You see those kids?" A'shai asked as he looked in the near distance.

"Yeah!" Liberty shouted.

"Run to them . . . go . . . we can blend in with them," A'shai shouted. He turned his head to look back at the man who had given chase and as he turned back around he collided head first into a woman, the impact sending him to the ground. He looked up into the eyes of the most beautiful woman he had ever seen. Like a model on a TV screen, her blue eyes made her angelic and he was momentarily star struck by her magnificence.

Liberty stopped running and looked behind her. The man was coming up on them fast.

"Stop them . . . stop them!" he shouted as A'shai scrambled to his feet and grabbed Liberty's hand as he looked around desperately for a way out.

"It's okay," the white woman said as she put her hands up. "Everything will be fine."

The man came running up, breathing hard as he finally caught up to them. "These two . . . stealing . . . stealing fruit . . ." He was so exhausted from the chase that he could barely get the sentence out. He put both hands on his knees as he sucked in air.

"He's lying!" A'shai shouted back defensively.

"It's okay. They're with me. They just got lost," the white woman insisted as she looked the two kids up and down. She pulled out money from her pocketbook and handed it to the man. "This should square things, right?" she asked.

The man grumbled something underneath his breath, snatched the money, and then walked away.

Confused and skeptical, A'shai looked at the woman as he stood in front of Liberty.

"Is this your sister?" the woman asked.

"She's my wife," A'shai stated proudly as he stuck out his chest all the while still shielding Liberty.

"Ohh," the woman responded with a slight chuckle, slightly caught off guard by his mature response. "Well I'm Ms. Beth, and your names are?"

"I'm A'shai, and she's Liberty," he responded.

"It's very nice to meet you both. You have a very pretty wife, A'shai," Ms. Beth responded.

A'shai nodded his head, his lip curled from mistrust as he eyed the blonde-haired, blue-eyed, Ms. Beth.

"Where are your parents?" Ms. Beth asked.

"They're around here somewhere," A'shai acted as though he was searching for them. "They're probably looking for us right now. We better get going."

Ms. Beth stopped them and said, "If you need some food . . . you know while you wait for your parents . . . I can help."

A'shai shook his head and replied, "We're fine. I told you our parents are coming soon."

Liberty tugged at his arm while whispering, "Come on, Shai. I'm hungry. Let's just eat something. She said she can help us."

Knowing that Liberty was running on an empty stomach put A'shai's back against the wall. He knew that they had drawn too much attention to themselves and he wanted nothing more than to keep moving, but he could withstand the hunger . . . however, he would never expect Liberty to.

"Okay," A'shai said.

Following Ms. Beth towards the crowd of children that were assembled in a single file, A'shai looked up at the large steel cargo boat. Graffiti decorated the side of it. The word . . . MURDERVILLE . . . had been tagged in black and red. Had A'shai been able to read maybe he would have understood where his feelings of apprehension were coming from. The boat's ominous moniker gave off all the signs, ringing a silent warning to the children standing in line waiting to board it. It was the worst decision that the two would ever make, and it was the ill-fated day that changed their lives forever.

FOUR

A'SHAI HELD LIBERTY'S HAND TIGHTLY AS THEY followed Ms. Beth and the other children onto the boardwalk that led to the ship. A'shai looked back, hoping not to see any of his father's rebels.

"Shai, I'm scared," Liberty whispered as she took a glance around also checking for Ezekiel's rebels.

"Don't be. Look," A'shai said as he pointed to the big ship at the end of the dock. Liberty looked at the boat and her eyes lit up. She saw more kids playing on the boat's deck. Balls were flying and laughter echoed through the air and the ship looked like a big carnival.

"Wow," Liberty said in amazement as she looked up at the gigantic ship and all the fun that was aboard. A big word stretched across the front of the ship: it read MYRTLEVILLE. Wide smiles grew on both A'shai's and Liberty's faces. The other kids giggled in excitement as they followed Ms. Beth down the boardwalk. The ship, in the children's eyes, looked to be one hundred feet tall and everyone couldn't wait to board the ship of fun.

Ms. Beth smiled as she stepped back, threw her arm around Liberty, and whispered. "We have games, food, and entertainment on the MYRTLEVILLE ship. We travel all across the world and do charity work for kids. You guys are going to love it," she said. Ms. Beth's smile was like no other and there was something about her that they both trusted. Anything was better than the life that they were living. A'shai was trying to lead them to safety and show Liberty that he could take care of them both but was falling short. He tried to plan their next move but came up with nothing. He was running out of ideas to keep them safe. *At least we can get some food on the boat and then I'll figure out what we will do next,* he thought as they neared the ship. Once the kids got within one hundred yards of the ship they cheered and took off running full speed. Everyone wanted to be the first one to get on the ship of fun that Ms. Beth described to them. A'shai watched as Liberty smiled, and it made his young heart warm to finally see her happy. He had yet to see her smile genuinely and when she did, it did something special to his soul.

"Come on slow poke," Ms. Beth said as she giggled and took off towards the ship with Liberty's hand in hers. A'shai smiled and ran to catch up with them. Although their day had been full of grief, they were about to get a brief moment of solace . . . or so they thought.

As they approached the boat, there were young soldiers passing out candy as each person walked in. A'shai caught up with the rest of the crowd but as soon as he walked in, everything changed. It seemed as if their world was taken right from underneath them.

"Get to the bottom now!" one of the soldiers yelled as he pointed the automatic rifle at the children. What was thought to be a ship of fun turned out to be a human trafficking ship. A'shai held Liberty tight in his arms as she cried and shivered in terror. Laughter and anticipation quickly turned to cries for help and screams as the harsh reality reared its ugly head. They were about to be trafficked and there was no turning back at that point. The ship's doors closed, and no one could hear their screams.

The two of them were waiting in line with the other children who were being forced one-by-one into the lowest deck of the ship. It was pitch black and nothing could be seen as they were shoved forward. The smell of human feces and body odor reeked from the door opening, giving the air a horrendous smell. The children were forced down the wooden stairs by two soldiers who all had skin that was as black as tar. The worn-out army fatigue uniforms and combat boots they wore intimidated the kids, and their brute force was severe. In between barking orders, they spoke amongst each other in a language that neither A'shai nor Liberty had ever heard before. The newly captured kids looked to Ms. Beth who stood back while smoking a slim cigarette. Her once warm, inviting smile had turned into a sinister stare as she looked at what were merely cattle to her. The children were nothing but future cash deposits that she would traffic through the exploited country of Mexico. She kept her eyes on Liberty as she noticed her beauty, knowing that she would be worth the most because of her beauty and youthfulness.

The children who had just been captured ranged from ages eight to fifteen. All of them were victims of their own naivety and had allowed Ms. Beth to lure them into a sinister operation. Once they entered the boat they were ambushed and whipped by the soldiers and forced into submission. The children who played on the ship's deck were only there for show and to bait other kids to the ship. Sadly, they were already trained and brainwashed to follow the orders of the soldiers, so they never tried to escape during the travels.

"Grab her! Take her to the second floor," Ms. Beth ordered as she blew out tobacco smoke and pointed towards Liberty. Ms. Beth didn't want her to go to the bottom of the ship where the rest of the children were being held. Throughout their voyage, Ms. Beth and her traffickers usually experienced a couple of deaths due to starvation or hypothermia. Liberty was too valuable to put at risk in such a way. Ms. Beth couldn't allow Liberty to die before she cashed in.

"No! Don't touch her!" A'shai screamed as he saw the soldiers focus on Liberty. A'shai tried to shield Liberty's body, and he held her tightly as she began to scream but it was to no avail. The soldiers tore them apart and forcefully grabbed Liberty by the back of her neck. Another soldier pushed A'shai to the ground immediately and stood over him.

"Don't try it!" he said as he pointed his gun at A'shai. A'shai quickly stood, trying to get to Liberty as they pulled her away. Liberty kicked and screamed to get to A'shai, but the soldier just flung her like a ragdoll, controlling her movements. A'shai gathered all of his strength and hit the soldier in front of him with a right hook to his pelvic area causing him to crumble on contact. He then ran over to the soldier that had Liberty in his grasp.

"Let her go!" A'shai demanded just before he punched the soldier catching him in the mid-section. The blow did not faze the man, but it did infuriate him. He loosened his grip on Liberty and focused on A'shai.

"You little bastard," the soldier yelled as he went for his sharp pocketknife. He stormed towards A'shai and slashed him across the face. A'shai cried out in pain as the right side of his face split open like the red sea. Blood began to flow out of the wound and A'shai held his face as his own blood crept between his fingers.

"Take him downstairs!" Ms. Beth ordered as she walked towards Liberty and grabbed her hand. Liberty cried hysterically as she reached for A'shai. The soldiers pulled him down the stairs, and A'shai began to scream for Liberty.

"Liberty!" he yelled as he reached for her. However, the men overpowered him and forced A'shai into the bottom deck where the others were. The soldier pushed A'shai down to the bottom of the ship and what A'shai saw blew his mind. It was total chaos. Three-dozen boys and girls were cramped under the ship, and a foul stench filled the air as A'shai looked around. He tried to run back up the stairs to exit, but the guards had closed the doors and padlocked them shut. No matter how much he kicked at the wooden door, it wouldn't budge and his frustration took over as he thought of what may be happening to Liberty.

A'shai cried as his young mind tried to take in what was happening to him. The sounds of the others' cries and sniffles overwhelmed the room. Ms. Beth and her traffickers preyed on the weak and homeless in third world countries, assuming no one would look for them, which worked in her favor. A'shai would soon be trafficked through Mexico and that's where his fate would be decided. He called for Liberty as blood continued to drip from his face. Rather than feeling sorry for himself, he worried about her.

"Liberty!!!" he yelled at the top of his lungs as he dropped to his knees.

A'shai's stomach rumbled as he clenched it tightly. He sat balled in the corner as he sniffled, wiping his runny nose with his hand. It had been three days and he had yet to receive any food. The damp, dark deck was full of feces and vomit from the severe conditions. The first couple of days A'shai heard children crying and begging for mercy but the cries eventually turned into moans and grumbles. The swaying of the ship only added to the torture as they waited to reach their destination. A'shai regretted betraying his father and replayed the scenario in his head a thousand times, wishing he would have thought of a better way to save Liberty than the one he opted for. A'shai wondered what Liberty was going through just a deck above him. For some reason, he felt like Liberty's protector. Their souls connected and it was something that his young mind couldn't fully understand.

He just knew for sure that he was supposed to keep her safe. It killed him inside that he was no longer able to. Although A'shai rarely thought about his deceased mother, his mind began to think about her. He saw an image of her when he closed his eyes and her beautiful face was smiling, which gave A'shai a brief moment of happiness. A'shai felt that he would die soon, so his short life was flashing before him. Liberty and his mother had the same skin tone, same smile, and the same piercing eyes. A'shai's mother died five years earlier of malaria and ever since then it was only A'shai and his disciplinarian father.

Weak and parched from extreme thirst, A'shai mustered what strength he had left and got on his knees. He put both hands together. "Please God, help us. Help us get out of this bad place. Please watch over Liberty and keep her safe. Amen," A'shai whispered as he looked up at the white light. *Is this what heaven looks like?* A'shai asked himself as the light shined down on him. It was too bright to see anything but white, and he knew that he was approaching death.

"Everybody out!" a guard yelled as he stood in the door, blocking the light. That's when A'shai realized that he wasn't dying, but the soldier had opened the door letting in sunlight. The soldier had a gun in hand as he barked orders telling everyone to hurry up. It was as if he was a sheepherder and the children were his cattle. Everybody scrambled to get to the door as the soldier stood by handing out bread as each person exited. A'shai was the last one in line to exit, and the soldier focused on him. It was the same soldier that slashed his face. The soldier smiled as he saw A'shai walk slowly while gripping his stomach in agony. A'shai's face had bloodstains on it, and the wound had slightly scabbed over.

"Your big mouth isn't so big now, huh?" the soldier said as he dropped the last piece of bread on the floor. He wanted to humiliate A'shai and let him know who was boss. A'shai looked at the soldier and then at the piece of bread on the floor. He wanted to step over the bread and keep walking to hold onto his dignity, but the hunger pains wouldn't allow him to. A'shai slowly bent down and began to gobble up the bread, stuffing the whole slice into his mouth. The soldier put his hand on his slight gut and began to laugh at A'shai's animalistic actions. Although A'shai was not in a position to say anything, he vowed that he would get revenge if the opportunity ever presented itself.

"That's right! Eat off the floor, you filth, and come to the deck when you're finished. We are almost to our destination," the guard said as he left A'shai there kneeling on the floor.

The bright lights nearly blinded Liberty as she stood in line to exit the boat and go onto the dock. Ms. Beth had kept her along with ten other girls on the upper deck in a dark room for the entire trip, giving them food every six hours. Liberty had cried so much that she had red marks beneath her swollen eyes. The soldiers hurried them off the ship at gunpoint. They had already explained to them before they opened the door that if they tried to run they would be shot. All of the young children were petrified, so running was not an option. Liberty looked for A'shai but his group had already been escorted to the warehouse where the kids were housed.

Ms. Beth shook the hand of El Garza, an overweight Mexican man. Then she accepted the bag with about six million pesos inside of it, which was about half a million dollars in American currency. She smiled knowing that she had enough to return to the States and relax off the money she had just made. She looked at what she did as nothing more than a job. She left her feelings and morals at home while she stole unknowing victims from their native third world countries.

The children were herded into a factory where the immigrants were kept. Liberty looked frantically for A'shai as she entered the gigantic, open-spaced building that had cots set up everywhere. It was full of people of different ethnicities. The loud chatter from everyone was overwhelming as Liberty timidly looked around. The armed men closed the door, leaving them in the warehouse amongst the pandemonium. Young Mexican guards walked around with guns to keep everyone in order.

"Liberty!" a familiar voice yelled, catching her attention. She looked around and saw A'shai heading her way. She hurried to him, and they hugged once they got close.

"Shai, I'm scared," she said as she broke down crying.

"I will protect you. I promise," A'shai stated as he hugged her tightly. He guided Liberty over to a less crowded corner and they sat down while holding each other wondering what was to come next. Their lives had taken an unexpected turn for the worse in such a short time and the only thing they had was each other. They both knew that things would never be the same again.

* * *

A'shai and Liberty had been at the factory for more than two weeks where they both were quickly put to work. They found out that they would be expected to help cultivate the cocaine fields. A'shai stayed close to Liberty as much as he could. He tried to protect her, not only from the Mexican drug cartel that ran the fields, but also the other trafficked prisoners who were hostile about the scarce food. A'shai remembered the day so vividly when Liberty was ripped away from him and their lives took two totally different paths.

Young Mexican boys, members of the infamous Garza drug cartels, patrolled the fields with shotguns in hand as they made sure the field workers were working and not horse playing. A'shai was side by side with Liberty as they held their individual sacks and stuffed them with coca leaves. The Mexican drug cartel used these leaves to produce grade A cocaine that would eventually be smuggled into the U.S. for wholesale. The hot sun beamed down on the workers as they toiled for hours under the tyrannous, watchful eyes of the armed cartel members. The coca leaves grew wildly and were limitless, and the cartel took full advantage. A'shai and Liberty worked frantically so that they could fill up their sacks. The rule was: no full sack . . . no food, so the children and women had to work quickly because they only had about an hour before the sun went down.

"Shai, I feel like I'm about to pass out. I'm hungry, and I can't do this much longer," Liberty whispered as she bent down to snap off a leaf.

"Okay, listen. Just walk next to me, and I will fill your

bag up," A'shai said as he noticed that Liberty's bag wasn't nearly as full as his own. He began to work overtime as he stuffed Liberty's bag as well as his own. After half an hour of hard work, he had finally gotten Liberty's bag nearly full. He sweated profusely but it was all worth it for A'shai. He just wanted to help and protect Liberty.

As they made their way down the row of leaves, a young boy of Haitian descent eased up on them. Neither A'shai nor Liberty ever saw it coming. The boy snatched Liberty's bag out of her hand while dropping his own half empty bag.

"Hey man!" A'shai yelled as he looked up and saw what the boy had done.

"Give me my bag!" Liberty yelled as she tried to grab it back but the boy slapped her hand away. The young Mexican guard heard the fussing and quickly fired a shot into the sky to regain order. He spoke in Spanish telling them to get back to work. A'shai wanted to tell the guard that the Haitian stole Liberty's bag, but he knew that it wouldn't make a difference. He had gotten caught slipping, and he would have to pay for it.

"Get back to work!" the guard said as he pointed to A'shai.

A'shai clenched his teeth and gave Liberty his full bag, while taking the half-full bag that the boy left. The whistle sounded off while A'shai tried desperately to make up for the leaves that were stolen but his attempt was futile as they had to make their way back to the warehouse. He looked at Liberty and she had tears in her eyes; one of them would not eat that night. A'shai had already decided that he would give Liberty his bag and would miss the only meal of the day.

He would do anything to keep her safe, including sacrificing his own well-being.

A'shai lay on the floor of the warehouse with Liberty in his arms trying his best to keep her warm. All of a sudden the sound of steel doors being opened awakened them. The lights clicked on, and a bullhorn sounded off as a group of men and one woman barged into the building.

"Everybody! Get up!" a man said in broken English on a bullhorn. The woman led the pack as her eyes scanned the place and everyone wondered what was going on. She began to point out girls who would then be grabbed up immediately by the guys. Obviously they were rounding girls up for some reason, and A'shai began to get nervous as they approached Liberty and him.

"Her!" the woman yelled as she pointed to Liberty. A guard rushed towards her, snatching her out of A'shai's arms.

"Nooo!" Liberty yelled as she reached for A'shai, lunging for him as the men pulled her away.

A'shai stood up quickly and yelled, "Let her go!" One of the guys pushed him down and caused him to fall on his back. The woman then signaled for them to go. She had gotten the girls that she wanted and was ready to leave. What they didn't know was that the woman had just gone shopping . . . shopping for prostitutes that she would soon exploit in the States. A'shai yelled for Liberty as they walked out, and he would never forget the look in her eyes as she was ripped away from him. It was the beginning of a painful path for Liberty, and all A'shai could do was watch helplessly.

FIVE

LIBERTY'S SENSES WERE SO HEIGHTENED THAT SHE could hear her own breathing. She dared not speak. The blacked-out windows allowed no light to enter the van and time stood torturously still as Liberty was transported to a destination unknown. Thirst plagued her, hunger gripped her tiny stomach, and fear stifled her as she cried silently . . . eyes wide but seeing nothing, soul crying while simultaneously muting all sound that escaped from her dried lips. The ride was so long that she had no choice but to defecate, soiling the little clothing that she wore. No food . . . no water . . . no fresh air. The lack of necessities tormented her young mind, terrifying her. The fact that A'shai was no longer by her side made her stomach flip-flop from vulnerability. She wondered where he was and if he was okay, but mostly she wondered where she was headed all the while praying for someone to rescue her. For three days she sat in the back of that van, starving; her knees folded to her chest as she held onto them for dear life. She tuned out the sounds of the whimpering girls around her. She didn't need to adopt any of their fears to know she was in trouble. The emptiness that she felt inside was unbearable. Flashes of her old village being raided raced through her mind. Her body battled with the overwhelming heat in the van as a chill came over her. She wanted to pray for GOD's mercy but as she thought of her current circumstance she concluded that HE couldn't exist. *This would not be happening to me if GOD was real,* she thought. Aghast with uncertainty, she never closed her eyes. She couldn't sleep, not when her heart was racing like she had stampeding thoroughbreds in her chest. She could barely hold her eyes open as fatigue plagued her, but her fear was constant and kept her awake the entire trip. The car finally stopped moving, and Liberty crawled to her knees unsure of what fate lay ahead of her. Anxious to stretch their legs, the women and young girls groaned as the doors were opened and they were freed from the back of the van.

"Get out! Hurry up! Get out!" one of the men shouted as he held an automatic assault rifle while moving them out of the vehicle like a herd of cattle. The sun's rays were blinding, almost painfully. After days of nothing but darkness, the light was just as foreign as this new place she had been brought to. Liberty's neck was on a swivel as she looked around for Ms. Beth. Even though the white woman was the very person who lured her into her current predicament, Liberty still hoped that Ms. Beth would help her . . . rescue her . . . free her.

"Line them up!" a man shouted.

Liberty was pushed into an orderly line. Her soiled clothes were ripped from her body, leaving her naked. At only ten-years-old nothing about her was womanly . . . nothing sexy . . . but despite this she could sense the inappropriate stares of lust as the men assaulted each of them with their eyes. To her captors this was business, big business at that. They could assess the value of each of the captives just by looking at them, and Liberty's youth actually worked in their favor. Not yet old enough to be sold, but young enough to work the streets and brothels, they had time to mold her. Her description, light African girl, was foreign for the region she had come from and would get the traffickers top dollar when the time came. It might take years before they received a big profit off her sale, but in the meantime she would work and become well versed in the art of sexual persuasion.

Out of nowhere Liberty and the rest of the girls were blasted with high pressure hoses, and the water was so icy that it took her breath away as it chilled her to the bone. The force was so strong it almost knocked her off her feet. As if she was a dog being washed, they sprayed until all of the dirt and grime had been removed and then left her shaking uncontrollably with nothing to keep her warm. She covered her privates as best as she could with her small hands as the men began to split the girls up into groups. They were being ranked, categorized . . . a price invisibly tagged on their toes. When they got to her, Liberty dropped her head shamefully, but the male trafficker that looked down at her smiled in satisfaction.

"A mulatto," he whispered, knowing that Liberty had the

blood of a white man somewhere in her African heritage. "Start her on the street. If she does well, upgrade her to the brothels. Keep her well. As she grows older her value will increase. No track marks! No scars! No diseases!" the man shouted, ordering the packaging and handling instructions for Liberty.

She was shoved out of the line and into a circle with the other kids that were to be put into street prostitution.

Everyone worked. That was the rule. If you didn't work, you didn't eat and Liberty was quickly learning that. As the hunger pangs gripped her stomach, she watched the other children eat. Most of them had fallen into submission fairly easily, but Liberty protested each and every time she was put on the corner. They lived out of a warehouse that had been sectioned off and split into different rooms. The children serviced every type of client, and even the little boys were expected to earn their keep. Being turned out before they even hit puberty, little boys were put on the track to attract pedophiles. Some of the young boys were even dressed like women, wearing short skirts with tape concealing their genitals, accessorized with half tops . . . being turned into transvestites before they even knew what sexuality was. Liberty lived in a sex-filled world that terrified her . . . one that she refused to participate in willingly. She was too beautiful to strike so the traffickers starved her as punishment, and it had gotten to the point where she was dry heaving uncontrollably from the empty feeling in her stomach. Two weeks had passed and her body was so weak that she lay curled in a ball of pain. The only thing that she had consumed was the dirty water that she caught in a bucket as it leaked through the warehouse roof. The time passed gruesomely slow as she cried endlessly, wishing that death would come for her. The sound of locks clicking let her know that someone was entering her room. She lifted her eyes to the door and noticed a woman enter the room. The male workers that ran the street operation stood behind her, and she raised her hand in dismissal.

"Leave me alone with her," the woman stated.

She walked over to Liberty, her high heels clicking across the floor.

Liberty cowered and closed her eyes, expecting the worst.

"I'm not here to hurt you, little girl," the woman stated. "Get up."

Liberty's small arms trembled as she pushed against the floor to lift herself.

"When is the last time you've eaten?" the woman asked.

"I . . . I . . . can't remember," Liberty said honestly. Her sunken eyes and bony frame caused a tear to roll down the woman's face. Human trafficking was a system of manipulation. Liberty didn't know that the young woman before her used to be in her shoes. Stolen from her home in Dubai, the young woman had moved her way up the ranks. From street whore, to brothel worker, to Madame, she had slept her way out of the misery. Now she helped to manipulate the other little girls that entered the business. Grateful for the dim light, she quickly wiped the tear away as she pulled a cigarette from her clutch. She lit it and slowly sucked in the nicotine, staining the tip in M.A.C. Viva Glam plum as she held the cancer stick between two seductive fingers. She walked to the door and snapped her fingers, immediately summoning a worker in the warehouse.

"Bring me food for her . . . good food. Go out and get a burger and fries," she instructed.

"She doesn't work, she doesn't eat," the man replied sternly.

"If she doesn't eat, she can't work, you imbecile. Look at her. Do you think anyone is going to pay to be with her in that condition?" the woman seethed. She was only twenty-four years old, but she was a veteran in the sex game. She was old news as far as the clientele was concerned . . . past her prime. She had once been the hottest name in the underworld, but her fifteen minutes had passed the moment her breasts had begun to require an underwire. She had become old news while girls like Liberty were on the rise. The worker reluctantly followed her orders, and she focused her attention back to Liberty.

"What's your name?" she asked.

"Liberty," she replied timidly.

"I'm Abia," the woman answered.

"Where's A'shai?" Liberty whispered. "I just want Shai."

"A'shai? Is that your brother?" Abia asked curiously.

Liberty shook her head.

"He came here with you?" she asked.

"They split us up! He said he would always protect me," Liberty answered. "Where is he?"

Abia noticed the look of infatuation in Liberty's eyes.

She recognized the love. "You love this boy?" Abia said in shock, as she silently wondered what a little girl so young knew about love. "Is he your boyfriend?"

"He's my friend!" Liberty shouted.

"I'm sorry that they took him away from you," Abia replied as she took a drag on her cigarette. A knock at the steel door announced the arrival of Liberty's meal. Abia retrieved it and then gave it to Liberty. She tore open the food, desperately stuffing it into her mouth, barely tasting it before she swallowed it quickly before they decided to take it away. "You have to forget about your past life, Liberty. You're here now, and all you can do is make the best of it. The only way to make it better is to work your way up. You're young, but you have to earn your stripes, Liberty. Work hard and eventually you will be upgraded to a higher, more sophisticated level of this business," Abia explained.

Liberty sat silently, feeling helpless. "I just want to go home," she whispered, referring to her old village as she thought of the family she had lost.

"This is your home now," Abia hissed. "And you better get used to it. The sooner you start following the rules, the easier it will be. They will only tolerate your disobedience for so long before you aren't worth the trouble. You can do this and be a part of this or do nothing at all," Abia said as she sliced one finger across her neck as if it were a sharp knife. "Do you understand?"

Liberty nodded, quickly knowing exactly what Abia meant. They would kill her if she didn't comply and assimilate to the way that things were done. Liberty's eyes misted as she watched Abia walk out of the room. She was the most beautiful woman Liberty had ever met, but Liberty was disgusted by her ugly soul. She listened as the clicking of Abia's stiletto heels echoed down the hall until the sound disappeared. She tucked her knees to her chest and laid her head on top of them as she cried a river. To survive she was going to have to sell her soul to the devil. Young Liberty may have given up on GOD, but she knew that the devil was real because she was living in hell.

Six months had passed and A'shai was getting used to the routine. He and a crew of other young field workers hid behind the dumpster in the inner city of Tijuana. It was another hustle of the Mexican cartel. They had the youth target the tourists in the area. They were trained to point out and rob Americans with money. It was just another day in the life, and A'shai scoped the busy city street for potential victims. What at first seemed cruel had become a way of life for the young workers, and A'shai somewhat adapted to the working conditions in the cocaine fields and on the streets. For some of the workers, the cocaine fields provided a better living than in their native countries where poverty was an everyday lifestyle. The Mexican cartel ran the governmental structure in Tijuana, so there wasn't any means of help. Life was what it was . . . hell.

As the boys hid behind the oversized dumpster, they watched as the wealthy American tourists walked the small strip were the local shops were located. They were looking for a mark that seemed to have money so that they could snatch a bag or purse. The field workers would do this every weekend in hopes of hitting a jackpot. A'shai was the youngest of the boys, but he was the fastest so they usually made him do the actual snatching.

"You see those diamonds?" the eldest said after they saw a beautiful woman come out of one of the shops. She was dipped in diamonds and blinged as the sun hit her ring, bracelet, and necklace. She had a fair complexion and her slim body was immaculate. She looked like she could be a famous super-model, and with the kind of jewelry she had on, she just might have been.

"Shai, she is the one. I bet you she has tons of money de' purse," the Haitian boy said in a heavy accent.

"I got it. I got it," A'shai said as he stared at the potential victim.

A'shai nodded his head as he rubbed his hands together, waiting for the right time. He came from behind the dumpster and began to walk towards her. A'shai put his hands in his pockets, trying to look as natural as possible as he neared the unsuspecting woman. His heart began to beat fast as he approached the woman who held her purse in one hand and a shopping bag in the other. He felt the adrenaline kick in and that's when he went for it. He ran up to the lady and snatched both bags from her hands and took off towards the alley where his accomplices were waiting.

"Hey! Come back here!" the lady yelled just before pulling off her stilettos to give chase. A'shai was running full speed as the boys cheered him on, but he stepped in a pothole in the road and twisted his ankle, drastically slowing him. He grimaced in pain and hobbled to the alley, giving the woman time to gain on him. Once he reached the alley, the lady had caught up with him and grabbed him by the back of his collar. The other boys emerged from behind the dumpster.

"Well, hello there, pretty gal," one Haitian field worker said as he circled the lady.

"I just want my things back," she said as she released her grip on A'shai. The Haitian boy began to fondle the woman, grabbing her butt and laughing as the other boys began to circle her also. A'shai stepped back unsure of what was going on. He just wanted her belongings, nothing more nothing less.

"What you want to give me for de' purse?" the Haitian boy asked as he looked at her with lustful eyes. He was the leader so the other boys followed suit and began to touch the lady inappropriately. She cringed and closed her blouse that showed a small portion of her cleavage.

"You can have the purse. I just want to leave," the woman said, backing down as she tried to exit the alley. The Haitian boy jumped in her path, stopping her.

"Why you rushing off? Let's have some real fun," he said as he grabbed his crotch and laughed sinisterly.

"Yo, what the fuck is going on? Let her go," A'shai said as he realized their intentions. He didn't want to sexually assault the woman in any form or fashion.

"Stop being a pussy, Shai," another boy said as he stepped forward.

"Let's just take the purse and go, man," A'shai pleaded. The other boys had already planned what they were going to do to the American beauty, and they weren't letting A'shai get in the way. Two of the boys grabbed A'shai and held him back while the other two began to rip off the woman's clothes. "Let her go!!" A'shai screamed as he tried to shake loose from their grasp. They were much too strong for A'shai's small frame. They managed to rip the woman's shirt completely off exposing her breasts and they muffled both her and A'shai's mouths as they prepared to rape her. The woman looked at A'shai, and both of them had tears in their eyes as they knew what heinous act was about to happen. There was a brief moment of silence just before the big boom. The sound of a gun being blasted echoed through the alleyway and blood splattered against the brick wall along with the young Haitian boy's brain. A tall slender black man stood holding the gun with a cigar hanging from his mouth. He was dark, well-built, and sported a $3,000 suit. Everyone jumped at the sound of the blast. The man was Baron Montgomery, the victim's husband and one of the biggest drug lords in the Midwestern states. He quickly grabbed the other boy that was abusing his wife and flung him like a rag doll against the building. Pure rage was written all over Baron's face as he caught the hoodlums trying to violate his wife. The other kids scrambled to get away but Baron let off another round into the air. "If anybody moves, I'm blowing their fucking heads off! Everybody get against the fucking wall," he demanded as his eyes were bloodshot red as anger overcame him. He knelt down and helped up his wife.

"Are you okay, Willow?" he asked as he took off his jacket and covered her up. She shook her head yes as she wiped her tears away. "I want you to see something baby," he whispered as he ran his hand through her hair and then gave her a kiss on the forehead. "Line up against the wall," Baron ordered as he turned his attention to the remaining three boys, including A'shai. He walked over to them and took a puff off his cigar. He then dropped it to the ground and stepped on it. "Do you know who the fuck I am?" he asked one of the young boys as he stood in front of him. Before the boy could answer, Baron pointed the gun to his head and squeezed the trigger, rocking him to sleep forever. His blood and brains splattered against the wall as his body fell limp and he eventually collapsed face down. A'shai and the last boy were petrified as they began to plead but Baron didn't care. He put the gun to A'shai's head and told him. "If you believe in a GOD, you better pray to him right now. Say your peace," he said as he tightened his grip on the gun.

"Baron, wait! He tried to help me. It was the others who tried to rape me. Leave him be," his wife said.

"Are you sure?" he asked as he looked back at her.

"Yes, I'm positive. He was the one trying to stop them," she said as she looked into A'shai's young eyes. Baron then pointed his gun at the other boy and fired two into his chest with no remorse. He put the smoking gun on his waist and looked at A'shai whose knees were trembling.

"Thanks for what you did for my wife, lil man," Baron said as he smiled trying to ease the kid's fear. He reached into his pocket and pulled out five crispy bills and handed them to A'shai who waved his hand rejecting the offer.

"I'm good. I didn't like these mu'fuckas anyway," he said as he looked down at their bodies. "Can I go?" he asked as he looked up at Baron.

"Yeah, you can go," Baron confirmed as he grinned at the wit of the youngster that stood before him. A'shai turned around and headed down the alley so that he could return to the fields. Baron and his wife watched him walk away. However, something in Willow's heart told her to stop him.

"Hey!" she yelled out. A'shai stopped and turned around. "Let us buy you dinner," she said, feeling that she had to repay him for his bravery to go against his friends for her honor. The sound of somebody giving A'shai free food was too good of an offer to let pass, and he headed back their way.

Baron and Willow watched as the kid in front of them stuffed his face like it was his last meal. They encouraged him to order anything he wanted and four different entrees were in front of him. A'shai didn't once look up and think about how barbaric he looked in front of total strangers. The Mexican restaurant was the most elegant one on Tijuana's downtown resort. It was one of very few upscale spots in the dilapidated town. A'shai had never seen anything like it and the food was the best he had ever had. He had already stuffed four rolls into his pocket, knowing that they would come in handy later.

"Slow down," Willow said as she burst into laughter. She looked at Baron who was also laughing at the young boy and that's when A'shai finally looked up. He had sauce all around his mouth and on his fingertips as he ate the food like a madman.

"What?" A'shai asked as an odd moment of silence filled the air. Baron and Willow just looked at him, both with grins on their faces.

"Nothing. So tell me, where are your parents?" Baron asked as he folded his hands on top of the table. A'shai focused back on his food and began to eat.

"I don't have any parents," he said as he thought about his deceased mother and his estranged father back in Sierra Leone. "I don't need any parents. I can take care of myself," A'shai said as he avoided eye contact with Baron.

"I can tell that you're not from around here. Your accent is too strong," Baron said noticing the strong African roots in the boy.

"I'm from Sierra Leone!" A'shai said proudly as he stuck out his chest and looked at Baron with clenched teeth. Willow's heart immediately dropped at the sound of the place because it was her homeland; she, too, was from the impoverished country. Willow reached over and rubbed A'shai's facial scar.

"How did you get that?" she asked hoping not to hear the kind of horror story that comes with having bad scars.

"It's nothing. Just a little scratch," A'shai said as he blew it off. A'shai began to grow uncomfortable with all of the questions and then he noticed that the sun was going down. He knew that he had to return to the warehouse before dark or risk being beaten. "Thank you for giving me dinner, but I have to go now," he said urgently as he stood up. The thought of being late and being punished made A'shai's limbs shake and he began to grow nervous. Baron caught on.

"Are you okay, lil man?" he asked as he frowned at the sudden change of behavior.

"Yeah, I just have to go before they notice that I'm gone," he said. Willow began to tear up as she thought about her childhood. She, too, was a human slave as a teen, but was lucky enough to have met Baron in the same town that they were in, Tijuana. They always came back to Tijuana on their anniversary to celebrate the day that he met her and purchased her freedom from El Garza. It may have seemed like an odd tradition, but Willow actually found peace by revisiting the place that she had been rescued from. She never wanted to forget where she had come from. It was therapeutic for her in a way. Each year she left a little bit of her painful past in Tijuana instead of allowing it to weigh down her heart. Baron was one of the most successful businessmen and drug kingpins in the Midwest, and El Garza valued their working relationship. Working for a man who trafficked humans initially turned him off, especially after rescuing Willow from his clutches, but he used his position of power to his advantage. Willow urged him to get the money and to continue to profit off El Garza, but she always made sure to give back. She opened a safe center in Tijuana for the women and children who were able to escape the modern day slave system . . . all with money that El Garza helped her husband make. So instead of Tijuana being a bad place with bad memories . . . to her it was a place that needed her presence and one that reminded her to cherish her freedom. Willow knew that A'shai was in the same boat she had been in years ago. Baron also picked up on it.

"Listen, do you work for the Garza family? You can tell me," Baron said as he stood up and walked around the table to A'shai. A'shai nodded his head yes.

"He is an old friend of mine. We should go have a talk with him," Baron said as he placed his hand on A'shai's shoulder. Baron was actually in town to discuss business with the Garza family and negotiate better cocaine prices. He had a great business relationship with the family and was sure that he could work out something.

They left the restaurant and headed over to the Garza warehouse. A'shai told them the truth about how he got to Tijuana, and it nearly brought both Willow and Baron to tears. Baron and Willow decided at that point that A'shai would return to the States with them. They had no children of their own, and it seemed like fate brought them to A'shai. Willow, because of earlier sexual abuse, was unable to have kids, so she was open to taking in A'shai. The fact that A'shai was from her homeland made bringing him home with them even more special to her. A'shai connected Willow to her roots, and Baron understood that. When he looked in A'shai's eyes he saw the eye of the tiger. They both fell in love with the young boy in that brief meeting, and the rest was history. A'shai left on Baron's private jet back to Detroit, Michigan with them that night. He had been one of the lucky ones. He had found a way out, however, Liberty's fate wouldn't have the same storybook ending.

* * *

The clanging of chains being unlocked awoke Liberty from her restless sleep as two of the workers entered her room and closed the door behind them.

"Be the lookout. Once I'm done you can take your turn," one of the men said as a slight bulge appeared inside his pants. Liberty scurried to the corner of the room and cowered as the man removed his gun holster and lay it gently near the door. "I'm going to make a woman out of you," the man said as he grabbed Liberty roughly and flung her fragile body onto the steel frame that served as a bed.

"No!" she shouted, seeing the same ill intent in this man's eyes as she had seen in Ezekiel's. Her feet went flying in the air and her fingers clawed at his face as he climbed atop of her, manhandling her into submission. She had no strength, but she came out like a lioness cub to protect herself. The scent of the man as he weighed her down with his body made her stomach turn and as his hands roughly parted her thighs, he forced his tongue into her mouth. Liberty bit down as hard as she could, drawing blood.

"Agh!" the man screamed as he brought his hand to his mouth in disbelief. "You bitch!" he screamed hysterically. The blow that followed made Liberty's neck snap so violently to the side that she feared her neck had broken. Dazed, her head fell back onto the bed and her body went limp momentarily. The room became hazy as she felt the man ripping her clothes from her body. She fought him, removing his hands from her body, but he was too strong for her. Determined to snatch her virginity away he entered her roughly. He penetrated her with so much force that he broke her pelvic bone. The pain was too much for Liberty to bear, and her body went completely limp as she gave up. She realized that no matter what she did, she could not stop this and the more she fought the more he hurt her. So she lay still as endless tears rolled down her cheeks, allowing herself to go far away to a state of mind where no one could touch her . . . withdrawing within herself so deeply that she found peace despite the evil going on around her.

SIX

EIGHT YEARS LATER

"I NEVER COULD UNDERSTAND YOUR PEOPLE," THE white, middle-aged Canadian said as he unfolded his clasped hands. He then grabbed the cigar out of the ashtray and took a pull. "Blacks always want it all. So selfish with what could be easily shared," he said with an arrogant smirk on his face. Baron sat across from him while A'shai also joined them at the table. They were on Baron's estate to discuss business. They sat poolside as an oversized umbrella loomed over them, blocking the beaming rays of the sun. Bonzi, the Canadian, wanted Baron to give up some of his territory so that he could move in. The name of the game was cocaine and that's what Baron sold wholesale to the streets. Bonzi was Baron's source of the illegal substance, and now he wanted to move his nephew in town so that he could get a piece of the pie. Needless to say, Baron wasn't having it.

"I'm sorry that you feel that way, my friend," Baron said as he took a sip of his cognac and then rubbed his neatly lined salt-and-pepper goatee. A'shai stayed silent as usual, as he sat back and listened. Baron always had A'shai sit in on his business meetings, legal or illegal, so that he could soak up the game. Since the day Baron had taken A'shai in, he began grooming him to be a better version of himself. Although the same blood didn't run through their veins, A'shai was Baron's boy. A'shai, now at the age of twenty-one, was a well-seasoned businessman and although he was a month away from receiving his bachelor's degree from Michigan State University, he had already gotten a Ph.D from the streets.

"So, what's it going to be? My nephew is a knucklehead from back home. I'm just trying to get his feet wet. I want to set up on the lower Eastside, and that's just a small portion of your region," Bonzi stated.

"I'm sorry. I can't do it. The Eastside is one of my most lucrative areas. I can set him up in a small city just outside of Detroit. Maybe Flint perhaps?" Baron said trying to be as diplomatic as possible.

"You niggers just don't know your place," Bonzi mumbled under his breath as he shook his head in disbelief. Still smiling, Bonzi put out his cigar. He couldn't take a black man telling him what he couldn't do. His hidden racism reared its ugly head. A'shai quickly slid his hand down to his .45 caliber pistol after hearing the insults from the millionaire druglord that sat to the left of him. Baron smoothly put his hand on top of A'shai's and tapped it, signaling for him to cool down.

"I guess our business is done here," Baron said as he smiled and extended his hand.

"Yeah, I guess so," Bonzi agreed as he downed his cognac. It was unspoken but it was evident that their business relationship had just ended. A'shai was burning up inside as he clenched his teeth and stared at Bonzi, displaying his chiseled jaw line. Bonzi paid the youngster no mind and focused his attention on Baron. "Are you sure you want to do this?" Bonzi asked. The underlying threat didn't go unnoticed by Baron.

"I'm positive," Baron said as he extended his hand to Bonzi. A'shai began to rub the scar on the right side of his cheek. He had a bad habit of doing that when he was angry. A'shai couldn't understand why his father was bowing down to Bonzi.

"Let me pour you a shot of my finest cognac, before you leave. I insist," Baron said knowing that Bonzi was a fan of good aged cognac. Baron threw his hand in the air as he motioned to his butler who was standing by the guest house.

"Winston, please bring me the special bottle that I have in the china cabinet," Baron yelled. Just as quickly as he said it, the butler disappeared into the house to retrieve the drink. A'shai was still boiling as he rubbed the side of his face. Baron patted his thigh under the table, signaling him to calm down. Baron unleashed his perfect smile at his son and then focused back on Bonzi who couldn't believe that Baron had refused his offer. A man of Bonzi's stature rarely received 'no' for an answer.

"You're going to learn, Baron. You have to change with the times. You have run the black market in Detroit for far too long. It's time for change. It's time for a new era," Bonzi said, already thinking about how he and his goons would move in on Baron's territory.

"I agree. It is time for a change. That's why my son is going to take over for me," Baron said as he patted A'shai's back and smiled. A'shai was still looking at Bonzi. *Just give me the word, I'll put two holes in his head,* he thought as he sat there tight-lipped. He hated to be disrespected and by Bonzi disrespecting Baron, A'shai felt it also. He couldn't believe that Baron was backing down and letting Bonzi's threats slide. At that moment, the butler came with the bottle of cognac on a sterling silver platter.

"Thanks Winston," Baron said as he grabbed the cognac and poured Bonzi a glass.

"Well, gentlemen, I think that's my cue. I will see you again," Bonzi said as he stood up and downed the cognac. Bonzi's bodyguard stood about twenty feet away and moved on request as Bonzi motioned to him, indicating that it was time to leave.

"I'm sorry it had to go down like this," Baron said as he stood up and buttoned up his Armani blazer. "Excuse us. Winston will see you out." Baron extended his hand and headed towards the house. A'shai followed suit and slid his hands in his pants as he walked alongside Baron.

"Pops, why did you let him talk to you like that? I was ready to body that mu'fucka," A'shai said as he expressed his anger.

Baron threw his arm around his son and stopped walking. "Look son, you have a lot to learn. Please believe I wanted to put a hole in his head right then and there. However, would that be smart? His bodyguard was about ten feet behind us . . . strapped. Plus, we're at our home. Your mother is in the house. Let me drop you some knowledge, Shai: bad boys move in silence," Baron said as he gave his son his infamous smile. "Now take a look over there." Baron looked back towards the pool where Bonzi was on the ground going into convulsions. Bonzi's bodyguard dropped to his knees and tried to grasp what was going on. Foam began to spill out of Bonzi's mouth as he shook violently. A'shai couldn't believe his eyes. He watched as Winston smoothly walked over while pulling a gun with a silencer attached to the tip. Winston walked behind the kneeling bodyguard and swiftly dropped two bullets in the back of the bodyguard's head.

"What Bonzi just drank is a special brew called Black Tea, a creole tea that can kill you slowly if sipped. In Bonzi's case, he drank enough to kill an army. I wanted him to suffer for talking to me like that. Like I said, bad boys move in silence," Baron repeated as he patted A'shai's back and turned him around towards the house. "Now let's go grab some lunch," he said smoothly. At that moment, A'shai realized that Baron didn't concede to Bonzi. He just outsmarted him. Baron handled the situation like a true gangster and he had just taught A'shai a lesson in the streets. That's why he admired Baron; he handled his street affairs just like he would a legit business deal: professional and with class. As they approached the door Baron added, "Guess I'm going to call up my old friend, Samad. Looks like we need a new coke connect."

* * *

A'shai tossed his car keys on top of the counter and began to pull off his blazer. He inherited his sense of style from Baron. Although, he was a street nigga he dressed as if he was a Wall Street banker, wearing top of the line Italian threads. A .45 pistol rested in his holster on his belt buckle. He had grown to be a strategic, intelligent young man. Baron and Willow groomed him for success and home schooled him until he was in ninth grade. At first it was rough for him to adjust because he had no previous schooling, but with Willow's persistence and patience he had caught up to other kids his age just in time for high school. He walked into his plush living room and stopped at the picture that sat on his end table. It was a photo of Baron, Willow, and him just shortly after they took him in. He smiled as he remembered that time so vividly. He knew that if it had not been for them, he would have been dead or in a dormant situation. He then noticed the scar on his face and then he began to think back on how he got the blemish.

"I hope you okay out there, Liberty," A'shai whispered to himself as he thought about his childhood friend. Frequently he would think about her and the more he did, the guiltier he felt. He had come from the same place as her, but he got lucky and met Baron and Willow. The fact that he didn't know where she was or how she was doing ate him up inside. Just as he finished his thought, he heard a noise coming from the back room. He quickly reached for his pistol and clicked off the safety. The first thought that crossed his mind was Bonzi.

Is one of his goons in the back?

Paranoia filled A'shai as he slowly crept to the back of the apartment. His killer instinct kicked in and he listened closely and noticed that the sound was coming from the master bedroom. As A'shai approached the door he gripped the gun tightly. He crept to the door and kicked it open with his gun pointed and ready to pop. What he saw blew his mind. Jenny, his current girlfriend, was in red-lace lingerie sprawled out on his bed waiting for him.

"Hey, Papi," the Latino beauty said as she posed as if she was in a photo shoot. A'shai slowly lowered his gun and smiled as he looked at her oiled up body.

"What up, ma?" he said, breathing a sigh of relief as he put his gun in his holster. "How did you get in?" he asked as he walked over to the bed.

"I have my ways," she responded in her heavy-accented tone. She was a full-blooded Latino with big brown eyes that always made A'shai melt. He wanted to inquire further about how she got in, but she began unbuttoning his pants and he figured he would ask later. She unbuckled his belt and then his slacks. His pants dropped to the floor and the bulge in his boxer briefs was on full display. She quickly pulled down the front part of his boxers, unleashing his slightly erect monster. His chocolate rod was very thick and began to rise at Jenny's touch. She quickly took him into her mouth and moaned while she tasted him. He threw his head back in pleasure as he rested his hand on the back of her head, guiding her.

"Damn baby," he crooned as he looked down, watching his rod appear and disappear over and over again. He reached down and released her breasts from her corset to rub her erect nipples. Her D-cup breasts sat up perky and firm, only adding to her already stunning beauty. Jenny worked her tongue like a pro as she made her tongue do circles around A'shai's rock-hard pipe. She grabbed his balls and massaged them as she worked her head game.

"I want to feel you, Papi," she whined as her hand made its way down to her neatly shaved love box, which was soaking wet. She pulled her panties to the side and began to slowly rub her clitoris in a circular motion. "Ooh, I can't wait any longer," she said as she sat back on her elbows and spread her legs. Her pinkness was exposed, and her slightly oversized clitoris was on full display. Her fat yoni lips were glazed with love juice, and A'shai slowly stroked himself as he looked on in pleasure. Jenny began to slowly scoot back, giving him room to get on the bed. The king-sized bed was about to become A'shai's den and he was the lion. The lioness, Jenny, was about to get what she had been waiting for all day. A'shai took off his clothes slowly while never breaking eye contact with her, understanding that he had to make love with her mind before he did so with her body. His piercing eyes and raven black skin were nothing short of beautiful to Jenny. She slowly raised her index finger and signaled for A'shai to come to her. A'shai smiled and climbed onto the bed. He slowly approached his prey, and the sweet smell of her love box invaded his nostrils as he neared his destination. He slowly spread Jenny's legs and raised them up in the air. That's when he attacked her love box with his tongue, slowly tongue-kissing her throbbing clitoris.

Instantly she came, releasing a small squirt out of her love box. The juices dripped down his chin as he continued to orally please her.

"Ooh. Don't stop, Shai," she said as her body quivered and her toes cracked in total pleasure. He eased his two index fingers inside of Jenny and began to pop her while he continued to orally please her clitoris. Jenny was going crazy as she grabbed his head and pushed his face into her love box. A'shai was a great lover and on top of that he was a powerful guy in the streets. That combination had her ready to nut again. Jenny felt another orgasm coming and her body tensed up, but just before she got off, A'shai stopped.

"Nooo, Papi," she screamed as she opened her eyes from what seemed to be a dream. A'shai stood up on his knees and grabbed his erection. She slowly rubbed his tip on her clitoris. Up and down, side to side, and round and round. He finally entered her love box, making her back arch in pure bliss. He gave her long and hard strokes as he pushed her legs over her head. A'shai worked his hips like a Latin dancer and let his balls swing, smacking her on the other entrance. Jenny placed her hands on A'shai's behind, urging him to go deeper inside of her. She screamed in pleasure as he went deep inside of her, filling all of her space. A'shai stroked her with authority but also with care. A'shai continued to make love to her until they were satisfied, leaving them both breathless.

SEVEN

"THAT'S $100," LIBERTY STATED AS SHE PULLED down the passenger seat visor and checked her make-up in the lighted mirror.

"For a blow-job!" the white man exclaimed as he adjusted his slacks. "I'm not giving you that. You must be out of your mind!" He rudely threw $20 at her and reached over her to open the passenger door. "Fuck out of my car!"

Liberty's eyebrow rose. She was enraged by the man's audacity. She had clearly laid out her prices before anything had gone down. The man had known what he was getting himself into. He was trying to play her. She tried to take the nice approach as she rubbed his penis gently, causing it to become slightly hard again. "Didn't you have a good time?" she asked seductively as she whispered in his ear, sticking her tongue inside slightly. The man grabbed her wrist tightly and threw her hand back at her.

"Not a $100 worth. Get the fuck out of my car," he

insisted. Liberty shook her head at the cheapskate beside her. Mu'fuckas always want to cheat you after they get theirs, she thought angrily as she went into her purse. She removed a small caliber pistol from her bag and pointed it directly at the john's crotch. "Gladly, as soon as you go in your pocket and pay me what I'm owed," she responded with a straight face.

Caught off guard the man's eyes instantly bulged in shock. "O . . . okay, you got it. $100," he complied as he reached into his pocket with a trembling hand and pulled out a cash-filled money clip. He began to peel off more twenties until Liberty snatched the entire thing from his hand.

"You're lucky this is all that I'm taking," she said. "You get to leave with your life." She got out of the car and hurriedly walked up the street. She half expected the man to protest, but instead he started his car and sped up the block. Her heart pumped wildly as she placed the empty pistol back into her bag. The gun was just for show . . . they were given to all of the girls just to ensure that they were protected from their johns. Despite the fact that there was always a 'shepherd' lurking on the block to watch over the working girls, the guns gave them an extra sense of protection. The unloaded .22 had gotten Liberty out of many bad situations and that night was no different. Liberty's hair whipped wildly on the windy L.A. night as she walked at a fast pace up Sunset Boulevard. She rushed into a party store and knocked on the bulletproof glass.

"Yo, Liberty! What's good, baby girl?" the counter boy asked. "You looking good, girl. When you gone let me get some of that?" he jokingly inquired. Liberty had been on the track for eight long years and since the first time the young Mexican kid had seen her, he had tried his hand with her.

"You can't afford it, Juan," she replied with an innocent smirk. No other girl on the block could even enter the convenience store unless they were spending money, but Juan had taken a liking to Liberty. He knew what she did but he didn't judge her for it. He allowed her to clean up in the store's restroom whenever she needed. He passed her the key and gave her a wink as she passed.

As soon as Liberty was inside the safety of the bathroom she locked the door and removed the money she had just made. Her hands flipped through bills efficiently. *$322*, she thought. She removed the $100 that she would have to turn in, before lifting the lid off the back of the toilet. She pulled out the small stash that she had made by overcharging her johns and added the extra money to it before putting it back and replacing the porcelain top. If she ever got the chance to escape, she wanted to have the funds to get out of town and although her chances were slim . . . this small hustle kept her hopeful. After stashing her money, she pulled out some baby wipes and propped one leg up on the sink as she cleaned her vagina. She had become so used to the routine that she was no longer ashamed of what she was doing. It was all in the name of survival. After eight years of being forced to sell her body and soul, every dick felt the same. She didn't know how to equate sex with love. She had stopped believing in fairy tales long ago. Her childhood had been flushed down the toilet the moment that Ezekiel had raided her unsuspecting village. Liberty was damaged goods and as she stared into the mirror all she could see were flaws. It was unreal how she was blind to a beauty that everyone else could clearly see. It didn't exist to her; she couldn't see her own mystique through her tainted vantage point. The everyday haze that she lived in made life almost bearable, and as she pulled out the small heroin-filled ziplock bag her stomach began to turn in anticipation. She wasn't allowed to shoot it up, despite the fact that it gave her the best high. She felt like she was flying on the rare occasion that she could sneak a needle into her veins, but because it left tracks marks on her arms she was banned from indulging in that way. Instead, she sniffed it and she popped Ecstasy as often as she could get her hands on it. Liberty had a nasty heroin habit, one that the traffickers happily maintained. Keeping her high kept her submissive as she worked the streets. She could never run too far away. Liberty was no fool. She had seen some of the other girls try to escape only to be lured right back by the monkeys on their backs. This is why she saved up her own money, little by little, so that if the day ever came she would be able to support her insatiable cravings and purchase a one-way ticket out of town. As a euphoric feeling crawled through her system she cleared the extra dust from her nose and left the bathroom. She returned the key, buying a pack of cigarettes on her way out before returning to the strip.

"Hey, Lib, wait up!"

Liberty turned toward the familiar voice. She watched her friend Trixie exit a vehicle and approach her. Liberty could tell by the strut in Trixie's step that she was in high demand that night. Despite the fact that they all were forced into prostitution, the women on the strip were still competitive with one another. Whoever made the most money had the most clout in the streets, and Trixie was winning that race by a mile. Her shoulder-length hair was naturally curly and framed her pretty face well. She was easy on the eyes. High cheekbones, naturally bronzed Brazilian skin, and chinky eyes made her seem so exotic. Her long, lean legs were like a web of seduction that men didn't mind being stuck in. Trixie had a figure that any woman would kill for, and she worked hard to maintain it. She knew that there were a million bitches that would love to snatch her spot, so she worked constantly . . . often going the extra mile for her clientele. It was no secret that once Trixie got a hold on a man, he was hers forever. She had turned out too many to count. The sex with her was just that good. While the working girls like Liberty had limitations to what they would do, Trixie had none . . . she performed it all . . . she sucked, fucked, welcomed anal, fulfilled fantasies and obliged fetishes all for the sake of making a dollar. She was the biggest diva that Liberty had ever met, and one of the only people that Liberty had grown close to over the years.

"Hey girl, you pulling it in for the night?" Liberty asked. "You meet your quota?"

Trixie went into her thigh-high boot and pulled out a nice-sized knot of dead presidents. "Don't a bitch always meet her quota?" she stated. She put the money back and removed a pack of cigarettes from the same boot.

"Damn, Trix, how much shit you got stuffed in that damn thing?" Liberty asked with a slight chuckle.

Trixie passed Liberty a square and then pulled one out of the pack before putting it back. "Bitch, as much shit as I need while I'm out here dealing with these niggas. I got rubbers, lube, and a blade in there too just in case a mu'fucka wanna get cute," Trixie said seriously. Liberty and Trixie weren't rookies on the block, and they acted accordingly, protecting themselves at all costs.

"I can't wait to come up out of this shit," Trixie complained as she wiggled uncomfortably while adjusting the thong out of the crack of her behind. "Where is this motherfucker?"

"Just take the shit off now, girl. You know they will leave us here all night to make sure the rest of these hoes earn their keep. It ain't easy to make a minimum of $500 when you only charging $25 to wrap your lips around some dick. Fuck that . . . my head too good. If a nigga pump his brakes to fuck with me he better be ready to come up off some dough," Liberty replied. She lit the cigarette as she leaned against a street sign and put her head back as she blew smoke into the air. She had been on the hoe stroll since she was ten years old and nothing surprised her at this point. She was a veteran, and her fuck game was out of this world.

"Hmm, hmm you know I need a mirror for that shit," Trixie commented as she danced uncomfortably in her stiletto boots.

"Girl, you don't need a mirror. Just rip the shit off. Go over there in that alley and handle your business," Liberty instructed.

Trixie disappeared down the darkened alleyway while Liberty stood on the sidewalk playing lookout.

"I can't see a damn thing back here! It's too dark! All of the fucking street lights are busted out," Trixie whispered harshly.

Liberty rolled her eyes and marched over to her friend. Liberty reached up and pulled down Trixie's black satin thong as she knelt on the ground in front of her. Reaching under Trixie's skirt she grabbed the piece of duct tape and slowly peeled it off, freeing Trixie's privates. Once it was completely removed, Liberty patted Trixie's package.

"It's a shame this big ol' dick was wasted on you bitch," Liberty joked as she stood to her feet.

Trixie stuck up her middle finger and exhaled as she finally was able to breathe. "Girl, please . . . ain't nothing going to waste over here. I be dicking these niggas down. They might not know what they are getting when they stop, but I've never had one man kick me out once they reach down there and find out what's between my legs. These down-low ass men are curious as hell. Shit, I get the occasional housewife too."

Liberty shook her head and tried to keep the disgust from showing on her face. Trixie was so feminine and beautiful that no one would ever guess that she was a transsexual. After years of being forced to live her life as a woman, Trixie now embraced it. "If I have to be a bitch, I'mma be the baddest bitch that has ever done it," she said.

"I'm just so sick of this. Every day it's the same thing . . . same bullshit . . . different men. I haven't figured out how yet, but the first chance I get, I'm leaving. I'm running as far as my feet will carry me," Liberty said honestly.

"That's what your little stash is for?" Trixie asked.

Liberty looked at Trixie in surprise as her brow lowered instantly. "How do you know about that?" she asked.

"Girl, please . . . Juan done sampled a little bit of this too," Trixie said.

"Juan?" Liberty shot back in disbelief.

"Juan, bitch," Trixie confirmed. "I told you these men be out here loving them some Ms. Trixie, baby!" She smiled and took a long drag of her cigarette before she continued. "He knows you keep some paper put up in his bathroom, and he mentioned it to me one night when we were hooking up. You know how that pillow talk shit goes," Trixie stated as she tapped the ashes that had accumulated on the tip of her cigarette, sending them flying into the sky. She noticed Liberty's disposition had gone sour, and she waved her hand dismissively. "Fix your face, mami. I didn't tell anyone else about it. Your secret is safe with me, Lib. You're my girl. It's not like you're stacking big paper, babes. Just a little nest egg in case you're able to break free. I respect it. You can trust me. I wouldn't play you like that. You're my bitch, Liberty . . . honestly, when you go I'm going with you. I wouldn't last a day without you out here with me. You keep me sane bitch!" Trixie stated.

Before Liberty could respond one of the 'shepherds' pulled up and all of the 'sheep' made their way to the van. The men who ran the operation were anonymous. It was a system of sexual enslavement that was run with such precision that they could never be caught. Even if one of the girls managed to escape she would never be able to name her captors. Every worker was referred to as shepherd and the working girls were the flock. After they were loaded into the back of the windowless freight van, they rode dismally back to the warehouse.

Once the girls arrived they were lined up one-by-one and the profit from the night's activities was quickly collected by the shepherds. Liberty stood unflinchingly next to Trixie. They had become accustomed to the routine. Liberty was still feeling the effects of her high and wanted nothing more than to be escorted to her cot so that she could fall into a comfortable sleep. Her lazy neck caused her head to wobble loosely as she fought the nod she was falling into. Trixie held onto her gently, discreetly giving her a shoulder to lean on. Liberty could feel herself drooling as her mouth fell open, but nothing could stop the drowsy haze she was stuck in.

As the shepherd made his way down the line he stopped at the young girl who stood to Liberty's left, causing her to straighten her back in attention and force her eyes to stay open.

The girl timidly handed over the money she had made that night. Four crumpled twenty-dollar bills were all that she had in her hand. Knowing that girl was new to the operation, Liberty instantly felt sorry for her.

"Let me ask you something? You speak English, no?" the shepherd asked.

The girl nodded fearfully.

"So you understood me when I said you were to bring back a minimum of $500?" he asked.

"I . . . I tried," the girl stuttered.

The shepherd acted as if he was going to walk away from her. "You tried," he mumbled as he rubbed his goatee. Liberty closed her eyes knowing that it would have been better for the girl to say nothing at all. The man turned suddenly on his heel and without warning blew a hole through the girl's head. Liberty felt the blood splatter onto her face and she stood frozen, her heart beating like a drum as she heard the girl's body hit the floor. Too afraid to look beside her, Liberty found a spot on the dirty wall in front of her and kept her eyes there. Tears fell down her eyes and mixed with the blood as it created crimson trails of sorrow on her cheeks. *I have to get out of here. It's only a matter of time before that girl on the floor becomes me,* she thought. Trixie squeezed Liberty's hand, but neither of them spoke a word.

"Clean this bitch up," the man ordered one of the other men. "And put the rest of them in their cages. Nobody eats tonight. Everybody meets quota . . . no exceptions . . . and until everyone does so, no one will be fed!"

As soon as Liberty was inside her closet-sized room she fell to her knees while frantically wiping the blood off her face. She knew that she could not take much more of this. It was only a matter of time before she would lose herself in this world. Her breaking point was nearing, and as she curled up on her cot she closed her eyes as the heroin lulled her back into a restless sleep.

EIGHT

"GET UP! EVERYBODY OUT OF BED!"

Liberty heard the voices of the shepherds on the other side of the steel door as they walked throughout the warehouse waking the girls. Liberty was still shaken from the events that had taken place the night before. It wasn't the first dead body she had seen. Over the years she had witnessed many gruesome things, but something about feeling the girl's blood on her face set off an intense fear within her. Anxious and weary, she was overwhelmed. As she opened her eyes, she instantly felt the itch to use. The crawling sensation that crept over her body caused her to dig her nails into her skin. She was on E and definitely needed a pick me up. The tumbling nausea building in her stomach wasn't from a lack of food but from a lack of heroin. She was jonesin' so bad that she could barely control her bowels. The shepherds kept the girls doped up most days, but on occasion they would make them go without the drug just to show their dominance. Liberty hated those days. The type of pain that she experienced from withdrawal was unbearable and she would do anything to feed her habit. She prayed that today was not one of those days. Liberty silently wondered why she was being disturbed. The girls never worked the boulevard in the daytime. They were creatures of the night so to be forced out of bed aroused Liberty's suspicion. The locks clicked on her door and she was wrangled out into the hallway, forced into a moving line with the other girls. She noticed Trixie ahead of her and she pushed her way to the front until she was directly behind her girl.

"What is going on?" Liberty whispered.

"What do you mean? This is the one day every year that we have a chance of getting out of here. They are choosing new girls to work the brothels today. How did you forget that?" Trixie asked.

Mixed emotions filled Liberty. She knew not to get her hopes up. Year after year she had been overlooked and bypassed. It only made her bitter to know that other chicks were moving up in the ranks while she was left to rot.

"This is a waste of time," she shot back with an attitude.

"Maybe, but at least you get to wash your ass for the occasion," Trixie stated. She knew that she would never be one of the girls to be handpicked for the brothels . . . she would never be more than a street walker. Lack of beauty was not the issue for Trixie because she was more than gorgeous. Her flawless looks rivaled those of any world-class super-model. It was the tool between her legs that kept her at the bottom, but she still welcomed the selection process . . . using it for what it was, a chance to take a real shower. Something as simple as that was a luxury.

They were herded into a large communal bathroom and one-by-one, pushed into the shower stalls. They stood still, arms outstretched as soapy water was poured over their heads and the workers washed them from head to toe with a coarse sponge. Like livestock they were processed until they were standing side by side in only their undergarments, shivering, as wind filled the drafty warehouse.

The doors were opened as two black limousines pulled inside. Liberty already knew who sat behind the tinted windows. They had only had one conversation, but over the years she had seen her come and go, each time choosing a few new girls but always leaving Liberty behind. The door opened and all that could be seen was the six-inch, red-bottom heel that emerged from the car. Finally Abia stepped out, looking more glamorous than ever before in a short mink jacket and a mini-dress that had come straight off the runway. Her eyes flew down the line quickly as she immediately pointed out a couple girls that appeared valuable. Her beauty was so intimidating that even the most arrogant of the streetwalkers became unsure. Those who covered themselves were instantly written off Abia's list of hopefuls. There was nothing she could do with an insecure young girl . . . she needed the sharks . . . the arrogant ones out of the bunch who were well-versed in the business of sex. She only wanted the bad bitches in her brothels because that's what it took to play the game at her level.

Liberty stood indifferent as she rolled her eyes slightly as Abia passed her. Liberty had been through this process many times before and her nerves were non-existent. As Abia was about to move onto the next girl, Liberty sucked her teeth causing Abia to halt mid-step. She looked sharply at Liberty and returned to stand directly in front of her. She smirked slightly, sensing a change in Liberty. Abia had purposefully bypassed Liberty over the years because she was soft. Liberty hadn't been ready. Her emotions had always betrayed her sensitive heart, but as Abia stood before her, this time she sensed a change. The streets had finally accomplished the act of hardening Liberty.

"I want her," Abia said as Liberty looked at her in shock. Abia kept it moving down the line as she chose more girls. Just as quickly as she had come she left.

"She picked me," Liberty whispered. She turned to Trixie in disbelief, but when she noticed the dismal look on her friend's face she realized what that meant. For the first time in eight years they were about to be split up. The devastation on Trixie's face caused Liberty's lip to tremble from grief as her heart broke in half. She hadn't felt this in so long, and as she gripped Trixie's hand her thoughts drifted to A'shai. She had thought of him often during her time on the streets but she always forced him to the back of her mind because she knew that she would never see him again. It was easier to just not think of him at all. A'shai had been her first love and best friend, but Trixie had been her only friend since him. She loved Trixie with all of her heart. They were brought together by circumstance and now they were being forced apart by a system that ranked Liberty higher simply because she was a real woman. She felt the same feeling of loss and the familiar hurt filled her as she looked Trixie in the eyes.

"I'm getting out of here, Lib. I'm not staying here without you," Trixie whispered as she shook her head from side-to-side. As Liberty was pulled from the line, she reached for Trixie.

"No, I'm not leaving her here!" she protested as she lunged away from the men while crying hysterically. Flashbacks of being torn away from A'shai ran through her mind. It felt as if she were reliving the same hell all over again. As Liberty was dragged towards the second awaiting limo all eyes were on her as the shepherds attempted to calm her down. Amidst the chaos Trixie grabbed one of the AK-47's from one of the men and began firing. The hair trigger caused bullets to fly as everyone ducked for cover. Trixie ran full speed towards the exit and out of instinct, Liberty snatched away from the men and took off after her. The screams of the other girls and the array of gunfire caused everyone to panic. It was the chance of a lifetime . . . the chance to flee and every girl took the opportunity. Scantily clad women and men ran in every direction, causing Liberty to lose sight of Trixie.

"Trix! Trixie!" Liberty called out into the crowd. She didn't see her girl, but she had to keep running. She was already too far gone to turn back now. Liberty ran in the opposite direction of the crowd, while covering herself as best as she could. It was broad daylight outside and she knew that she wouldn't get very far without any clothing.

Once she was a few blocks away she ran down a deserted alley and cowered behind a dumpster. She would have to wait until nightfall before she could run any further. In the meantime she looked up and down skid row, making herself aware of her surroundings just in case she needed to find a quick escape.

Liberty burst into the corner store, causing a scene, as she pushed past the customers at the counter. She knocked on the bulletproof glass causing Juan to look at her like she was crazy.

"Liberty? What the . . . ?"

"I need the key . . . the key, Juan, please," she said desperately as she looked around nervously. She knew that she was taking a risk by coming to collect her stash, but without it she would be stuck. She had gone all day on E, and her body was craving a fix so badly that every part of her ached. He passed her the key and watched as she frantically headed to the bathroom. Once inside she locked the door and rushed to remove the back from the porcelain toilet, but when she looked inside and saw nothing but clear water the contents of her stomach came up. The money was gone and although it had not been much, it was all she had to get by. There was only one other person who knew where her money was stashed.

I trusted her, Liberty thought, knowing that Trixie had gotten to the money first. A knock at the door interrupted her thoughts. "Just a minute!" she called through the door.

"It's Juan!"

Liberty unlocked the door, and he opened it slightly. "I've got some clothes for you. Nothing fancy . . . just some sweats," he said.

"Did Trixie come here?" she asked as tears fell down her cheeks.

"I don't know. My shift just started not too long ago," Juan said. "You need some help a' something?"

"No . . . the clothes are enough . . . thank you." Her voice cracked as she spoke and he wanted to press the issue, but decided that he didn't want to become involved in whatever problem she had gotten herself into.

"Lib, I don't mean to put you out but the customers. . . ."

"Don't worry. I'm leaving," she whispered as she wiped her nose. A shiver ran down her spine. She quickly dressed and dropped her head as she headed towards the exit. She didn't even see the black limousine that was sitting curbside outside of the store until it was too late. She was snatched up before she could protest and stuffed inside the car.

"Don't make a scene, Liberty," Abia said as soon as Liberty's behind hit the leather seats.

"Am I going to die?" Liberty asked. She didn't want to beat around the bush. She had seen girls be killed for much less.

"No," Abia answered shortly. "The bad days are over Liberty. I told you a long time ago that you had to earn your stripes. You have done that. Now you're ready . . . I'm about to introduce you to an entirely new world. The pain is over. It's time to enjoy the spoils of this business."

"And Trixie? Where is she?" Liberty asked.

"You mean the guy who grabbed the gun?" Abia asked.

"Don't call her that. She's more woman than you'll ever be," Liberty shot back.

Abia smiled at Liberty's loyalty, knowing that men paid top dollar for that type of dedication.

"She wasn't caught, and she better hope that she never is. They will kill her for a stunt like the one she pulled," Abia replied honestly. "Now I don't have time to babysit. At this level it's no longer enslavement, Liberty. You're not trapped here, but most of the girls choose to stay. Spend one day with me . . . let me show you the ropes . . . if you don't like what you see you can walk away free and clear."

"I can leave?" Liberty asked in a disbelieving tone.

"You've worked the boulevard for eight years. You've earned the right to make your own choice . . . but at least know what you're walking away from before you decide. One day. That's all I ask of you," Abia stressed. She reached into a compartment inside of the limo and pulled out a silver dish filled with heroin. As soon as Liberty saw it, her breath caught in her throat. She needed to hit that as soon as possible. Her body was yearning for it.

Liberty nodded as her tense body remained on pins and needles. She did not know what to expect, but she decided to go with the flow. At that point she needed a pick me up and without any cash of her own, Abia was the only one who could fulfill her craving. "Okay," she agreed.

"Okay," Abia said with satisfaction as she opened her legs and placed the drug-filled dish on the seat in between her legs. "Come get it."

Liberty got down on the limo floor, positioning herself between Abia's thighs and as she indulged in the drug, Abia stroked her hair. Liberty was stepping into a completely new world, one where her destiny would be in her own hands. One where eroticism and seduction was enjoyable instead of forced. As Abia's fingertips massaged her scalp, Liberty's entire body began to tingle. Her hands felt like silk feathers as Abia kneaded and stroked the contours of Liberty's neck. She was a woman with much experience. At thirty-two, she had experienced every aspect of the game and although she was retired from servicing clientele, she mentored every girl who came under her wing. They each admired her, and Liberty would be no different. Abia was a legend in the business. With every new girl that passed through her hands, she established a pecking order. Abia was the head-bitch-in-charge, no exceptions, and she seduced each new girl so that they understood who was the lead dog in the pack. It was Abia's extravagant world, and she was the queen. Liberty set up lines of heroin, filling up with as much as possible to avoid the empty feeling that had just tortured her. Her eyelids fluttered from pleasure as Abia caressed her.

"Have you slept with a woman before, Liberty?" Abia whispered as she rolled up the window that separated them from the driver.

Liberty nodded her head as she continued to snort the powder between Abia's legs. Abia reached down and removed the dish, then pulled her thong to the side. "Are you good at it?" she asked suggestively.

Completely caught up in the orgasmic feeling of her

high, Liberty's curiosity got the best of her. Numerous women had paid her for her services during her days of tricking, but none had ever been like Abia. Her essence was different from any woman Liberty had ever encountered. She possessed a mystique that made Liberty's body react to her. Abia lifted Liberty's shirt and rubbed Liberty's hardened nipple as she repeated, "Show me."

Liberty pulled Abia to the edge of the car seat and put her hands beneath Abia's behind as she dipped her tongue inside her warmth. Liberty was no amateur. She knew how to make any human being cum. Women always paid the most so Liberty had made sure that she was good at it. She pulled Abia's clit in between her lips and licked it with just enough pressure to make Abia squirm.

"Oooh," she moaned, surprised at the pleasure that Liberty was giving her. Liberty sucked and pulled while softly nibbling on Abia's flesh button. Liberty knew that she was being tested but was confident that she was passing with flying colors. The way that Abia was contracting her ass let Liberty know that she was doing her job. She flicked her tongue back and forth, fast and then slow . . . slow and then fast before sucking it with just enough pressure to make Abia's eyes roll in the back of her head. Liberty was so into it that she reached one hand into her own panties and played with herself as she brought Abia into ecstasy. Abia smiled in complete bliss as she caught her breath, and Liberty sat back on the seat, directly across from her. Liberty's head fell back as she wiped her mouth.

"Is that good enough for you?" she asked.

"That was the best," Abia replied with a smirk. She was surprised at Liberty's ability to pleasure a woman and could only imagine the skills she had acquired for sexing a man.

There was no way that she could let Liberty slip through the cracks. She needed her as an addition to the brothel. It was a money game and with a working girl like Liberty, Abia knew that she couldn't lose.

Liberty was flying high as a kite and her soul was content as the heroin took her to a temporary sanctuary of euphoria. Her neck was on a swivel as she looked out of the limousine's windows at the multi-million dollar homes that were nestled in the hills of the city. Beverly Hills seemed like light years away from where she had just come. The manicured lawns, privacy fences, and opulent mini-mansions were breath taking.

"Where are we going?" she asked.

"Home," Abia replied simply as she placed oversized Gucci glasses on her face.

NINE

WHEN THE CAR PULLED UP TO THE mansion Liberty was in a state of disbelief. When she had thought of working a brothel, she had pictured something completely different. This was luxury at its finest. She immediately felt out of place in the sweat suit she was wearing. She looked down at her threads.

"Don't worry, Liberty. No one is here to judge you. These girls came from the exact same place that you did. They know what it's like. Let's just go inside and freshen up before I show you around," Abia stated. The driver opened the door for them, and Abia exited the vehicle. Liberty hesitantly followed. She felt like she had just been sent to Emerald City. She may as well have been on another planet—that's how foreign the opulence was. She pulled nervously at her clothes as she followed Abia inside.

"There are twenty girls that live at the mansion. Ten are veterans and ten are new girls like you," Abia explained while giving Liberty a tour of the estate. "We understand the importance of personal space and privacy here so each of you has your very own master suite." Abia opened two French doors and spread her arms wide to show Liberty her room. She gasped at the beautiful décor. "This is your room if you want it," Abia continued as she spun around, showing off the lovely space. Liberty couldn't wait to soak in the deep-jetted bathtub or sit at the vanity and brush her hair. Although it seemed trivial, those were things that she had never done . . . to be a true woman, in control of her own destiny. She had no idea what that felt like. Liberty was speechless at how things had changed in the blink of an eye.

"There has to be a catch," Liberty stated.

"No catch, Liberty. This is the life. We don't deal with bullshit johns that make you feel worthless. Our client list consists of politicians, stockbrokers, judges, athletes, oil tycoons . . . the elite of our society. Many of our ladies don't stay in the business long. Many have been turned into the wives of the men that frequent here," Abia stated.

"What's the split?" Liberty asked as she weighed the pros and cons of the situation. Part of her wanted to leave and never look back, but there was something so intriguing about Abia's offer that Liberty could not refuse her.

"60/40," Abia replied frankly. "But all of your other needs are taken care of . . . you get to live in this fabulous home rent free. You get to drive foreign cars and rock designer clothes. You get to live the life that most people only dream of."

A knock at the door interrupted their conversation as another girl entered the room.

"The glam squad is heeerre," the girl announced excitedly as she clapped her hands together.

Abia smiled knowing that her team of professional stylists was right on time.

"We'll be down in a minute," Abia told the girl. She turned back to Liberty. "There are clothes and toiletries in the walk-in closet. You should be able to find something that can fit you. If you decide to stay you'll be given a stipend each month to update your wardrobe to your tastes. You get yourself together while I go freshen up. I'll meet you downstairs in a few and then I can introduce you to everyone."

Liberty nodded as Abia left her to soak it all in. Liberty immediately entered the adjoining bathroom and ran herself a bath. She hadn't been allowed to ever relax and unwind. Bathing was a rare occurrence back at the warehouse and as she entered the steaming water, her body melted from appreciation. The tub was large enough for a group of people to sit inside and she stretched out as the scent of shea butter entered her nose. This is crazy, she thought. 24 hours ago she didn't even know that something like this existed . . . now here she was thrust in the middle of it all, feeling slightly overwhelmed because she was unsure of what was expected of her in return. It all seemed too good to be true.

Liberty soaked her body until the water ran cold and hurried to the closet to dress. She was taken aback when she stepped inside. It looked like a fashion boutique. She had never owned more than one outfit a day in her life and as she thumbed through the racks of designers she was floored. She picked out a long-sleeved, backless, mini-dress, with studded shoulder accents and matching designer shoes. The expensive fabric felt so foreign on her skin, and she felt slightly out of place.

A knock at the door caused her to turn around.

"It looks good on you," Abia said. "You ready? The others are waiting for us."

All of the ladies gathered in the personal salon and for the first time Liberty saw the type of women she would be working with. They were a completely different breed than the ladies on the track. Everything about these new bitches shined. It was obvious that they were getting money; even after the house took its cut, the girls were stacking paper. Everything from their Brazilian blowouts to their perfectly manicured hands and feet indicated that they were far from amateurs. This wasn't a hobby . . . this was a career, a lucrative one. Abia put her hands on Liberty's shoulders and escorted her to one of the styling stations. As she stood behind her looking at Liberty's reflection she saw a gold mine. Once Liberty was cleaned up she would undoubtedly be the most valuable girl in the house.

It took hours for Liberty to make her transformation. Her long bone straight hair and Chinese bangs accentuated her face perfectly. Abia had gone all out . . . no expense had been spared. By the time the makeovers were complete the new girls couldn't be distinguished from the old. Even Liberty was in awe of her own beauty and tears accumulated in her eyes as she looked at her reflection in amazement.

"This is unreal," she whispered, unable to quit staring at herself.

"It's real Liberty . . . you just have to embrace it," Abia whispered as she handed her a crystal wine glass. Abia turned to the group of women and raised her voice so that everyone could hear her as she addressed all of the new girls that she had just rescued from the warehouse. "You all have a choice to make. You can stay or go, but this is the time to decide. If you would like to walk away . . . there is the door. You can do so without any repercussions, but if you would like to stay and live this life then lift your Pinot Grigio in the air."

Abia waited and noticed that every single glass was lifted in the air except for Liberty's. She turned towards her and asked, "What do you say? You can go out into the world and be ordinary, or you can stay here and live extraordinary."

Liberty lifted her glass and Abia smiled in satisfaction. They sealed their agreement with a toast . . . it marked a new beginning for Liberty. It was the next phase for a young woman whose life was predestined for tragedy.

A'shai pushed the all-black Range Rover down I-75 on his way to East Detroit to check on his father's crack spots. Baron quickly introduced him to the family business, and he took to the streets like a duck took to water. A'shai had quickly moved up the ranks and became his father's eyes and ears to the streets. By day he was a college student but by night he ran the most sophisticated and lucrative drug operation Detroit, Michigan had seen in years. He couldn't help but to think about how Baron handled Bonzi earlier that day. It made him reevaluate his tactics. Baron was a strategic thinker and it was as if he had played chess with Bonzi . . . and won.

A'shai pulled into the housing projects that sat just off the highway and parked. He made his way to the 'trap spot' and knocked on the door in a five knock rhythm that was the only way to gain entry. A woman opened the door and the aroma of cooked crack cocaine hit him in the face.

"Oh, it's Shai!" the young redbone yelled enthusiastically as she stepped to the side to let him in. She gave him a flirtatious smile and cocked her hip to the side in hopes to get extra attention from him. However, A'shai paid her no mind, despite the fact that she wore no clothing. He stepped into the apartment and a wave of greetings and stares came his way. A'shai remained silent, only nodding to the girls acknowledging him. All the girls were naked with doctor's masks on; all of them doing their part in the elaborate drug operation. A'shai didn't allow them to wear clothes while working in order to prevent theft. Some cooked the crack, some chopped it up, and some girls weighed it. It was all a smooth operation that trickled down from Baron's regime. The trap spot was one long apartment that was originally three apartments until Baron knocked down the walls, combining them. Baron owned the building so it didn't throw up any red flags to the authorities. On top of that, the handsome pay that he bribed the local police department with kept the law out of his business.

"Yo, where's Nico?" A'shai asked after he glanced around the spacious apartment.

"He's in the money room," one of the girls said as she

bagged up the product while sitting at the table. He headed towards the back where the profits were counted and the closer he got to the money room, the louder the sound of the money machine got. The sound of bills running through the machine was like a sweet melody to A'shai's ears. When he opened the door he saw Nico sitting at the table with a smile on his face while he put a rubber band over a stack of money. A smoking blunt hung from the left side of Nico's mouth and the smell of Kush weed filled the air, accompanied by smoke. A'shai looked over and also saw a young lady sitting at the table with him. He instantly frowned and looked at Nico and shook his head in frustration.

"Who is this, Nico?" He asked as he pointed at the slim, chocolate girl. Nico took a pull on the blunt and winked at the girl.

"This is my friend, Bunny. Bunny, this is my cousin Shai," Nico said proudly as he blew the smoke out slowly. He then passed the blunt to the girl. She looked at A'shai and extended her hand.

"Hi, Shai. I've heard a lot about you," she said as her hand lingered in the air. Nico saw the way that the girl's eyes lit up when she found out the man before them was the infamous A'shai Montgomery. The girl saw A'shai and money bags seemed to appear in her glazed over eyes. She was finally in the presence of the man the streets claimed to be the next boss. All of the girls in the city wanted A'shai and had heard about him in some shape or form. A'shai looked down at the girl's hand and didn't budge.

"Look, I'm sure you're a nice girl . . . but you have to

go, ma," he said sternly as he stepped to the side so she could have a clear pathway out. The girl's smile quickly turned upside down and the rejection slightly embarrassed her. She looked at Nico, waiting for him to say something but it never happened. Nico actually pointed to the door, signaling her to go because he knew that he was in the wrong. Baron had made it clear that he didn't want anybody in the money room except A'shai or Nico. He ran his drug operation as if it was a Fortune 500 company and that very reason alone attributed to his success.

The girl smacked her lips and quickly stood up and stormed out. A'shai watched as she left and closed the door behind her.

"I wanted to smash shorty. Why you tripping?" Nico asked A'shai as he picked the blunt back up and put it in his mouth. A'shai walked over to Nico and snatched the blunt out of his mouth and snuffed it out in the ashtray.

"Why am I tripping? You don't get it do you? You know only me and you belong in the money room. But somehow you let a stripper bitch in and you ain't even on your shit. You back here smoking weed when you supposed to be getting the count ready," A'shai said as he as he placed his hands on his hips and shook his head.

"Relax. We were just chilling. How do you know she was a stripper anyway?" Nico replied.

"For one, the bitch name is Bunny," A'shai shot back as he sat down and sifted through the money. Nico didn't admit it, but he did meet her in a strip club just two nights before. A'shai looked at Nico and noticed the diamond encrusted chain on his neck and he clenched his teeth tightly. He had explained to Nico many times before about where most diamonds in America came from. Conflict diamonds usually came from Sierra Leone. The hardship and horror stories that were behind the blood diamonds bothered A'shai. Slaves were forced to search mines night and day to find those stones. Families were torn apart and people's blood shed over the diamonds that Americans wore freely. They had no knowledge of how the jewels got to them and around their necks. Nico noticed that A'shai stared at his necklace and he quickly tucked it in his shirt, not wanting to hear A'shai preach to him the origin of the blood diamonds.

"Thank you," A'shai said as if he had read Nico's mind. "So, what the count look like?" A'shai asked as he began to put the money in the duffle bag by his feet.

"One hundred stacks," Nico said confidently as he ran the last stack through the machine.

"Perfect," A'shai said as he began to put the money into the duffle bag. The average take per day was $100,000 and that was on a slow day. He loaded the bag up and tried to get out of the trap spot as quickly as possible. He felt that just being around Nico made him dumber. Honestly, the only reason he even tolerated Nico was because he was Baron's nephew. Baron was a family man and always believed in looking out for blood so he let Nico run the projects, which was one of the hottest drug areas in the city.

"I'm about to bounce. Yo, I'm going to be out of town for a couple days. Drop the cash off to Pop's house while we're gone. Listen, the safe combo is 7-11-55. Ma will be expecting you. Got that?" A'shai said as he stood up and put the last of the stacks inside the bag.

"Yeah I got it. 7-11-55. No problem," Nico responded. "Yo, where you going?" Nico asked nosily.

"Pops and me are heading out to L.A. this weekend," A'shai replied unenthusiastically as he motioned towards the door. "I need you to hold it down while I'm gone."

"You know I got you. What you need to do is put a good word in for me with Unc. Tell him I'm trying to come up. Sitting in the crack house all day ain't what I want to do. I'm a boss nigga like you. I should be doing pick-ups and going to business sit downs with y'all," Nico said as he stuck his chest out. A'shai didn't even bother to respond. Although he and Nico were the same age, A'shai was twice his age in the mind. A'shai knew that a clown nigga like Nico wasn't built for being a boss but only a worker. A'shai walked out the door, leaving Nico there to tend to his own pipe dreams.

"Bitch ass nigga," Nico said as envy overcame him. He picked up the blunt that A'shai had put out and lit it. He never could understand why Baron had placed A'shai in charge and not him. Nonetheless, while Nico was smoking, A'shai was on his way to the next spot to pick up money. While Nico slept, A'shai was up thinking and that's why A'shai was in the top position.

"Thank you," Baron said smoothly as he grabbed the Remy on the rocks from the stewardess. They were thousands of feet above land as they made their way to the West Coast to visit a new coke connection. The private jet rode smoothly and was just as comfortable as Baron's living room. The plush seats, light jazz, and soft carpet created a relaxing environment for the drug lord. He sat across from his son, A'shai, and smiled. "How does it feel to be nearing the finish line?" Baron asked referring to A'shai's upcoming graduation from college in a couple of weeks.

"It feels good. I just have finals next week, and I will be done. It's been a long time coming," he answered as he also received a glass from the stewardess.

"I'm proud of you. You are making your mother so happy by getting that degree. I always knew you were going to be special. You had the eye of the tiger even as a young boy," Baron said as he took a sip of his drink and gave A'shai his infamous smile. Baron always could light up a room with his smile. It was always sincere and real. People felt that from him.

"Thanks Pop," A'shai replied modestly.

"Now, you are coming to a forked road in your life. You can take the business world by storm, and I know you will be successful in anything you put your mind to. The other option is to follow in my footsteps. I know morally it would be right for me to tell you to leave the streets alone and fly straight. But your pops is a smart man. I know the streets are harsh, and I would much rather you not make it a career. But I also know that you're going to do what you want to do regardless of what direction I want you to go in. I just want to let you know that I have your back in anything that you do. If you want to be a Wall Street banker . . . I'm with you. And if you want to move coke . . . I'm going to show you how to do it the right way. It's all on you," Baron said, dropping his adopted son some mental gems.

A'shai smiled and loved his father's gangster. He knew that Baron wasn't one to judge and would ride for him on any decision he made.

"You know what I want?" A'shai asked as he looked into his father's eyes, returning the stare.

"No, son. I don't know. Tell me. What do you want?" Baron asked as he sat up and looked A'shai straight in the eyes.

"I want to be like you. That's all I know," A'shai said just before he downed the liquor.

Baron nodded his head slowly and knew at that point that he had created a monster and there was no turning back for A'shai.

After a four hour flight they felt the jet begin its descent over the city of angels. The palm trees were visible beneath them as soon as they crossed the city's limits, and it was a far cry from Detroit's dilapidated scene. Samad, Baron's new coke connect, had arranged for a limo to pick them up. As soon as they landed a chauffeur was waiting at the clear port for them at the bottom of the steps. Quickly Baron and A'shai exited the jet, looking like they had just stepped out of a GQ magazine. The Italian threaded suits, designer loafers, and natural swagger made them look like street royalty. Just as quickly as they entered the limo, they were pulling off on their way to meet the notorious West Coast drug kingpin . . . Samad Sadat.

Baron was impressed as he walked into Samad's mansion. The marble floors and wrap around porcelain stairs were immaculate to say the least. It would be his first time meeting Samad face to face, but they both were well familiar with each other off their reputations for moving weight. They had been involved in a few business deals through their various mutual contacts in the past, but this time the two bosses would come in contact personally. The butler escorted them to the spacious living room where marble stone accented the Italian leather furniture.

"Please, have a seat. Samad will join you shortly," the elderly Caucasian butler said as he waved his hands over the sectional sofa. Baron nodded and took a seat. A'shai followed suit and sat next to Baron. They both looked around and admired the palace that Samad called home.

Baron planned on letting the drug game go and intended to pass the crown down to him. After hearing that A'shai wanted to follow his path, he decided right then that this trip would be his last on any drug business. Baron looked over at A'shai and knew that he was leaving the game in good hands. Baron looked down at his Movado watch and saw that it was a couple ticks before noon, the time when they were supposed to meet Samad. Just like clockwork, the sound of the front door opening and closing echoed through the mansion and moments later a slim, athletic Arabic man came walking into the room. He had on a Nike jogging suit and a towel was draped around his neck. Sweat dripped from his brow as he approached them, wiping his forehead.

"Good afternoon, gentlemen," he said as he approached them with a smile and extended hand. Baron and A'shai stood up and both of them were surprised at Samad's youthfulness. He looked to be in his early thirties. To be that young in that position of power was very surprising. "Excuse my dress attire; I just finished my daily jog," Samad said as he smiled.

"No problem. Pleasure to meet you,'" Baron said as he was the first to shake Samad's hand. "This is my son, Shai," Baron said as he opened his shoulder towards his son. Samad shook Baron's hand with a smile and then looked towards A'shai and did the same.

"Please have a seat," Samad said as he walked around the glass coffee table and took a seat. His butler brought him bottled water and he immediately opened it up and took a sip. He then opened up negotiations. "I've heard great things about you, Baron," Samad said as he sat back and got comfortable.

"Likewise," Baron replied as he studied Samad's movements, trying to read him. A'shai, like always, just sat back and watched a master at work. Baron was a genius at mental chess and negotiations; always choosing his words and actions carefully.

"You made a lot of people unhappy with your move against Bonzi," Samad said.

"Well, it was time for a change. I stand behind my decision, and I always will," Baron said firmly, not having any regrets and prepared for anything that came from his decision to knock off a boss.

"He was a racist prick anyway," Samad said lightening up the mood. Samad actually was happy that Baron had done what he did. Baron only got rid of the competition for him, which meant more clients for him. "That mishap brought you here, so I'm not complaining," he added.

"Right. That's how I see it too," Baron said.

"So let's get down to business. I know you didn't fly across the country to shoot the shit, my friend," Samad stated.

"Indeed," Baron said as he clasped his hands and leaned forward, interested in what was about to be said.

"Coke is your game, right? I will give you kilos of the purest fish scale in the country for sixteen a key," Samad said as he rubbed his rubble light beard. Baron immediately liked the sound of the price because he had been paying sixteen-five with Bonzi for years. Being the businessman that he was, Baron still attempted to negotiate so that he could get the best price possible.

"How about fifteen a key, and we will buy one hundred per month . . . consistently?"

"I can't do that. That's too low." Samad said as rubbed his hands together. "I can go fifteen-five, but that's the lowest I can go."

Baron liked the sound of that price and just as he was about to answer, A'shai sat up and stepped in. "We are going to pass but thanks for your time," he said with a no-nonsense expression on his face. He extended his hand for Samad and stood up. *What the fuck are you doing?* Baron thought as he scolded his son in his head. He was silently cursing A'shai but Baron's facial expression never changed. He also stood up as he wondered what his son had up his sleeve. Samad shook his hand and then Baron's as they ended the meeting abruptly. A'shai turned to head out and Baron followed. "I don't what the hell you're doing, but it better work," Baron whispered as they headed to the door. Baron was totally taken off guard as he thought about the great price Samad had just given them.

"Trust me, Pops. We won't make it to the door," A'shai whispered back as he put his business skills on full display for his father. A'shai thought about the fact that Samad needed them and not the other way around. A'shai thought about how Samad had gotten in touch with Baron as soon as he heard about Bonzi's death. He also thought about how Samad had flown them out just to have a sit-down with him. A'shai's business savvy was beginning to peak its head and A'shai hoped like hell that his plan would work.

"Hold up!" Samad yelled as he thought about how much money he was potentially letting walk away. "Deal!" he yelled as he smiled, knowing that A'shai was a young shark. A'shai smiled and winked at his father as they turned around. A'shai approached Samad with his hand out and they shook.

"I want it for fourteen-five," A'shai said knowing that he had Samad wrapped around his finger.

"Deal. You have a shark for a son. The two of you have to come back out and join me at The Gentleman's Ball. It'll be a great way to kick off this business friendship," Samad said as he looked at Baron and shook his hand. Baron smiled and looked on at his protégé. Baron hadn't been to The

Gentleman's Ball in years and he figured it would be a great way to introduce his son to the heads of the underworld.

"We'll be there," Baron replied. It was the perfect rite of passage for A'shai, and he would establish many contacts at the exclusive event. He knew at that moment that A'shai was built for this game and was on his way to being the boss of all bosses in due time.

TEN

LIBERTY PULLED HER AUDI A8 UP TO the Geisha House sushi bar in Hollywood and stepped out of the car. It had been two months and life was obviously good. She was in high demand at the brothel and had quickly stacked enough money to live comfortably. The first thing she had purchased was a brand new vehicle. She paid the foreign whip off in full . . . not even realizing that she didn't know how to drive it until it was time for her to pull it off the lot. She quickly learned with the help of Abia, and the vehicle became her most prized possession. She had a fetish for the finer things. Because she had never had anything, now that she could afford it . . . she wanted to buy everything and as she walked into the popular restaurant she felt accomplished and as if no one could touch her.

She gave her name to the hostess, knowing that her date was already seated and awaiting her presence. As she walked across the room, most heads couldn't help but to turn her way. She was killing the dress she wore . . . the fabric fitting her curvaceous body like a glove. She spotted her date and gave him a smile as he stood to welcome her. He pulled out her chair for her and she pecked him on the cheek before she sat down.

"Good evening, handsome," she greeted.

"You look beautiful, Liberty," he replied.

"Flattery will get you everywhere, your honor," she whispered over the candle-lit table.

Judge Collin Bridges had presided over the federal district in L.A. for the past twenty years. A 60-year-old gentleman, he was quite attractive with his salt-and-pepper beard that he wore neatly trimmed. Everything about him was distinguished and there was nothing more attractive to Liberty than established money. Judge Bridges radiated confidence and power. A widower and father of two adult children, he lived a lonely life. The women at the brothel had become the companions that he chose to keep time with. Liberty had been instructed to treat him very well. He had requested her in particular because after seeing her portfolio, she had sparked his interest.

"So how much is a night with someone like you going to cost me?" he asked.

"$5,000," Liberty answered. "I'm worth every penny though."

The judge smiled and sat back as he took her all in. He had been with many women in his day, but Liberty was a rare beauty. There was something about her that stood out amongst the masses. It was more in the way that she carried herself than in her actual looks. He watched as she picked up her champagne flute . . . so graceful as if she were a prima ballerina and life was her stage.

"I'm sure you are," he replied. "So where are you from?" he asked.

Liberty could tell that the judge was there for companionship. She had learned to read her clients and to provide them with whatever void they were missing in their lives. Whether it be a night of mind-blowing sex or just a listening ear, Liberty could provide her men with all that their hearts desired as long as the price was right.

Liberty no longer felt like a two-bit whore. She was clocking a salary that rivaled that of physicians and attorneys. Instead of hating what she had become, she embraced it. There was no point in dwelling on the things she couldn't change so instead she buried her past, vowing to never think about it again. With Abia's help Liberty was given a new life. The right palms had been greased to make Liberty's presence in the states as legal as if she had really been birthed there. All of her paperwork was legit. With a phony social security card and birth certificate she had all the makings of a new life, and it was up to her to make the most of it. Instead of chasing an education or developing a trade, she was living the fast life. It was all she knew. Seduction was the only skill that she had ever developed and with connected friends like Abia, she was going to let it take her straight to the top.

Her past was not something that she ever spoke about so instead of answering the judge's question she replied, "I'm really not in the mood to talk, Collin. I could think of some other things that we could be doing right now."

She smiled sexily as the judge moved his chair closer to hers and she slid her hand in the seat of his crotch, massaging his stiffening manhood. A job that she used to hate had become one that she appreciated. She loved the power that she held over her clients. Instead of being the one that was taken advantage of, she felt like the manipulator . . . the black widow that trapped men in her web. She could see the lust in his eyes and it gave her a natural high because she knew that all of the cards were in her hands.

"Let's get out of here," he whispered.

Liberty rose from her seat and grabbed the judge's necktie and held onto it as she walked out of the restaurant, dragging him playfully behind her as he became hypnotized by the natural sway of her hips. He was in for a long night. It was his first time requesting her company, but Liberty knew how to hook a man. After she put her thing down on him he would become just another regular on her rotation.

Liberty entered the mansion just before dawn. She crept inside to avoid waking the other ladies. She hadn't made many friends in her time there, but it didn't bother her. She was there to make the money . . . fuck the bitch standing beside her. The way she saw it, they were her competition. Her cut-throat mentality was a direct result of her sordid past. Everyone she had ever let into her heart was always ripped away from her so she had closed and locked it to avoid losing someone else she cared for. She didn't even give anyone the opportunity to get close to her.

"Long night?" Abia's voice cut through the pitch black mansion, causing Liberty to gasp unexpectedly as she dropped her handbag, spilling the contents of it onto the floor. Abia flicked on the light and bent down to help Liberty pick her things up. She noticed the white powder that dusted the floor and then she looked up to notice that Liberty was high. Abia wasn't naïve to the fact that most of the girls in her stable indulged in one drug or the other, but Liberty went hard on narcotics like a true addict. The last thing Abia needed was a junkie bitch. She was known for having a high quality operation. She wasn't about to allow Liberty to ruin the reputation of a brothel she had worked years to establish. Her clients didn't pay to be around the likes of base heads, crack heads, or dope heads and if Liberty didn't tread lightly she could easily become one.

"You might want to slow down on this stuff, Liberty. You're not working the streets anymore. You don't need this to cope. I can help you wean off this shit if you want," Abia suggested as she handed Liberty her bag. Both women stood and Liberty shook her head.

"No, I'm good. I can handle it," she replied. She was only nineteen years old, but had been snorting heroin since the tender age of ten. She noticed the sympathetic look on Abia's face. "Don't judge me, Abia. You gave me this habit . . . people like you led me down this road. You don't get to look at me like that," Liberty spat as she snatched her clutch.

Abia knew that Liberty was right, but she had been in

the business long enough to notice when one of her girls was headed towards self-destruction. Liberty had only been at the brothel for a couple of months and already she was bringing in more money than even the most experienced girl. Liberty was going on two, sometimes three dates a day, making her the highest earner out of the group. It was good money, but she was going so hard that she would eventually burn out. Most days Liberty only came home to shower before darting right back out the door to meet another client. Her body and mind needed a break. It took a lot of drugs to keep a person flying non-stop the way that Liberty was doing, and Abia could tell from Liberty's constantly running nose that she had graduated to snorting cocaine. It was Abia's job to keep the inventory in good condition and Liberty was no exception.

"I'm not judging you, hun, but you need to slow down. The Gentleman's Ball is coming up soon, and I need you to be at your best for that Liberty," Abia replied.

"The Gentleman's what?" Liberty asked in irritation. All she wanted to do was sleep at this point. She hadn't known that Abia was going to be watching her every move, and she wasn't feeling the authority that Abia was trying to put on her.

"The ball, Liberty. I've been telling you ladies about this since you stepped foot inside this house. It's the most important event of the year. The men who come to this event make our regular clients look like blue-collar workers. It's like an auction. Girls get sold to the highest bidder," Abia explained.

"Like slaves," Liberty said dismally.

"Like rarities," Abia shot back. "Some men pay for one night . . . they fly out and leave their wives at home so that they can enjoy a single night of pleasure . . . but some of the men pay to keep you long term. Those men are so rich that you won't have to lie on your back another day of your life. They spend big money, and I can't have you walking in there with bags under your eyes from these sleepless, drug-filled rendezvous. So like I said . . . slow down before you crash and burn."

ELEVEN

WILLOW SAT IN THE LARGE STADIUM AND tears of joy filled her eyes as she looked at the sea of square hats. It was a significant day in her life . . . it was the day that her son, A'shai, would receive his degree. Her heart swelled with pride as she blew him a kiss. A'shai gave her a charming wink and then held up his hand giving her a sign that only the two of them shared . . . a hand gesture that meant 'I Love You'.

"I am so proud of that boy," Willow stated to Baron who sat to her right.

"Me too. Today is a big day . . . it's his day," Baron replied.

The prestigious couple held hands as they admired their son for his tenacity and drive. Willow knew that A'shai would do something great with his life. She had connected with him from the very first time she lay eyes on him. She was well aware of the life that he had come from because they shared a common past; that made this day even more joyous. A'shai had done quite alright for himself. He had defied the odds.

When his name was called, Willow stood to her feet excitedly, clapping and smiling with class.

A'shai accepted his honor and then walked over to his mother to plant a kiss on her cheek. "This is for both of us," he whispered in her ear. Willow had urged him to pursue an education more than anyone else in his life and had helped him see it through until the end. She was his biggest supporter and he paid homage to her by sharing his greatest accomplishment with her.

She gripped his face and kissed his cheek before he walked back to his seat.

After the ceremony Willow and Baron greeted their son with love. A'shai was beaming from ear to ear. His usual serious demeanor was overshadowed by the triumph he felt.

"Congratulations, son," Baron stated as he gave A'shai a firm handshake.

"Let me get a picture with my baby," Willow said as she pulled him close and fixed his silk neck tie.

Baron chuckled as he shook his head. "Come on, Will, you're embarrassing him," he said.

A'shai was not really one for picture taking, but he would do anything to please Willow. He pulled her close, wrapping his arm around her shoulders and posed for the shot.

"Get one of me and my favorite girl," he said, making Willow feel like the love of his life.

"I think me and a few of the fellas are going to go out to celebrate," A'shai said as he removed the cap from his head.

"What? Oh no! I made you a big dinner. I thought you could celebrate at home with us," Willow said.

Seeing the disappointment on his mother's face A'shai kissed her cheek and said, "Dinner sounds like the perfect way to celebrate, ma."

They took a few snapshots and then headed home. A'shai walked into the house and was shocked when he heard . . .

"SURPRISE!"

He smiled as he recognized all of his closest associates and classmates. Even the hood had come out to show him love.

"Congrats, son!" Baron shouted as he patted A'shai on the back.

He turned to Willow and Baron. "Dinner huh?" he said with a chuckle.

"I had to get you back here somehow," Willow said. "I've been planning this for weeks. I want you to have a ball and live it up. You deserve it!"

Willow walked away to play hostess to her son's friends while A'shai stood next to Baron, completely taken aback by how many people had shown up. He knew that he had love in the streets but this was like a real live block party.

"Enjoy yourself tonight, Shai. This is your gift from your mother. I have a different surprise for you tomorrow. I love you, young man," Baron stated.

"I love you too, Pop."

An old Teena Marie slow jam came on and A'shai immediately recognized Willow's favorite song. He went and found her and then pulled her onto the dance floor.

"Boy, what are you doing? There are plenty of fresh tail

little girls here for you to dance with," Willow said as she threw her head back as they two-stepped.

"Nope I don't see nothing but the most beautiful lady in the room," A'shai replied. They danced the night away and although normally A'shai wasn't the dancing type he indulged his mother, showing her the time of her life. He truly shared his big night with only her, turning down girl after girl who tried to steal his attention away. "Thanks for this, ma. Thank you for everything," A'shai stated, knowing that he would be nowhere if it had not been for her generous and kind heart all those years ago. She had pulled him from the trenches and changed his entire life.

"You don't ever have to thank me. You are my son, and you mean the world to me."

Baron smiled as he looked over at his son, A'shai, who sat across from him. A'shai had just graduated the day before in Michigan and already they were across the coast in L.A.

They sat in the back of the luxury stretch limo, sipping champagne while waiting on the "special call." They both wore black tuxedos accented with silk bowties and diamond cufflinks. Presidential would be an understated way to describe the way the two men looked on that night. It was a special night and both of them could feel the electricity in the air. It was the night of The Gentleman's Ball, the single most exclusive ball of the year. Only politicians, millionaires, and bosses attended the private affair. The location of the event was kept secret for up to twenty minutes prior to the start time. Each man or entourage was told that they would receive a phone call to notify them of the location and only people on the guest list would be allowed to enter. It was very private and Baron had the pleasure of attending the same ball a few years back. He thought bringing A'shai was a great way to celebrate his accomplishment. He also knew that it was a good way to get A'shai's feet wet in the corporate black market.

"You know, your mother was very proud of you yesterday," Baron said as he poured champagne into the flute. A'shai smiled and nodded his head as he remained silent. They sat in parking lot of the Hilton that they were staying in and like clockwork, the phone rang exactly twenty minutes before 10 P.M. Baron picked up his phone and pushed the talk button.

"Hello," he said as he waited for the voice on the other end. A man told him the address to the ball and hung up. And just like that, they were headed to the secret location.

The prestigious hotel was closed down for the night. The sign out front read:

CLOSED FOR CONSTRUCTION

However, the hotel was actually about to host L.A.'s most exclusive event. Limos lined up in the back of the hotel as men entered through the rear entrance. It was a black tie affair so every man wore a black tuxedo with black tie. As Baron's and A'shai's limo pulled to the back curb, both men admired the beautiful women who stood outside acting as personal hostesses, one for each car that pulled up. A tall blonde beauty opened the door for them and stepped to the side so they could walk on the red carpet that led to the back entrance.

"Welcome to The Gentlemen's Ball," the exquisite woman said.

"Thank you," Baron said as he stepped out of the car and reached into his pocket. He slid a crispy $100 into the woman's hand, and she accepted it gladly. She placed the bill inside of her cleavage and smiled. A'shai stepped out and fixed his cufflinks, and they headed into the building. As they walked inside, masquerade masks were handed to them, and they were ordered to put them on to conceal their identities. As soon as they put the masks on, they were greeted by another hostess who handed them each a hand-rolled Cuban cigar along with a flute of the finest champagne. She then pulled a lighter from her cleavage and lit the cigars for them both. Baron took a puff and smiled.

"This is good right here," he complimented as he tasted the expensive cigar. He was a consummate connoisseur of cigars and could smell good Cuban smoke from a mile away. A'shai also hit his cigar and they proceeded through the room. The immaculate showroom was nothing short of amazing. An immense stage sat in the middle of the floor that had a runway attached to it. The theme of the ball was black and white. The porcelain floors on the stage were checkered black and white as well as the abundance of balloons around the stage, which made it a sight to see.

"Follow me, gentlemen," their hostess said to them as she led them to their seats right below the stage in the first row. The sounds of Ol' Blue Eyes, also known as Frank Sinatra, serenaded the ball.

"What you know about Ol' Blue Eyes," Baron asked, being a fan of a wide range of music. A'shai chuckled and nodded his head to the sounds of "My Way." Baron took a glance around the room and although the men had masks on, he was able to recognize a lot of his business partners and associates and even some celebrities. Baron looked across the room and began to give A'shai some game.

"See that cat right there," Baron said as he discreetly nodded his head in the direction of the man he saw. A'shai nodded his head as he followed Baron's eyes.

"That's the mayor of New York City," Baron said and then looked to the other side of the room. "And over there . . . that's one of the biggest hip-hop moguls in the world." A'shai looked over and couldn't believe his eyes. The flamboyant, brown skinned rapper was dapperly dressed in an expensive suit and sat discreetly amongst his entourage.

"Damn, you ain't bullshitting. That's crazy," A'shai said as he looked over noting the hip-hop mogul's attendance. He was still noticeable even though he wore a mask.

"You're in the big leagues now, son. All millionaires travel in the same circles. It doesn't matter how you get it as long as you got it," Baron said as he smiled and nodded his head at his son. Just as A'shai was about to respond, a voice on the loudspeaker sounded.

"Fifteen minutes to show time," a female voice announced

over the intercom. A man was seated about three chairs down from them, also masked.

"Hello my friend," he said discreetly to Baron. He was accompanied by a beautiful black woman on his arm. He raised his mask to reveal himself. It was Samad.

"Hello," Baron said to his new coke connect. Samad also nodded at A'shai, who returned the gesture. Before they could engage in any conversation, the announcer stated that the show was about to start. A skinny white man with a Zorro-type mask walked onto the stage with a microphone in his hands.

"Welcome to The Gentlemen's Ball. Let the bidding begin!"

Liberty looked in the vanity mirror as she applied mascara to her face, preparing for the biggest night of the year. Butterflies fluttered in the pit of her stomach. Abia stood behind her with her arms crossed, watching the beauty doll herself up.

"You look gorgeous," Abia complimented as she placed her hands on Liberty's shoulders.

"Thank you," Liberty answered. She had heard about this ball for so long and wondered what to expect when she went out to the showroom. She could hear the chatter from the men and the soft music playing and it only added to her nervousness. Liberty's hand began to tremble as she applied the eyeliner to her lids.

"Don't be afraid. You are going to do great," Abia said as she took notice of the young damsel-in-distress. "It's just like any other trick, but it's for a lot more money," Abia said as she thought about the high ticket price that Liberty would demand. Hands down, she was the most stunning woman in the building and Abia understood that. Abia already knew whom she would get the attention of and that was Samad Sadat, one of the biggest cocaine distributors in the country. Samad always purchased the belle of the ball each year, and she knew this year he would be amazed. Inside Abia's head, she knew that if everything went as planned Samad would buy Liberty, not only for the night. . . .

Since the ball was held in a hotel, it acted as a gigantic brothel for the night and soon the rooms would be filled with men. Some left wives at home, some simply needed a dinner companion, others were looking for long term affairs, but they were all there seeking one of Abia's girls. That night they would engage in various sexual acts and all types of fetishes. Abia already began to think about how she would make $1 million in one single night. She closed her eyes and smiled and prepared for the biggest trick of the year.

The hostesses assigned each man a bidding fan as they circulated throughout the room. A'shai passed and just decided to watch. Little did he know that he was about to witness high-priced prostitution at its finest. The show began and a slim Asian woman walked down the runway with seductive lingerie that was see-through, immediately getting oohs and ahhs. The bidding started and people began to discreetly raise their fans in an attempt to purchase the girl for the night. The bidder stood at the end of the stage with a microphone in his hand.

Baron had already planned to buy his son a girl for the night and looked over at A'shai and asked him, "You want her?" as the girl walked out and stood on stage. A'shai couldn't believe what he was witnessing. He quickly turned down the offer . . . but that would soon change when he saw the only girl that would ever hold his heart.

Liberty watched as the girls went in and out of the dressing room, and Abia monitored them like a hawk. Abia made sure that their stomachs were sucked in as tightly as they could go. She had far exceeded her expectations and nearly banked $1.5 million. Her operation was flawless and had a level of discretion that men in high places respected. Their purchases of the girls' services would be deducted on their annual taxes as a charity donation, making their actions that night easier to justify. There were no strings attached for the men unless they wanted there to be; it was a politician's dream.

It was time for Liberty to go onto the stage. She took a deep breath and with a small nudge from Abia she walked out with all eyes on her. She wore a silk La Perla robe that hugged her enticing frame and plump assets. Her perky breasts sat up and her long nipples seemed to protrude through the silk's fabric. There wasn't a soft dick in the house. Liberty was the last girl to hit the stage, and Abia knew that she had saved the best for last. Liberty saw all the masked men in the audience, which caught her off guard as she walked down the runway. The bright lights shined down on her face and every set of eyes looked in her direction.

"Let the bidding begin!" The man on stage said. That's when the place erupted. Everyone wanted a piece of the African-born beauty with the body of a model and ass of a horse.

A'shai's heart dropped when he saw Liberty. He was speechless and felt a lump form in his throat. As she walked down the runway with black circles around her eyes, she had the stare of a girl with no soul. It pained A'shai to see the men yelling and whistling at her like she was some sort of meat and they were starving lions. She looked older but hers was a face he would never forget . . . he was looking at his girl. He almost jumped onto the stage to snatch her off, but he restrained himself while remaining seated. He quickly leaned over to his father and whispered, "I want her," trying to get his love so that he could save her. A'shai watched intensely as his heart beat rapidly, and he stared at Liberty, hoping she would look his way but she never did. The price got to $50,000, and Baron and Samad were the only ones left in the bidding war.

"We have to get her, pops," A'shai urged as they bid against each other. Samad refused to lose the woman that he came for. He smiled at Baron in between bids, loving the competition. A'shai waited on pins and needles as the two continued to bid. The bidding kept getting higher and higher and everyone in the room began to get excited at the two men bidding on the belle. They were on their feet, watching the two men go back and forth. Neither of them were budging or batting an eye and the bid got up to $125,000.

In the beginning, Samad enjoyed the friendly competition, but when he saw that Baron wasn't budging he began to grow impatient. He was tired of the games and stood up and yelled, "A half a million!!!" as he looked over at Baron and winked. The crowd erupted and began to clap at the unprecedented bid. The place was on fire. Baron shook his head. He wasn't prepared to pay that much for one girl for one night.

"We can't take her home like some of these men. This is only for one night, and it's not worth it," Baron said explaining why he decided to concede.

"Pops, you have to get her," A'shai said as he began to worry. Baron conceded, and the announcer closed out the bid.

"Going once . . . going twice . . . sold to number 23! That was amazing! Give both of these gentlemen a hand. This has broken the record for the highest bid ever. Give them a round of applause," he said just before the two gentlemen got a standing ovation. While everyone was laughing and clapping, A'shai clenched his teeth and fought back tears. He began to put together a plan in his mind to get his girl. He wasn't about to let her slip away again.

TWELVE

LIBERTY HAD NEVER BEEN SO NERVOUS IN her life. She had a $500,000 price tag on her head and even she knew that she wasn't worth that much. *How am I supposed to live up to that price? What does he expect of me?* she thought as butterflies danced in her stomach and she wrung out her fingers tightly while pacing back and forth in Samad's great room. She closed her eyes and inhaled deeply as she tried to calm her nerves. *I know how to satisfy a man . . . he's just like the rest of them. I can do this. Stop tripping Liberty,* she told herself. She was trying to put Samad on the same scale as all of her previous clientele, but it was obvious that he was in a league of his own. She had messed with many men before, but Samad's wealth ran deep. As Liberty walked around the room looking at all of the antique furniture and expensive artwork she knew that Samad's money was old. He wasn't new to this. There was nothing gaudy or flashy about the way that he lived, but everything about the remarkable property indicated that he was royalty. It was quite intimidating. She heard the doors clang open and watched as Samad entered the room. He was far from handsome . . . in fact his looks were quite unattractive. His lean figure was too slender for her tastes and his large nose took up too much space on his small face. He turned her off, and as he approached Liberty she tried to erase the look of contempt that crossed her face.

"Welcome to my home . . . your home," Samad stated. "You're a very beautiful girl, Liberty."

Liberty lowered her eyes to the floor to avoid staring at his face. "Thank you.

"Umm . . . my things. All of my clothes, my jewelry, and my car are back at the mansion. When can you take me to go get them?" she asked.

Samad put a finger beneath her chin so that she would look him in the eyes. He turned her face to the left and then the right as if he were inspecting her. "You won't need those things here," Samad replied. "You will have an entire wardrobe fitted personally for you and you will have a personal driver to take you wherever you would like to go. Someone as special as you deserves to be catered to."

Liberty smiled slightly, blushing as she warmed up to him a bit. His ugly appearance was rivaled by the charm of a Casanova.

"I don't want you to feel uncomfortable here, Liberty. I would like for you to be my mate. Get to know me and I think you will like the situation that you have been brought into," Samad stated. "You hungry? Would you like some food?" Samad held out his hand and waited for Liberty to grasp it.

Liberty sighed, figuring that she may as well become accustomed to Samad. She grabbed his hand and smiled as he led her into the chef's kitchen.

"I'm going to make you a native dish that my mother used to make me," he said.

"Where are you from?" Liberty asked curiously.

"The Middle East. I was born in Egypt but I was raised in Iran," he responded.

"Do you have any family?" Liberty asked.

He looked her in the eyes and reached out to touch her cheek. "You are my new family," he said seriously. "And you will give me my first son I hope."

Caught off guard, she didn't know how to respond. She hadn't expected him to request a child from her. It wasn't even something that she had ever thought of. The world was too corrupt to bring another soul into it, but she knew that her opinion did not matter. She cleared her throat and nodded her head in compliance while giving him an unsure smile.

"That's my girl," he answered.

Despite the fact that he had personal chefs on call, he fixed her a homemade Persian meal from scratch that she actually enjoyed. The fact that he was trying to impress her made her relax slightly, and she found herself having a genuine conversation with him. As they sat side-by-side at the dinner table, he wiped food from the side of her mouth.

"I'm sorry. I'm not very good at this formal dinner thing," Liberty said as she blushed in embarrassment.

"Don't apologize. I know the places that you have been, and the conditions under which you were forced to live. Those days are over. You are mine now. You no longer have to use your back to provide a lifestyle. All you have to do is be my woman, and I will take care of everything else," Samad said.

She was surprised at how nicely he was treating her. His hand rubbed her shoulder gently, massaging her stress away. He looked at her clothing . . . the expensive couture dress that she had worn to the ball. "We have to get you some clothing . . . something more suitable for your new life here with me," he said. Unable to contain himself he leaned in to kiss her. Liberty's back stiffened at first, but the feeling of his hand stroking the nape of her neck so gently caused her to relax. She reminded herself that he had paid too much for her to turn him down. She opened her mouth and invited his tongue inside as she kissed him back, throwing her inhibitions to the wind. She reached for him as her fingers skillfully began to unbutton his Ralph Lauren dress shirt, but he stopped her as he took her hand inside his. He kissed the back of her wrist.

He helped her up from the table. "For the next few days I want you to rest. Your body has been through enough for now."

Not used to being rejected, Liberty frowned in confusion. "You don't want me?" she asked.

"Of course I want you, but I want you to want me back. This is no longer a job, Liberty. Become my woman," he whispered. He led her upstairs to the master bedroom where he unzipped the back of her dress. "Rest for the night. I will see you at breakfast in the morning."

Liberty watched as Samad left the room, leaving her head spinning in confusion. If he didn't want sex, she didn't know what to give him. It was all she had to offer. She hadn't given her companionship to anyone since she was a little girl. She didn't even know how to love a man anymore. In her eyes they all wanted something . . . including Samad . . . she just hadn't figured him out yet.

Liberty awoke to the sound of people talking around her and as she slowly opened her eyes she noticed two women standing at the foot of the bed. The doctor's masks they wore over their faces let her know that they were medically trained but she felt violated as one of them said, "Put her feet in the stirrups," without even acknowledging Liberty.

"Stop! What are you doing?" Liberty shouted, kicking her legs in protest as two women tried to force her legs into the stirrups. "What are you doing?!"

One of the women came to the side of the bed and spoke calmly. "Relax, Liberty. My name is Dr. Kapoor, and I am here to give you a medical examination. The woman at the foot of the bed is one of my nurses. We are not here to harm you in any way. In fact, it won't even hurt. You will feel a slight discomfort, but it isn't painful. We are just giving you a pap smear," the woman said.

"A pap what?" Liberty asked as she panted angrily and sat up fully.

"It's a medical test that will tell us if you have any sexually transmitted diseases or any issues with cervical cancer. It's just a precaution to make sure that you are healthy. We will also perform a routine physical when we are done," the doctor explained. "Lay back and try to relax. I promise it will not hurt."

Liberty reluctantly lay on her back as her legs were hoisted into the stirrups at the end of the bed. She cringed as they performed the procedure feeling more violated than she had in a long time, but as promised there was no pain. Samad entered the room while her legs were spread wide open and she turned her head in shame. She didn't even know him and he was standing at the foot of the bed, peering at her insides as if he was entitled to.

"How does everything look?" he asked the doctor.

"Looks good. Very healthy considering," the doctor replied discreetly. "I'll have to test her cultures to verify, but this one is in good shape."

The instruments and fingers were removed from Liberty's womanhood, and she quickly snapped her legs shut as she watched Samad walk to the head of the bed.

He stroked her hair gently but she jerked her neck to the side, clearly upset.

"You're displeased with me?" he asked.

"You could have let me wake up first before you had them pry my legs open," she snapped.

"I could have, but I did not," he answered simply.

"I don't have AIDS or no bullshit like that," she said, slightly insulted. "If you even thought so why would you pay so much for me?"

"I did not get where I am today by making assumptions, Liberty. The only thing I know to be fact is what I witness with my own eyes and ears. You are addicted to heroin, am I right?" he asked. Liberty lowered her eyes and didn't respond. "And you have slept with a lot of men for money?" Samad continued, asking probing questions that pointed out just how seedy Liberty's life before him had been. Still she didn't answer, but her silence was all Samad needed to know that he was speaking the truth.

"I am just taking the proper precautions, Liberty. Please understand," he stated. Seeing that she was upset, Samad grabbed her hand. "Come on. I have a surprise for you. A new wardrobe and some expensive jewelry always make a woman feel better."

Liberty got out of the bed and followed Samad to the walk-in closet. He went over to the wall where a 42-inch LCD monitor sat. A number pad was displayed on the screen, and Liberty watched as he punched in a four-digit code. One of the walls in the closet slid to the right, opening up a hidden room that was illuminated in blue light. Liberty gasped as she looked at the showcases of jewelry that sparkled inside. Beautiful stones of rubies, emeralds, diamonds, and onyx, lay inside. Her hands shook as she walked around the room, her fingers lightly touching the glass cases that held the expensive pieces.

"Is this all yours?" she asked in amazement.

"Now it is all yours," he answered, while standing with his hands clasped behind his back.

She stopped when she got to a necklace that caught her

eye. The black diamonds set in platinum called out to her. "It's so pretty," she said.

Samad reached into the case and removed it before stepping up behind Liberty and putting it around her neck.

"I can give you the world beautiful," Samad whispered in her ear. "All it takes is your cooperation and obedience."

The things he whispered in her ear were so enticing that she found herself spreading her legs as he reached his hand between them and began rubbing her clit. There was nothing attractive about Samad, but his lifestyle was gorgeous and the authority that he held when dealing with her made her wet. She loved his take-charge attitude and as he dipped his fingers in her love box she moved with his rhythm, fucking his hand and growing hotter by the second. The mirrors that surrounded the room reflected their heated sex session as Samad bent her over the glass showcase and entered her from behind. She had never had raw sex before. She always made her clients strap up and when he entered her without protection she tensed slightly.

"Relax," he said. "I want to pump you full of babies. You are mine now."

Liberty closed her eyes remembering that Samad had purchased her for the long term. *He's right. I am his. He wouldn't have paid so much money for me if he didn't want to keep me around,* she thought. She threw her hips back onto his shaft as he stroked her from behind. His uncircumcised penis felt strange and his extra skin felt out of place as it rubbed against the lips of her vagina but she pushed all of that to the back of her mind as she put on a performance.

She went to work, going through the motions, but deep inside she felt cheap. Not even the half-million dollar price tag on her head helped to increase her self-worth. She went through the motions until she was sure that Samad was satisfied.

"Go get cleaned up and then meet me in the garment room. I have a completely new wardrobe for you," Samad said. "Nothing but the world's best fabrics is good enough to grace this skin."

She did as she was told and as she washed her body she realized why all of the other girls had dreamt about being chosen by Samad. He treated her well, but her heart wasn't in it. She would meet his expectations, but she couldn't help but wonder when a man would live up to hers. It had been so long since she had felt the nervous butterflies that came with new love that she had forgotten how good it felt. She knew that her life was missing something, however. Even with her newfound independence she still felt trapped . . . cheap . . . worthless. Not even Samad's abundance of wealth could buy back the pieces of her soul that she had sold over the years. She enjoyed the shower so much that she let the water run cold and then quickly exited the bathroom. She noticed a short silk kimono lying on the bed and she wrapped herself up in it before going to search for Samad. The estate was so enormous that she didn't waste time going from room to room. She hit the button on the intercom system and said, "Samad . . . where are you?"

"I'm in the garment room on the west wing. Come out

of the room and make a right . . . just keep walking until you get to the end of the corridor," he explained.

Liberty couldn't help but chuckle as she shook her head and went to find the room. Expecting Dolce, Prada, and Fendi she grew excited thinking about all of the fine threads that Samad had waiting for her. As she stepped into the room her face fell in confusion as she saw the odd looking clothing hanging off the many racks.

"What's this?" she asked.

"These are called burqas," Samad said as he removed one of the full body coverings. "I made sure the seamstress made them of the highest quality."

Liberty frowned slightly as she looked at the traditional Muslim garment. The room was full of them.

Where are the designer clothes . . . my Gucci and Louboutin? she thought as she tried to hide her shock. This was definitely not what she had expected. Samad had thrown her for a loop.

Samad pulled a head covering off the rack. "This is a hijab," he said. "Whenever you leave the house you are expected to wear the full dressing. When you are here with me you are only required to wear the hijab."

"But I'm not Muslim," she said.

Samad gave her a sharp look that caused her to stop speaking. For a brief moment his face turned cold and a dark glare came over him as he stared at her.

"You are what I say you are," he said with authority. "You belong to me, Liberty. You are mine now and no other man needs to see what is mine. I've invited you into my home and in my home you are expected to worship two things . . . Allah and me." He held one of the burqas out for her. "Put it on."

Her heart pounded furiously as anger overtook her. How dare he force his beliefs on her? She wanted to give him her ass to kiss but he held her entire livelihood in his hands.

"Can I ask you what the jewels are for? If I have to wear these they will be covered anyway," Liberty protested.

"That's the problem with women like you. You always want to be seen. So much flash . . . you require so much attention. The jewels are for you, not for the world to see. This is non-negotiable. Now let me see you in it," he insisted, this time more sternly.

Liberty took the garment and hesitantly slid out of her kimono robe before dressing in the burqa. The fabric swallowed her shape, hiding her curves and concealing her beauty. The only thing that could be seen were her eyes, which were pooled with fresh tears. She now realized what the catch was. Her life was not entirely her own to live. Her time with Samad would not be as glamorous as she had thought. She didn't see the point of having money or beauty if she could not flaunt it for others to see. The venomous look she had seen in Samad's eyes let her know that he was a snake and if provoked he was capable of spitting his venom her way.

THIRTEEN

LIBERTY TOSSED AND TURNED ON THE SILK sheets, her mind refusing to unwind. She had a hard time sleeping in her new environment. There was something about Samad's estate that made her restless. The vastness of the halls seemed to carry a constant echo, making it impossible for her to be at ease. She looked over at the empty space that Samad rarely occupied. Their night-time routine was the same. He expected sex from her, engaging her body into the wee hours of the night. When he was done he would stroke her hair until she pretended to fall asleep. When he thought she wasn't looking he snuck out of the room and went into his office until the early morning hours. It was the one room in the entire house that she had never explored, and she silently wondered what secrets Samad held inside. It was clearly off limits to her, but as much time as Samad spent locked away inside that room, her curiosity was piqued. She crept out of bed and went to his office door, putting her ear to the wood. Her prying ears picked up on Samad's conversation, and she frowned as she thought, *Who is he talking to this early?*

She listened closely, spying because while she lived under the same roof as him, she barely knew him. Although he never intentionally mistreated her, something didn't feel right when she was in his presence. It was the way he looked at her that intimidated her. He was hiding something, and she needed to know more.

"This one is working out much better than the last," she heard him say. "She is adjusting much quicker. It shouldn't be long before she gives me a son."

Her eyes widened, and she gasped knowing that he was speaking of her. A child was not in the cards for her. She would never bring one into the world with a man who didn't love her. To Samad, Liberty was a prized possession . . . a trophy . . . a human souvenir for all to admire. A baby had not been a part of her plan.

"Ahem!"

She heard the sound of someone clearing their throat and she turned around to find one of Samad's servants standing behind her with a kettle of hot tea on a serving platter.

Liberty quickly lowered her head and rushed back down the hall as the woman gave her a stern look. She hurried to the master bedroom and sighed as she closed the door, leaning against it for support. Hearing Samad express his intentions for her made her see things more clearly. Liberty had thought that Samad was insatiable in the bedroom. As often as he bedded her, she could barely keep up . . . but now she knew why he was so persistent with his lovemaking. He was trying to get her pregnant and that was something that she refused to allow. He owned her, but she refused to birth a child for him. She may have been his property, but no child of hers ever would be.

The next day Liberty awakened to breakfast in bed. She sat up and stretched her arms as Samad placed the wooden tray across her lap. He kissed her on the top of her head, and she gave him a weak smile.

"I have some associates coming over this evening to watch the big game. You feel like entertaining tonight and being my rising star?" he asked.

If Samad actually allowed Liberty to be herself, she wouldn't mind being with him, but the rules he established for his woman were too strict for her. She always felt like a scolded child when he was around. He intimidated her greatly but she nodded her head anyway knowing that she didn't have much of a choice in the matter. Samad was a wagering man and an avid gambler. He didn't have many friends . . . only business relationships, so she knew that the evening to come was important to him.

"I'll be on my best behavior," she said.

Hours later she stood at his side in her burqa as he introduced her to his guests. She hadn't known it would be a couple's event and as she admired the gorgeous attire of the other women in the room she instantly felt as if she would suffocate in her Muslim gear. She never understood how Samad expected her to be arm candy when no one besides him even knew what she looked like. She felt uncomfortable and unattractive as she watched the other women socialize with one another, while leaving her out. She didn't blame them. She would have done the same thing. Liberty couldn't respect her attire when she knew nothing about its origin. It wasn't her religion. She did not embrace it . . . Samad had forced his beliefs upon her. How did he expect her to be a trophy wife if she couldn't flaunt what she had or the things that he had given her? Liberty sat down next to Samad and listened in on the conversation. Samad grabbed the remote control and flipped on the national news.

"This man," Samad commented as he nodded his head towards the TV screen where the president was making a speech. "He is too nice. He'll never be re-elected if he continues to give out all of these handouts. He sympathizes with the peasants," Samad said as he sipped his red wine. Liberty looked around the room at Samad's associates who all seemed to agree with him. She had been given strict instructions to only speak if directly spoken to, so she kept her two cents to herself. She found it funny that these spoiled heads of society would speak about something that they knew nothing about. They came from money. They had never experienced life at the bottom . . . all they knew was the bird's eye view from the top.

"At the end of the day, he's still one of them," one of the women said. Liberty couldn't help but to shake her head and chuckle slightly. *So this is what they talk about when we are not around,* she thought in disbelief as they spoke candidly as if her skin wasn't black.

"You disagree?" one of the men asked her.

Liberty looked at him and then glanced at Samad nervously before she spoke up. "I do actually. I don't think that people should speak about things that they have not experienced. You have no idea what it is like to scrape and fight for everything that you have. The people put our president into office . . . they need him. He is their voice. He doesn't spite the little people in order to please people with opinions like yours," Liberty said in a low tone.

There was a long silence in the room until Samad's associate raised his glass at her and nodded his head. "Very well said," he complimented. "Samad, it's about time you have a lady with something to say."

Samad raised his glass and replied, "I told you she's something special."

One of the wives waved her hand in dismissal. "Nobody cares about his politics. As long as he keeps looking like that, he will have my vote forever," she said with a laugh.

Liberty laughed slightly and replied, "I'm with you."

"Oh is that how he got elected?!" Samad's associate said slyly.

Liberty's eyes went to the TV screen as she took in the president's appearance.

"He definitely has an aura about himself that is attractive," she whispered to herself. She looked up and noticed Samad watching her closely. There was something cold about his stare, and she turned away quickly as she refocused on his friends.

The dinner lasted well into the night and when the last car finally pulled off the estate Samad turned to her. "Did you enjoy yourself?" he asked.

"It was interesting," she answered. He removed the Muslim garb from her head, exposing her striking face.

"I will never give you to another, Liberty. You are the only woman I see. I need to be the only man that you see," he said. He stroked her cheek before walking away leaving her standing in the foyer, wondering what he meant.

The next morning Liberty awoke to her normal breakfast in bed. She performed the same ritual every morning. Samad ensured that her every need was met. She took a few bites of her food and then made her way inside the plush bathroom where she normally watched her judge shows while soaking in the tub. Her water had already been run and she immersed herself as she reached for the remote control that controlled every feature in the room. Dimming the lights and closing the shades with just a click of a button, she set the atmosphere for relaxation. As she hit the button that caused a flat screen to flip out of the wall, she frowned when nothing occurred. She hit the button once more and again, nothing happened.

"Did he take the TV out?" she asked aloud as she quickly washed her body before getting out. She walked back into their bedroom and opened the entertainment center only to find that television was missing too. "What the fuck?" she said in irritation.

She stalked from room to room searching for televisions until she realized that every single one had been removed from the premises.

"Samad!" she called out as she entered the living room where he was sitting calmly, sipping a cup of coffee with his feet kicked up in his leather recliner.

"Good morning," he responded.

"What's good about it?" she shot back. "Where are all of the televisions?"

"I told you I need to be the only man that you see," he responded. "You take too much interest in the men you see on that thing."

"Is this about last night?" she exclaimed. She couldn't believe that Samad was being so irrational. She had known that he was possessive but this was crossing the line. He was trying to cut her off from the world.

"I will be the only man that you see," he repeated, this time more sternly, never looking up at her as he picked up the morning newspaper.

Tears accumulated in her eyes and she felt powerless. He had a way of making her feel cheap despite the excessive amount he had spent on her. He dominated her and controlled her every action.

"Go upstairs. I'll be up in a moment. You're ovulating," he said.

Liberty's nostrils flared slightly in pure rage. She wanted to tell him to go to hell, but restrained herself knowing that she would only be making things worse. The longer she dwelled beneath his roof, the more she learned what type of man Samad really was. She turned around and retreated to their bedroom as her tears began to flow. When he joined her in the bed, her skin crawled. When he touched her, she cringed in disgust. She felt like an abused child, helpless and defenseless. She shut her eyes tightly as he began to kiss her. He was so delicate in the way that he handled her that her growing fear towards him almost seemed unwarranted. She was his obsession, and she could see the signs of his fixation with her. He was no ordinary man. His attraction to her was no longer flattering, he wanted her too much. Even the smell of him was starting to make her sick. *He wants to control me, but there is one thing that I won't ever let him control. I'll never give him the child he wants. I'm going to make sure of it,* she thought bitterly as he entered her. He wore no protection and Liberty swore to herself that it was the last time she would ever allow him inside of her without taking precautions. She just had to think of a way to do it undetected.

Liberty lay in bed moaning in pain as chills plagued her body. She felt sick to her stomach and as she inhaled deeply she closed her eyes in an attempt to relieve her discomfort. Samad walked into the room and went to her bedside.

"You've been in bed all day. Is everything okay?" he asked.

"I'm hot . . . everything's blurry. I don't feel good," she whispered as she rolled on her back in agony.

He noticed that the color had drained from her face. She

looked pale and he felt her clammy skin. A light sheen of sweat glistened on her forehead.

"You need a doctor," he concluded. "I'll send someone in to help you dress. The driver will be waiting for you out front."

He reached down and touched her stomach. "This could be the day. Maybe you are carrying precious cargo. You could be pregnant with my child," he said. He bent over her and kissed her head before walking out of the room.

As soon as he was gone, Liberty sat up in bed and kicked the covers off herself as she rushed to dress. She threw on one of her burqas, not even caring at this point what she was putting on. She just wanted to get out of the house and from underneath Samad's thumb. She was sick alright, sick of him and his rules . . . sick of his lifestyle . . . sick and tired of being controlled. She hurried and dressed then weakly walked down the stairs where Samad was waiting for her.

"I would come with you but I have an important conference call," he said. "Do you mind going alone?"

Samad wasn't the only one who had eyes . . . she had been watching him as well and had learned his routine. Liberty already knew about the conference call. In fact, it was the exact reason that she had gotten 'sick' on that day. She was counting on him not being able to tag along.

"Don't worry about me. I'll be fine. I probably have a virus or something," she said.

"You call me if it's something more serious or if there is something to celebrate," he instructed.

"Of course," she replied.

As she walked out of the house she could feel his eyes following her. They burned a hole through her back but she never turned around. Instead she got into the black Cadillac Escalade and melted into the backseat as the driver pulled out of the gates. When Liberty was out of Samad's view she turned around and sighed in relief. She felt as if she had escaped from prison. Everything in her wanted to run . . . to shake the driver and leave for good, but she had nowhere to go. No friends . . . no family . . . no plan. She was stuck, but as the city streets passed her by she enjoyed the time away from Samad, no matter how short lived.

Liberty walked into the doctor's office where she waited nervously. Samad's money was too long to keep secrets. She knew that the doctor she was about to visit was on his payroll but this was her only hope. Liberty desperately needed the doctor's help and hoped to appeal to Dr. Kapoor woman-to-woman. Her foot bounced off the ground as her nerves got the best of her and when her name was finally called Liberty stood slowly, feeling faint.

"Hello, Liberty. Samad called me. He said you aren't feeling well," Dr. Kapoor said as she washed her hands and then put on a pair of latex gloves.

"I feel okay now . . . I . . . I'm here because I need your help," Liberty stated as tears accumulated in her eyes. She began to hyperventilate as she leaned over and grabbed the examining table. She was besieged with stress, and this was too much for her to take. Abia hadn't schooled her on this part of the game. She snatched the Muslim attire off. "I can't breathe in this shit," she whispered in disgust and impatience as she tossed it on the floor in frustration. She breathed in . . . breathed out . . . inhaled . . . exhaled as if she had been deprived of oxygen. Dr. Kapoor turned around and froze when she looked at Liberty. She could see the desperation in her eyes and as she looked at the young girl she could sense Liberty's entrapment. She knew that Liberty was Samad's paid-for-hostage, and she turned a blind eye to the situation because Samad paid her royally, but as Liberty stood before her, guilt began to eat away at the doctor. She remembered the oppression that she had come from, growing up in India. Liberty's circumstance was much different but still all the same. Samad was oppressing her and when Liberty broke down in her examining room, Dr. Kapoor had to fight back her own emotions.

"I need your help . . . I know that he pays you, but you are the only person who can help me," Liberty sobbed as she fell into the doctor's arms. Uncomfortable and in an awkward position, Dr. Kapoor hugged Liberty reluctantly. She wanted to help but also did not want to lose the independence that she had earned by making connections with men like Samad. He had the power to shut down her entire practice if he ever found out that she had helped Liberty. Her conscience tugged at her heart because Liberty was so young. She had seen more than the average woman would see in her entire life. Liberty had lived through more struggles than the privileged children of America would ever be burdened with.

"What can I do?" Dr. Kapoor finally asked, deciding that as a woman she owed it to Liberty not to contribute to her downfall.

"He's trying to get me pregnant. He controls everything I do . . . I don't want to give him a baby. I never want to have a child for him. I don't love him," Liberty cried.

"If I do this and you get caught . . . you cannot tell him that I helped you with this," Dr. Kapoor stated seriously.

Surprised that the doctor was even willing to help her, Liberty nodded her head repeatedly. "I won't . . . I would never sell you out. I just need something . . . birth control . . . I'll do anything to stop him from planting his seed in me," Liberty whispered.

Dr. Kapoor sighed as she wondered how she had even become involved in this life, but she was too far in to turn back now. "Okay. I can't give you a pill. He might find them, and my name will be on them as the prescribing doctor. I can plant a small rod called Implanon into your arm. It has hormones that will prevent you from becoming pregnant for up to five years," Dr. Kapoor stated.

Liberty nodded her head eagerly and replied, "Will it hurt? Will he see it?"

"No. It doesn't hurt. It'll barely leave a mark, and he will not be able to detect it," the doctor answered.

The doctor performed the quick procedure, and when she was done Liberty felt as if a huge burden was taken off her shoulders. Relief washed over her, and she looked at the doctor in appreciation.

"Thank you so much," Liberty said. "You helped me more than you know."

"You're welcome," she replied. The doctor knew that she

had done a good thing, but she felt on edge as if she had just risked everything she had worked so hard for. "I'm glad that I could help you this time Liberty but do not come here again. I don't want to be put in this position by you a second time. I will keep this between us, but let's not make this a habit. This bridge has been crossed . . . now burn it." Liberty nodded her head and walked out of the office. She wasn't expecting the doctor to become her ally. If life had taught her anything it was that she could only depend on one person and that was herself.

Liberty soon realized that her new life was not all that it had been hyped up to be. Samad didn't know how to love . . . all he did was control. His leash on Liberty was so tight that she could not breathe. What had started out as a fairy tale had quickly transformed into a nightmare. The clothing that he made her wear ate away at her self-esteem, making her feel invisible. No one spoke to her directly; instead Samad's servants, chefs, and maids spoke to her through him. She felt like a child, stifled by a tyrannous parent. It was an extravagant existence indeed, but the loneliness she felt outweighed all of the glitz. Samad was an important man who kept his property secure, but the longer she was there the more she felt like a prisoner. The guarded estate, security cameras, and perimeter boundaries were not there to keep strangers out . . . Liberty felt as if they were set up to keep her in. She was stuck and although Samad treated her fairly, depriving her of nothing, she still felt out of place. He intimidated Liberty, and she hated the stern rule he watched over her with. He was a ruthless dictator, and she was too afraid to go against the grain for fear of what the repercussions might be. She had every material possession at her fingertips, but when it came to having money of her own she was penniless. He never put a dime in her hands, but instead sent one of his men with her if she needed to go shopping. He inspected her purchases, making sure they met his approval before she even came into his home. And just in case the thought ever crossed her mind, he took away her every opportunity to escape. Samad wasn't new to this. He realized that Liberty had been Americanized for way too long and that it would take some time for her to become accustomed to his ways. So he kept a watchful eye over her to ensure she stayed in line.

He purged her body of the drugs she had been abusing, forcing her to go cold turkey for weeks until she no longer craved them. Those had been the hardest days of her life, but once the hazy cloud of addiction was lifted from above her head it was the one thing she did appreciate Samad for. He was overbearing and gave her no independence, but his intentions were good most days. Liberty knew she had nowhere else to go. With no family, no friends, and limited resources at her immediate disposal she was stuck. So she did what she had to do, which was assimilate to Samad's lifestyle and cause no fuss to avoid confrontation. She had died on the inside a long time ago. Compared to some of her previous circumstances, life with Samad was simple and she wanted nothing more than to keep it that way. She had seen Samad's temper when it came to his dealings with different associates and she never wanted to be on the receiving end of it. She complied with his house rules and made sure that she was seen but rarely heard. When it was just she and Samad, he was more relaxed. The pressure for her to behave just right was taken away when they were alone, but whenever there were others in the room Liberty felt a thick tension from him.

He had been working increasingly hard at getting her pregnant. He disguised his motives by calling her beautiful and setting the scene for romance, but he no longer had Liberty fooled. She couldn't help but smirk at his frustration because if it was up to her she would never get pregnant by him. He was clueless to the measures she had taken to ensure that it didn't happen, and as the days moved on he grew insecure from what he assumed to be his impotence. She could sense his apprehension, and it made her days a bit easier to know that she had a little bit of control back in her own hands. He was beginning to tire of her. It was as if he only wanted her to procreate . . . and if she didn't fulfill that desire then she was worth nothing.

Samad secluded himself inside his office more and more, which sparked a curiosity in Liberty. *What is he hiding?* she thought as she watched him out of the corner of her eye as he slept beside her. Her eyes darted to the red numbers on the clock that read 4:53 A.M.

I have to see what is inside of that room.

Liberty slowly pulled the silk comforter back as she slid her body out of bed. She hoped that he did not notice her absence, and she cringed as she cautiously lifted her body weight from the mattress. She knew that she was taking a risk, but she no longer cared. She had been in that house too long without knowing what lay on the other side of that door. Moving in silence, with the stealth of a cat, she tiptoed to the bureau. She pulled open Samad's drawer and retrieved the set of keys that he kept hidden there. There wasn't much that Liberty missed, and she had discovered his amateur hiding spot shortly after moving in with Samad. She nervously snapped her head back as she heard Samad's breathing pattern change. Frozen in paranoia she prayed that he didn't awaken, and she didn't move until his snoring resumed. She hurriedly left the room and walked quickly to his office. Time wasn't on her side and her hands shook terribly as she placed the keys inside the lock. Letting herself in, she closed the door behind her and turned on the lights. She moved quickly, going over to his desk as she opened each drawer and frantically flipped through his papers. Liberty was careful to put things back as she had found them. She didn't want to leave any trace of her intrusion behind.

Things inside the office seemed normal and she grew frustrated when she couldn't find anything out of the ordinary. He doesn't keep this room locked for nothing, she told herself. *What are you hiding in here?* she asked as she stood with her hands on her hips while turning in a full circle as her eyes inspected the space. All she saw was executive furnishing fit for a businessman such as Samad. She had no reason to be suspicious but the nagging feeling in her stomach told her that something was awry.

Warning bells had been going off in her head when it came to Samad, and it was time she started listening to them. Just as she was about to give up her search, she noticed a dim light shining beneath the closet door. She rushed over to the closet and quietly opened the doors. The light was coming from the back of the large walk-in. She noticed burqas in assorted colors hanging in the closet and an eerie feeling passed over her as she made her way towards the light. Her hands began to sweat. She didn't know exactly what she was looking for or even what she expected to find, but she was afraid and the frantic beating of her heart rang in her ears.

She finally came to a glass display that sat in the back of the closet, tucked away in a corner.

"What is this?" she whispered as she looked at what appeared to be a collection of vases. But as she peered closer she noticed that each vase had a different woman's picture framed above it. Her hand shot to her mouth and her heart sank into her stomach as reality slapped her in the face. Vomit built up in the back of her throat as she shook her head back and forth. The beautifully decorated vases were not vases at all . . . they were urns. The letters R.I.P were printed on them along with a time frame. Her shaky hand reached up to retrieve an urn. Liberty already knew what was inside, but she just had to look. She didn't want to believe that the women in these pictures were dead, especially at the hands of Samad. But as she looked inside and saw the powdery dust she knew that it was true. She read the dates below each picture:

Mercedes
RIP
2007–2008

Joanna
RIP
2008–2009

Samantha
RIP
2009–2010

There were more than ten urns on display dating back a decade, and Liberty couldn't help but notice that none of the girls before her had lasted for more than a year. One way or the other all of the women had ended up dead with no one to even miss them. She knew that they all shared the same circumstance. Abia had made it clear that Samad was a valued customer of hers. He had been purchasing girls and getting away with murder for years. The shrine put a fear in her heart that she had never felt before and as she backed out of the closet she sobbed uncontrollably. Flustered and with her nerves on edge she fumbled with the keys as she locked the office. Terror filled her as she began to put a countdown on her own life. She could sense Samad's disinterest in her and she now knew where it would eventually lead. She had been with Samad for six months and knew that it wouldn't be long before he disposed of her.

I'm going to end up just like them, she thought as the faces of the beautiful young women flashed through her mind, haunting her psyche. She quickly replaced the keys and breathed a sigh of relief when she found Samad sleeping soundly. As she stood above him she knew that there was no way that she could lay beside him. I should get him before he gets me, she thought. Liberty wished that she had the soul of a killer, but she knew that it was something that she did not possess. Her heart wasn't black enough to commit murder. She had seen it before with her own eyes. She knew how much blood could come out of one human being, and it wasn't something that she wanted on her conscience.

I have to find a way out of here, she thought. *I have to leave him before he kills me.*

FOURTEEN

A'SHAI COULDN'T STOP THINKING ABOUT LIBERTY. SHE had been on his mind for months. She had grown into a woman, but she still looked exactly the same to A'shai. When he saw her, his heart felt as if it had skipped a beat. Feeling possessive over her, he was prepared to bid until his bank ran out, but Baron had stopped him. Seeing her on the platform had saddened him because after all the time that had passed, she was still stuck in the system. A'shai felt as though he had been her downfall. He was the one who had led her onto a prisoner's ship, and she was still plunging into the darkness all these years later. He had tried to take his mind off her. He hustled tirelessly in the streets, stacking his paper and going hard in the game. Getting money was the perfect distraction to keep him from pining after the childhood love from his past. It was the moments that he stood still that he saw her face . . . moments like now when he was laying in bed with his girlfriend Jenny that he wished the girl next to him was Liberty.

"What's wrong, Shai?" she asked. "You've been so distant."

A'shai pulled his arm from behind her head and replied, "I'm just tired. I'm not trying to be cold towards you. I've got some things to take care of today though so don't make any plans to hang around here," he said. He wasn't fond of the way she was slowly becoming a fixture in his life. She was trying to plant roots on him, and he wasn't interested in cultivating their relationship. His connection with her had been interrupted the moment he laid eyes on Liberty at the ball. He wanted a sincere love . . . something genuine, and Jenny couldn't provide that. Women wanted him now because he had the world in the palm of his hands. He was young, rich, and powerful, which was attractive to them . . . but Liberty had known him before all of it . . . she had loved him without any of it . . . and wouldn't see him any differently because of it. He wanted her and as he thought of her being sold and purchased like an item he felt a great pain in his chest. If Liberty was anything like the little girl she used to be, then she was an amazing woman, and A'shai needed her in his life.

Jenny, on the other hand, was high maintenance and required a lot of attention. She was used to being spoiled. She was one of the hottest chicks in Detroit, and many men wanted what A'shai had, but she was addicted to him. His power and prestige was like a magnet to her and ever since he had returned from L.A. the attraction had been less than mutual. He was Baron Montgomery's heir and that alone brought women out of the woodwork . . . women like Jenny who were opportunists who saw A'shai as their new sponsor. He saw them as pieces of ass. He wasn't into cuffing or upgrading no chick. He was about getting money, and Jenny was just something to do in the meantime. She was nice arm candy and good company on lonely nights. In fact he was quite fond of her, but he didn't see her in his future. Ever since losing Liberty as a child, he never made plans to keep a chick around because none of them could ever measure up to his childhood love. The affection that he had built up towards Liberty in such a short time was so great that when he lost her his heart broke. No girl after her had been able to repair him and since he had located her, all of his feelings for Liberty had resurfaced. They may have only been kids when their paths crossed but she had left an everlasting imprint on his life. He couldn't shake the memory of her and now that he had seen her again he was itching to check for her.

He couldn't get Liberty out of his head and ever since The Gentleman's Ball he had been counting the days until it was time for them to re-up. Baron usually sent his workers to cop at the re-up, but A'shai already had it in his mind that he would be making the trip this time. He blew through his portion of the first batch of bricks just to get back to L.A. more quickly. He wanted to find Liberty. Now that he had a clue about where she was he refused to lose her again. He felt Jenny's hands rubbing his chest and what would normally make him feel like a king merely aggravated him. He removed her hands and climbed out of the bed. "I've got an important meeting to get to. I've got to go," he said. "Where you want me to drop you?"

"I can wait here for you till you get back," she offered.

"I'm not coming back," he replied quickly.

He could see the disappointment on her face, but A'shai didn't care. He only had one woman in his line of sight, and he was too preoccupied with memories of her to think of anyone else.

A'shai sat across from Baron as they drank coffee and read the Wall Street Journal. It was a ritual and both were silent and in deep contemplation as they calculated their wins and losses in their head. Willow walked into the room with two huge breakfast plates and placed them before the men in her life.

"Thank you, baby," Baron stated without looking up.

"Thanks, ma," A'shai said. He kissed her cheek as she leaned over to greet him.

"You look like an old man, Shai. Don't let this one make you dull like him," Willow said with a striking smile. A'shai loved the way her curly, wispy hair stuck out of her dreads. Her hair wasn't even the right texture to wear the ethnic style, but somehow it fit her.

"We've been doing this since he was fourteen years old," Baron defended. "I've made quite the businessman out of him."

"So you have," she answered while shaking her head at her son and husband.

Willow kissed the tops of both of their heads and then walked out of the room.

As they sat over breakfast, A'shai said, "I think it's time I made the re-up trip to L.A."

Ever since A'shai had begun working in the streets with his father he hadn't been interested in little work. If he was going to do it he had wanted to do it large. Even as a young boy he hadn't wanted to put in the footwork. He was interested in cutting deals so his sudden interest in re-upping threw Baron off slightly.

"Since when do you like doing the grunge work?" Baron asked.

"Since we had that talk about me taking over. I started at the top of the business. If you are going to pass all of this down to me I want to make sure I know the operation in and out . . . even the grunge work," A'shai stated.

Amazed at his son's exceptional reasoning Baron nodded his head in agreement. Normally Baron wouldn't even consider sending A'shai. In his opinion it was too big of a risk. If A'shai was caught his entire future would be deaded with a prison sentence, but Baron knew that he couldn't protect him forever. A'shai was right. He did need to know every aspect of the game. "Okay," Baron conceded. "You'll fly in and out on the jet. I don't want you riding back with the work. Two of the workers can meet you there so that they can drive the semi back to the Midwest."

"I can handle it, pop," A'shai said.

"I know you can, but why risk it if you don't have to? You would never catch me riding with that much product. That's what you have soldiers for, Shai. You call the plays, and they execute them," Baron answered. "Put the call in and tell Samad to expect you next weekend."

"Why wait an entire week?" A'shai asked. He was tired of

waiting. He was trying to get to Liberty as soon as possible and another week felt like an entire year.

Baron peered curiously at his son, sensing something was up. "Well, our people out of Flint haven't run dry yet, and we're still waiting for Pontiac too. There isn't a rush. We move smart, not fast. Unless you know something I don't know?"

A'shai shook his head and replied, "I'll put the call in."

The week crept by but A'shai kept himself immersed in the streets to keep his mind from going crazy. His anxiety was high as he thought of seeing Liberty again. He didn't even know how she would react or if she would even recognize him, but this was something he had to do. He would never know if he didn't try.

A week later he was sitting alone on the private jet headed for California. He had no game plan; he was just stepping out on faith hoping to lay eyes on Liberty. He couldn't predict what the future had in store . . . he only hoped that she was included in his.

A'shai stepped off the plane and entered the black town car that waited for him on the ground.

"Greetings, Mr. Montgomery," the driver said as he held open the door for A'shai.

A'shai stepped inside and immediately checked beneath the seat for the handguns that were stored there. He removed a .9mm Ruger and popped out the magazine, checking to ensure that it was fully loaded. He quickly put it back in place and cocked it back, placing a bullet in the head. Putting it on safety he tucked it in the shoulder holster beneath his suit jacket and leaned back comfortably as the driver pulled off and headed for Samad's.

The car pulled up to the massive estate, and A'shai stepped out of the car. He tipped his driver and then walked up the stairs to Samad's front door. He rang the bell and was greeted by Samad.

"Shai . . . how was your flight?" Samad asked as they shook hands and he welcomed him inside. A'shai's eyes scanned his surroundings, searching for Liberty or any sign that she lived there.

"I wasn't expecting for you to return so quickly. Business must be good in Detroit," Samad commented.

"Business is good everywhere if the right person is running it," A'shai replied as he took a seat in Samad's great room. He sank into the expensive leather seat and placed his elbows on his knees as he leaned forward.

"Touché," Samad remarked. "I take it the order will be the same this time around . . . since that was the stipulation that allowed me to give you the product at such a discounted rate." Samad spoke freely, not worried about the repercussions of his words. He never had to worry about anyone walking into his home under false representation. If A'shai was wired up, Samad would have known as soon as he walked through the sensors on his front door. The alarms would have sounded off as if A'shai had stolen something.

"My word is good. We will never decrease our order. If the quantity does change . . . we'll be copping more and that means good money for everyone involved. I don't think you would have a problem with that," A'shai stated.

Samad laughed and said, "No problem at all. How long are you in town for?"

"Not long at all. Just here to take care of a few things then it's back to Detroit," A'shai said.

"That's a shame. I could have shown you a good time. Taken you to see some of the beauty that the West Coast has to offer," Samad said, referring to some of the finest strip clubs in the city.

A'shai smirked and shook his head. "I doubt anything could top what I've already seen out here. The ball was a good time. You shelled out a nice amount for one of those girls," A'shai said throwing out the bait to get more information. "Was she worth it?"

Samad smiled mischievously and replied, "Let's just say she's still around and I usually bore of the same pussy after only a few weeks. It's been what? Five months now? That should answer your question."

A'shai's stomach turned and he began to rub the scar on the side of his face in irritation. He was tight at the thought of Samad and Liberty's intimacy.

"Yo, where shorty at now? I don't want to be discussing business while prying ears are around," A'shai said, trying to get Samad to reveal Liberty's whereabouts.

"She's out with my driver, running errands. I know that you and your father value your privacy so I sent her away for a few hours," Samad replied.

Normally A'shai would have had it no other way, but this time it worked to his disadvantage.

"I like to know my associates. I hope to have a lasting

friendship with you and your father. You should consider extending your trip by a couple days. We could discuss some big business. I see the future. I see past your father's reign," Samad said. He knew that he was on the border of being disrespectful, but he had to test the line. He had seen a spark in A'shai during their initial meeting and knew that there was no reason to deal with Baron on the long term. Samad could put A'shai over his own operation, which would cut him in on some of that Midwest profit.

A'shai wanted to slap the taste out of Samad's mouth. A'shai peeped the subtle disrespect that Samad threw at him. He was trying to divide and conquer, A'shai was no fool, he knew that Samad was an opportunist who wanted a piece of the pie. A'shai wasn't about to let Samad eat off his plate. There was nothing that Samad could offer A'shai that would make him turn on Baron. A'shai was itching to speak up and put Samad in his place, but he knew that entertaining the thought would buy him more time to wait for Liberty. Even though he would never cut Baron out, he leaned forward as if he were interested and replied, "We should talk. Maybe I will extend my trip by a day or two."

Samad nodded and smiled as if he had just baited a prize winning catch. "Good. Let's have a drink."

Not fully trusting Samad, A'shai let the glass of fine brandy sit in front of him untouched as Samad fully indulged in his own. Everything that Samad was proposing went in one ear and out of the other as A'shai impatiently waited for Liberty to arrive back home. She was whom he had come for . . . everything else that Samad was speaking about was irrelevant, and he was beginning to rub A'shai the wrong way. All money wasn't good money in A'shai's eyes and Samad as a connect might not have been the best idea.

When A'shai heard the front door open his heart nearly stopped.

"Samad?" Liberty called out in search for him. Her voice was unfamiliar and as A'shai awaited her appearance he sucked in air, forgetting to let it back out as his chest swelled anxiously.

"I'm in the sitting room," Samad called out. He took a sip of his brandy and turned towards A'shai. "Let me show you what $500,000 buys you," Samad bragged.

When Liberty walked into the room she thought her eyes were playing tricks on her. He couldn't see her through the fabric of the burqa, but she saw him clearly. The man before her looked like an older version of A'shai. His presence took her off guard. She had no clue that Samad was affiliated with her childhood friend. It had been so long that Liberty figured it to be too much of a coincidence. This can't be him, she thought as she looked at Samad's business associate, examining him from head to toe. Her hands shook as Samad embraced her, groping her and kissing her sloppily. She put her head down in embarrassment and put her hand on his chest to push him away slightly. "You've been drinking," she whispered, thinking of how hypocritical he was. He indulged in whatever sin he wanted too, but he made her cover herself from head-to-toe because it was the traditional Muslim way. He disgusted her because she knew that Samad was no more Muslim than she was . . . he just embraced a controlling nature.

Samad took her face in his grip, squeezing her chin between his thumb and four fingers. Liberty closed her eyes as he pinched her tightly. She grimaced but didn't dare move as he looked down at her.

Anger filled A'shai as he watched. "We gon' finish discussing this business or what?" A'shai asked in an attempt to interrupt Samad.

Samad loosened his grip and turned his attention back to A'shai. "She's obedient . . . you have to make them obedient so they don't stray," Samad said, speaking as if Liberty was his pet instead of his woman. A'shai didn't answer and Liberty looked at him briefly before diverting her eyes away. She was enthralled by his presence. He was dark and handsome . . . strong and confident. For the first time Liberty was grateful to be concealed beneath all of the fabric because it helped to hide her smile. Everything in her wanted to call out to him. His name was begging to fall off her lips, but she contained herself. Her heart fluttered nervously and she kept telling herself that this wasn't real. *This is not Shai sitting here in front of me. It can't be . . . can it?* Her suspicions were confirmed when Samad spoke his name. "A'shai, you need to get you a bitch like that," Samad said.

Liberty's breath caught in her throat as tears filled her eyes. It's him, she thought as she looked him in the eyes. He met her gaze and stared intently at her, unable to turn away.

"Excuse me. I can't be rude to the lady of the house. I'm A'shai Montgomery," he introduced as he stood and held out his hand to her. Liberty wanted to grab his hand and never let it go. She reached out her hand and as soon as her fingertips touched his palm, her adrenaline sped up . . . she could feel the heat rising from his grasp as he shook her hand.

"I'm Liberty," she replied as she continued to look in his eyes. She saw the glimmer of recognition in him, and her heart swelled as tears fell behind her covering.

"It's very nice to meet you," he said. He held onto her hand a little longer than necessary then finally let her go before Samad noticed anything out of the ordinary. Over the years they had been so far apart but had remained a fixture in each other's mind and heart. Neither could believe this opportunity to reunite. Liberty had blocked him from her thoughts because it had hurt too much to think of their short time together. She couldn't believe that he was standing less than ten feet away from her. His dark skin and beautiful deep eyes were so striking to Liberty. She stood back proudly as she took him all in. He was 100 percent man, and it was obvious from the jewels he wore along with his Italian suit that he had made it to the side of the game that she knew nothing about. He was successful and somehow he had made a life for himself. MURDERVILLE hadn't hindered him the way that it had done Liberty and on the inside she was glad for him. At least one of them had known happiness. She smiled, knowing that no one could see her face behind her garment. Liberty wished that she could reach out to him . . . that she could tear the cloth from her face and greet him with a smile. She wanted to rush him and become tangled in his embrace, but she knew that none of those things would ever happen. Samad stood between them and there was no way that she could acknowledge A'shai in Samad's presence. Her heart was beating so fast that she felt as if she would have a heart attack. It ached as she stood frozen before him, taking him in . . . breathing the same air as him. Her face was soaked with emotion beneath the fabric and as they became lost in each other's presence she could tell that he remembered her.

A'shai felt a mixture of rage and love as he realized that Liberty was still living with the consequences that came with ever stepping foot on MURDERVILLE. *She's never been free,* he thought. He could feel his chest caving in at the mere thought of what she had been through. A'shai wanted to embrace her, but he had to play his hand correctly. He couldn't react impulsively. A'shai knew that Samad was a powerful and dangerous man. A'shai would have to think out an entire plan in his head before he implemented anything. He yearned to see Liberty's face. She was so covered . . . so subdued . . . so trapped beneath all of the bullshit. They were so close to one another but could not speak without inhibitions. He could see her chest heaving frantically and her eyes pleaded with him.

Help me, they begged.

She didn't have to speak the words in order for A'shai to understand. He heard her, and he nodded his head acknowledging her request. The silence was thick and if Samad had not been under the influence he may have noticed the tension in the room.

Samad snapped his fingers at Liberty, breaking her out of her daze and she quickly regained control of her emotions as she gave her attention to Samad.

"Yes?" she answered.

"We need some privacy so that we can discuss some things. Disappear for a while," Samad stated without looking Liberty's way. Hesitantly, Liberty stepped away from the table as her weary heart sank into her stomach. It ached so badly that she could practically hear it breaking. She discreetly watched A'shai in her peripheral vision. He was so close, but at the same time seemed so far away. Disappointment filled Liberty as she retreated to her room. *I have to talk to him,* she thought as she paced back and forth. Little did she know, he was thinking the exact same thing. A'shai was just as desperate to get to her as she was to him. Samad had no clue that they even knew one another. They were connected in a way that he could never understand. Liberty's mind spun as she dreamt of being whisked away by A'shai. She didn't know where he had come from or how he had finally found her, but she would go anywhere with him. She used to trust him and something told her that she still could. Fear of Samad kept her from speaking up. Liberty was very perceptive and she could tell that A'shai was connected. He represented a larger entity than just himself. His confident stature told the story of a man with clout, but she wasn't naïve . . . she knew that not many could match Samad's reign. A'shai couldn't trump Samad and although she wished that he could, reality was that he probably didn't have enough power to save her without facing harsh repercussions himself.

A'shai waited almost an hour before he made an effort to separate from Samad. "Yo, can I use your bathroom?" A'shai asked.

Samad nodded his head and motioned towards the stairs. "At the top of the stairs take the east hall. It's the third door on your right."

A'shai stood and walked up the stairs and then followed Samad's instructions. He located the bathroom but bypassed it as he peered over his shoulder cautiously. He peeked his head inside room after room in search of Liberty until finally he saw her. She was no longer covered from head to toe but, dressed in a black silk slip and black lace bra. She sat in the middle of a plush king-sized bed crying her eyes out, her face buried in her hands.

In awe of her appearance, he paused momentarily to take her in. With no make-up and no fancy clothes she was beautiful. Natural. But A'shai could hear the pain emanating from her soul as she sat unaware of her audience.

"Liberty," he said as he stepped into the room.

She looked up stunned and then looked behind him for Samad.

"He's downstairs . . . drunk," A'shai said.

She exhaled a sigh of sadness and relief as she leapt off the bed and ran to him. A'shai embraced her tightly, wrapping his arms around her securely as she heaved tormented wails into his shoulder.

"It's okay ma . . . it's okay Liberty. I'm here now," he whispered. She gripped him desperately as her body trembled fearfully.

"He's going to kill me, Shai. I saw the urns . . . the other girls . . . he killed them," she rambled.

A'shai looked over his shoulder and then turned to her, holding her face in the palms of his hands. "Shhh . . . shhh. Nothing's going to happen to you. I'm here now. I won't let it," he assured.

"Take me with you, Shai. Please . . . get me out of here," she sobbed, clasping her hands together as if he could walk on water.

She was too frantic, and A'shai knew that they didn't have time for a lengthy conversation.

"Calm down, ma. He'll hear you. You have to give me a few days to get things in order. I have to leave but . . ."

Liberty cringed, her knees buckling slightly as she bounced up and down desperately begging him. "Shai, please noooo," she cried. "Don't leave me here. Take me with you . . . noooo. Please, Shai, please."

A'shai could see the fear in her and instantly grew hot. "Does he hit you? Has he hurt you?" he asked, slightly raising his voice as he reached for his pistol.

"No . . . but he will do a lot worse if you don't save me," she said solemnly. "If you leave here without me, you won't come back."

"I'mma always come back for you Liberty. That's my word, ma," he said. He kissed the top of her head and looked into her face as the seconds ticked by. Knowing that he couldn't remain with her for much longer without arousing suspicion he said, "I'm coming for you. I promise. When does he leave the house?" he asked urgently as he gripped her shoulders.

"He doesn't . . . he never leaves. He watches me like a hawk," she explained. She was so emotional that she could barely speak without yelling.

"Shhh . . . calm down, ma. Think. Is there ever a moment when he doesn't have you under a scope?" A'shai asked.

"He runs . . . every morning he goes for a jog," Liberty said.

"How long?" A'shai shot back.

"Half hour . . . an hour at the most," she said.

"I'mma come back for you. Just be patient. I won't leave L.A. without you," he said. He kissed her cheek and then walked out of the room.

Liberty's lips trembled so badly it appeared as though she had the shivers. When he disappeared from her sight she broke down. Her knees hit the floor, and she bent over in grief. She needed A'shai to come back for her this time . . . she needed to be rescued more than she needed the air in her lungs. He was her only way out.

A'shai sat down the block from Samad's estate and watched as Samad exited his gates in full running gear. He waited until Samad was out of sight and then instructed the driver to pull the limo onto Samad's grounds. He hopped out of the car and rang the doorbell. He was greeted by one of Samad's many service workers. The maid stood before him.

"Samad is expecting me. I'm A'shai . . . his business partner from Detroit," he announced.

"Mr. Sadat isn't here, but if you are expected you can wait for him inside," the woman replied.

A'shai followed her to the sitting room, and she motioned for him to have a seat. "He will be back shortly," she stated. "I have many chores to do, but, please, if you need anything just call me. My name is Sarah."

A'shai nodded and watched her leave the room. As soon as she was gone he slowly snuck up the stairs and headed for the bedroom that Liberty shared with Samad. He opened the door and found Liberty staring blankly out of the window. She was uncovered and in normal street clothes.

"Liberty," he said, making her aware of his presence.

As if her ears were playing tricks on her she snapped her head to the right as she looked at him in disbelief.

"You came back," she whispered as she rushed to him. She wrapped her arms around him and kissed him sensually as he hugged her, lifting her slightly from the floor.

"Get your things. Let's go," A'shai instructed.

Liberty rushed to the closet and grabbed the few pieces of clothes that she had that weren't of Muslim heritage. She threw them into a small suitcase and A'shai grabbed it from her hands. He put his hand on the small of her back and led her out of the house. They smoothly re-entered the car. "Drive," A'shai called out to the driver. Liberty's eyes widened in surprise when she noticed that the vehicle was loaded with weapons. It looked like an artillery closet with all of the different assault rifles and hand pistols.

Liberty was so afraid that she thought she would pee her pants. Being caught was not an option. The penalty would be too great if Samad knew of her insubordination.

"Relax," A'shai said, sensing her apprehension.

A'shai gripped her knee and leaned in to kiss her cheek but was interrupted by the barrage of bullets that rained down on his car.

"Shai!" Liberty screamed as she covered her ears.

"Get down!" he shouted as he pushed her to the floor of the vehicle and grabbed one of the assault rifles. The windows in the limo shattered as Samad's goons drove beside them, firing relentlessly. A'shai came up blazing as he pulled the trigger of his AK. "Drive this mu'fucka! Go!" he shouted in the midst of the all out gun battle. A'shai noticed that the car was zig zagging back and forth, making it hard for him to let off a clean shot and when he glanced at the driver he discovered why. His head was blown half way off and the car was going at full speed with no one to control it. "Hold on!" he said as he crouched over Liberty and waited for the impact as the car rammed through the showcase of a store front. Customers screamed and ran in every direction as A'shai and Liberty gathered their bearings. Slightly dazed by the impact the couple sat up as A'shai peered out of the back of the car. The goons were pulling to a stop in front of the store. "Let's go!" A'shai said as he pulled Liberty from the car. He handed her the .9mm in his waistline and they made a run for the back door figuring if they got lost in the frenzy it was hard for them to be spotted. A'shai knew that one of Samad's men would be waiting for them at the back exit so he came out shooting first. He had no time for questions and when he hit one of the goons dead in the forehead he felt no remorse. They ran back out to the busy city street and luck was on their side as A'shai raised his hand and stopped a cab.

Scratches covered them from the impact of the crash and A'shai could see the cabbie peering at them suspiciously. "There's a big tip in it for you if you mind your business, fam," A'shai stated. He looked out of the back window making sure that no one was following them before turning to check on Liberty. "You okay?" he asked.

She nodded her head as her shaky hand gripped A'shai's gun. "Let me see that, ma," he stated as he gently eased it out of her fingertips.

A'shai gave the cab driver directions to the private airstrip and when they saw the plane, both of them let out a sigh of relief. They were home free and once they were back in the city of Detroit, Liberty would be safe behind the protection of Baron's organization.

A'shai held Liberty's hand as they ran up the stairs of the jet. He went to greet his pilots and stopped when he saw the two white men slumped over the control panel with two bullet holes in the backs of their heads.

"Oh GOD, Shai . . ." she gasped as she covered her mouth. "He's going to kill me. I shouldn't have left!" She was beginning to panic, and A'shai grabbed her shoulders and looked her in the eyes.

"I'm going to get you out of here. Trust me, ma!" he stated aggressively, adrenaline pumping through his body.

She nodded her head and he disembarked the jet with her right behind him. When they got to the bottom of the steps they saw Samad's Audi A8 pull up. Liberty froze like a deer in headlights as time—for her—stood still. A'shai pointed his gun at the car as Samad emerged from the vehicle.

"A'shai, my good friend. It seems we have the same tastes in women," he commented as he got out and lit a cigar.

A'shai wasn't looking for conversation. He was fully prepared to go out blazing on Liberty's behalf and as he gave Samad the screw face he pointed his gun unwaveringly. A'shai didn't hesitate. He fired, spraying bullets everywhere and killing the bodyguards that had stepped out of the car with Samad. What Samad didn't know was that A'shai had a marksman's aim and was a killer at heart. Samad reached for his waistline, but A'shai fired a shot so close to his head that it halted Samad instantly.

Samad's hands shot into the air. "Calm down, A'shai. This . . . we can work this out."

"Put your keys on the ground," A'shai stated.

Samad did as he was told and then said, "You are going to ruin your father over one bitch?" he asked.

"Get on the ground," A'shai said.

Samad smirked and then put both knees in the dirt. "It doesn't matter where you take her. I'm going to find her . . . I'm going to find you both and when I do, you'll wish that you never saw her pretty face," Samad threatened. As A'shai walked up on Samad he wanted to put a bullet through his brain, but he thought of the backlash that he would get from Baron.

"You're going to die for some pussy, A'shai," Samad stated.

A'shai hit him forcefully with the gun, knocking him out cold and then grabbed the keys to the Audi. He opened the door for Liberty and instructed her to buckle up, then ran to his side of the car and drove away, leaving one of the West Coast's biggest drug bosses bleeding in the dirt.

A'shai and Liberty drove to the nearest bus station and caught a long ride back to Detroit. As the bus pulled away from the station Liberty began to bawl silently, putting her face in her hands to muffle her cries. A'shai reached over and wiped away her tears as he leaned into her ear.

"I love you, Liberty. Nobody is ever going to harm you again. I promise you on my life. I will die before that happens," A'shai stated.

"What did you do?!" Baron barked as he stood before A'shai. He had never raised his voice at his son before, and Willow looked on in shock but didn't interrupt. "Do you know what this has done? What you have done? All over a girl."

"She's not just some girl," A'shai responded calmly as he stood before his father.

"Do you know the danger you have put yourself in? She has to go back! You will not be affiliated with her," Baron demanded. He was so furious with A'shai that he couldn't control the tone of his voice. This was by far the stupidest thing that A'shai had ever done.

Willow tried to peer out of the windows of her home to view the young girl that had made her son act so uncharacteristically. She couldn't make out the figure in A'shai's car. It was too dark outside, and the night time concealed her identity.

"She cannot stay here!" Baron hollered. "You went into that man's home, murdered his workers, stole his woman! Did you not expect him to retaliate?! This is interfering with business, A'shai. She goes back."

"She's not going back," A'shai said maintaining his position. "I thought you would help her the way you helped me."

"No, you didn't think at all! I will not go to war over a whore," Baron charged. "She is not welcome here."

"Then I guess neither am I," A'shai stated. "She's not going back to him. She's with me now." His arrogance enraged Baron, and as A'shai walked away Willow tried to intervene.

"Baby, think about what you're doing," she reasoned.

A'shai stopped and kissed his mother on the cheek. "I have thought about it, ma. She was all I thought of since the day you brought me here. I love you," he said.

His statement floored Willow and revealed the depth of his attachment to Liberty.

A'shai turned his back on his mother and walked out as Willow called after him.

"Let him go!" Baron bellowed. "But if you walk out of those doors with that girl . . . you're cut off! You hear me, Shai?! He's the connect and your actions were disrespectful! He could have killed you!"

A'shai turned and rubbed the scar on the side of his face. "He should have . . . because now I'm gonna murk him."

FIFTEEN

A'SHAI REACHED OVER AND GRABBED LIBERTY'S HAND. His tires screeched against the stone driveway as he pulled off Baron's property. He was torn and his disloyalty plagued him as he thought of how he was turning his back on the only family he knew. But as Liberty intertwined her fingers with his, he remembered that he was the only family she knew and he could never leave her out in the cold.

"I'm going to take you somewhere safe . . . we need to lay low for a few days until I can come up with a plan. I need some time to think," A'shai said.

Liberty looked out of the window feeling truly free for the first time. She had not seen A'shai since they were kids, but being with him felt right. It was the only thing that had ever felt right in her entire life.

"Thank you," she said sincerely as she turned towards him. "You don't even know how you saved my life."

A'shai pulled her hand up to his mouth and kissed the back of it gently.

"I'm sorry for pulling you into this mess with me," Liberty whispered. "It seems like your life turned out okay . . . like maybe MURDERVILLE benefited one of us. I can tell you getting on that ship was the biggest mistake I have ever made in my life. But you . . . you were lucky. Things got better for you."

A'shai could hear the sadness in her voice as she spoke, and he couldn't help but feel guilty for the way things had ended up. He hadn't seen the type of struggle that she had and he silently wondered about the things that she had been through over the years. Liberty had gotten the short end of the stick and despite the fact that they were both kids when they were taken, A'shai felt as if everything that had happened to her was his fault.

"Don't apologize for anything. I owe you this. I didn't protect you. All of those years ago, I should have just admitted that I didn't have a plan. I was running scared just like you. Instead I led you right into hell. That's what that ship was Liberty . . . it was hell and I took you there," A'shai admitted.

"It wasn't hell until they took me away from you," Liberty replied under her breath. She didn't think that A'shai had heard her, but his ears intercepted every word. He tightened his hold on her hand as he eased his Range Rover onto the interstate.

"Get some rest, Liberty. We will be driving for a while," he said.

"Where are you taking me?" she asked.

"Up north. My family owns a winter home near Boyne Mountain. It's secluded. You'll be safe there," he responded.

Liberty closed her eyes and the peace that settled over her was so foreign that she immediately popped them back open. She had never gone to sleep with a serene mind and heart. There was always a threat lingering in her life. She was used to being preyed upon by others who wanted to hurt her. With A'shai it was different. It was as if time had stood still for them because she still felt the same love for him that she had so many years ago. In his presence she felt safe. He noticed her hesitation and put his hand on her shoulder as he rubbed the tension out of her neck. "Relax. I got you," he said. She closed her eyes and went to sleep without reservations.

The five-hour drive north gave A'shai time to clear his mind. He knew the risk that he was taking but felt that he didn't have a choice. It was his obligation to protect Liberty . . . he had promised her and he had broken that promise once before . . . he couldn't do it again. Baron had been calling his phone for hours, but he refused to answer. His father couldn't understand the connection that A'shai and Liberty shared. He didn't know their back story. All Baron saw was a girl who had been for sale. He was blinded by Liberty's lifestyle, but he had no clue what had brought her to that point. A'shai gave his father the 'fuck you' button, sending him to voicemail as he finally arrived at his destination.

He shook Liberty gently. "Wake up, we're here," he said as he reached over and unbuckled her seat belt.

She looked up at the beautiful winter log cabin that sat amongst the mountains. The 3500-square-foot home was impressive real estate and the two of them had it all to themselves. A'shai grabbed her hand and escorted her into the house.

"It's late and everything is closed right now, but there's a storm headed this way tomorrow. I'm going to have to go stock up on food and a few supplies to last us about a week," A'shai told her.

Liberty nodded her head and sat down on the couch as she put her hands in her face, overwhelmed.

"I thought I was going to die in that mansion. This feels so good . . . just being free . . . you know? I have spent so much of my life being under someone else's thumb. I've never had control of my own destiny," she said. She was crying heavily but her tears were a direct result of mixed emotions. She was mourning her past and all that she had been through but also shedding tears of joy, considering that she had made it through. "Did you ever think of me?" she asked.

"Every day," A'shai replied honestly. "I always hoped that you were okay."

She smiled, slightly flattered that he had never forgotten about her.

"You're far from the knock-kneed, bony little girl I used to know," he commented.

"You have no idea," she said as she shook her head in disgrace. "I don't even remember that little girl."

A'shai had so many questions for Liberty. He knew the expectations that were placed upon him simply by being Baron's son. Liberty was not the type of chick that he was expected to be with. She had a stigma attached to her name.

He knew that she had been with many men. He wanted to ask her how many had parted her thighs, but he knew that more than likely she had lost count. He did not want to embarrass her or make her feel badly. *I can't think about who she's been with. She was forced to live that lifestyle. She was doing what she had to in order to survive. Any nigga that came before me doesn't matter,* he thought as he convinced himself that her past was irrelevant.

A'shai had always been mesmerized by Liberty and as he sat staring at her, enthralled by the changes he saw, he realized that his feelings toward her had not changed.

He sat down beside her and she leaned back, resting her head on his chest as she exhaled deeply.

"Relax . . . you're safe now. Put all of your burdens on me. You don't have to worry anymore, ma. I'll take care of you," he stated.

A'shai had left home so quickly that he only had the money that had been in his pocket. He knew that he would need big paper in order to stay off Samad's radar. Nothing about him was afraid. He would war with any nigga that wanted to bring it to his doorstep, but with Liberty by his side he couldn't afford to move reckless. He had to align his chess pieces and think strategically before he acted—the way that Baron had taught him. He needed the money out of his safe and knew that there was only one person he could ask to bring it to him. They hadn't always seen eye-to-eye but Nico was the only person he trusted with his paper. He wasn't the smartest man A'shai had ever met, but he wasn't a broke nigga. A'shai knew that he wouldn't have to worry about his paper coming up short if Nico brought it. Once Liberty was asleep he slid from beneath her and armed the alarm system to ensure that he wasn't caught slipping. He went into the next room and picked up his cell to call Nico.

"Fam, what's good baby? Fuck type of shit you on? I know you not running away with bitches now? Not you, kid," Nico teased, letting A'shai know that he had spoken to Baron.

"It's not like that. Look I'm not calling to rap with you, fam. I need a favor," A'shai stated directly, not wanting to beat around the bush.

"Anything . . . just say the word. You need me, I'm there. I didn't like that pussy ass mu'fucka Samad anyway," Nico stated, ready to pop off.

"Nah . . . nah. This isn't your beef, family, and this isn't just some broad. We go back," A'shai stated. "Look, I need you to bring me my paper out of my safe."

"No doubt, baby. Where you at?" Nico shot back without hesitation.

"I'm in Boyne," A'shai stated.

"I'll be up there in the morning. What's the combo?" Nico asked. A'shai gave him the numbers to open his safe and with that the two ended the call. A'shai knew that Nico would come through and he felt relieved to know that some serious cash flow was headed his way. The thought of the $275K was enough to calm his spirit. A'shai removed his shirt and then sat on the floor next to the couch that Liberty slept on. He took his pistol out and clicked it off safety, placing it in his lap for easy access. As he listened to the soothing rhythm of Liberty's breathing, it relaxed him. He closed his eyes and drifted off to sleep feeling as if the void in his life had been filled simply by being in Liberty's presence once again.

A'shai was awakened by the sound of the doorbell chiming and he shot up out of his sleep, grabbing his pistol instinctively. Liberty didn't even budge, and he stood as he walked cautiously over to the front door.

"It's Nico . . . open up it's colder than a mu'fucka out here," Nico said, his voice quivering from the winter hawk.

A'shai still looked through the peephole before opening the door and lowering his weapon. The two men embraced slightly, and Nico slid A'shai a duffel bag full of cash. A'shai didn't feel the need to count it. Nico was fam and was getting major money. He had no reason to pull grimy on A'shai, so he took the duffel bag and put it in the front closet.

Nico moved further inside of the house, looking around until he spotted Liberty. Used to sleeping without clothing, she had stripped down to her bra and panties in the middle of the night, giving Nico a perfect view of her assets while she slept.

"Damn, that's shorty?" Nico commented as he admired her body, but not really getting a good look at her face. He stared a little too long, irritating A'shai.

"Watch ya' mouth, fam," A'shai spat, seriously.

"No disrespect," Nico replied. "You really ready to war over her? You know the position you putting us in?"

A'shai shook his head. "Nah . . . this is on me and only

me. I don't move sloppy. You know I wouldn't have played it like this unless it was absolutely necessary. I couldn't leave her there," A'shai said.

Nico glanced over at Liberty once more. He understood what A'shai saw in her physically. Her body was undeniable, but her track record was marred. Any man with a $100 bill could have had her. She was damaged goods, and Nico couldn't understand why A'shai was putting it all on the line for this particular woman. A'shai was usually so selective in who he kept time with. If a chick had been smashed by too many niggas she wouldn't get the time of day with him. Liberty on the other hand had sex with random men on the regular, yet he dismissed that indiscretion.

"I don't understand this, fam, but it's not for me to understand. You let me know if you need anything. It's nothing. You know how we do. There is a storm coming your way so I can't stay, but don't hesitate to call me, bro," Nico stated sincerely. Not many niggas would have taken the hard drive without receiving anything in return, and A'shai appreciated Nico's loyalty.

"You haven't talked to me," A'shai reminded as his cousin walked out of the house.

"No doubt," Nico answered.

A'shai watched Nico pull away and then went to awaken Liberty. He stood over her watching her sleep for a few minutes before getting on his knees in front of her to stroke her hair.

"Wake up for me baby girl," he whispered in her ear.

She opened her eyes but felt so weak that she closed them right back.

"Get up, ma. We've got to go to the store. You need clothes and we need food," he whispered.

"I can't, Shai. I'm so tired," she moaned. She was extremely fatigued, and she attributed it to all of her years of living the fast life. Now that she was able to slow down everything was catching up to her.

A'shai could tell that there was no rousing her so he decided to let her rest, figuring that she probably needed it after all that she had been through. "I'm going to go get what we need then, Lib. Don't open the door for anyone but me . . . nobody!"

"I won't," she mumbled.

Willow wiped the tear that fell from her eye as she looked at a picture of herself with A'shai. He was the only son she knew. From the moment he came to her aid when he was merely a boy, she had loved him. It didn't matter that their bond wasn't formed by blood . . . it took more than the act of birthing a child to be a true mother. Her heart ached for her son as she thought of the wall that his back had been pushed against. She had never questioned her husband before and normally stuck by his side, always wanting them to appear as a united front, even when she didn't agree with his ways, but this time Baron had taken things too far. He had excommunicated their son, and for that Willow would never forgive him. She was sick with worry because she knew the game. Although she rarely spoke, Willow often listened and she was well aware of the danger that A'shai had placed himself in. The fact that Baron was feeding him to the wolves further aggravated her anxious heart. Willow stared out of the second story bay window and watched as the snow fell outside. She closed her tired eyes as she felt another presence enter the room.

"I'm so mad at you right now, I can't even look at you," she said aloud, knowing that her husband was standing behind her. He wrapped his strong arms around her slim waist and buried his face in the nape of her neck. Her long fine hair was kept in dreadlocks that smelled of vanilla, and he inhaled her angelic scent.

"Shai is hard headed. That girl he's with is no good for him. He is just like me. My blood doesn't run through his veins but my mentality is cemented in his heart. You don't start a war over pussy . . ."

Willow scoffed and looked at him incredulously. "Oh? How quickly we forget," she commented sarcastically.

Baron chuckled and shook his head as his hand traveled to the jewel between her legs. "This pussy was worth it," he whispered seductively as his deep baritone caused her panties to become soaked in anticipation. She squirmed out of his reach and turned to face him.

"Besides your pussy wasn't for sale," Baron stated, his tone heavy with judgment.

"You don't know the first thing about this girl, Baron. She may be a good girl. If she came from where Shai came from she may not have had a choice in the matter. There is a difference between being a whore and being a victim," Willow reasoned.

"Either way, she's not good enough for him. You can't turn a girl like that into a housewife," Baron said. "And he's going to have to learn that the hard way."

"But Samad is dangerous Baron," Willow stated.

"So is A'shai," Baron replied confidently as he thought of the killer instincts that his son possessed. Coming from Sierra Leone, A'shai was ruthless simply because of his environment. Baron was more than positive that A'shai could hold his own. Samad would be in for a surprise if he thought that touching A'shai would be easy. He was young in years but nothing about A'shai was naïve. He was skilled with his hands and deadly with the gunplay. Not to mention he was superior by far when it came to rational reasoning. He was a thinker . . . a sharp young man who could think himself out of the stickiest of situations. "He's your son so you don't see the ruthlessness in him. He's put in enough work to know how to handle himself just fine. A'shai is stubborn. I have to love him tough. It's the only thing he can comprehend. He wants to be a man and do his own thing so I'm going to let him. Everything will be fine."

Willow sighed and whispered, "I hope so because if something happens to my baby, you and I are going to have some very serious issues."

She gave him a stern look, her mouth set in disapproval, and her eyebrows arched in displeasure. He knew that her threat was real. Baron had been the man who held the key to Willow's heart until they brought A'shai into their world. Now he was second place in her life, but Baron completely understood. A'shai was her son, and their bond was unbreakable. Baron loved how she mothered him. The last thing he intended was to tear their family apart, but there was no room for Liberty. She was a liability, one that he couldn't afford to take on.

* * *

Willow just couldn't sit still. She tossed and turned all night, her gut clenching painfully from the fear of the unknown. Her stomach was in knots and tears came to her eyes each time she thought of A'shai being outnumbered, overpowered, and outgunned. And despite what Baron told her, she could see in his eyes that the situation was bothering him more than he let on. He played tough, but she knew that he was broken up about his blow out with A'shai. She couldn't numb her heart the way that Baron could. She constantly called A'shai's phone, praying that he would answer but each time she got his voicemail. Fed up and in need of answers, she called Nico.

"What's up, Auntie Will?" He answered on the first ring.

"Where is my son?" she asked, cutting to the chase.

"I don't know. I haven't heard from him in a couple days," Nico replied.

Willow detected the lie as soon as it slipped off his tongue. "Boy, I've known you since you were running around pissing in diapers. You come out of your mouth with another lie and I'm going to knock your teeth down your throat the next time I see you. Now where is he?" she repeated.

Nico had never heard Willow so angry, but he knew that she was not one to fuck with. She may have seemed gentle in nature, but he knew better and was well aware of her ruthlessness. She was a black widow who was capable of eating someone alive if she had to. She only played the back because she had a good man who was capable of handling the front.

"He's up north at the house in Boyne," Nico stated reluctantly. "But you shouldn't drive up there for a few days. There's a snowstorm coming in, and the roads will be rough going up. If you wait I'll take you myself as soon as the weather clears. He's hiding out, playing house with that bitch. . . ."

"Watch your mouth," Willow said quickly before she hung up the phone.

She grabbed the keys to her E-550 and headed out of the door. The horrible intuition that she was experiencing was torturing her and would not allow her to wait until the storm passed. She felt that her son needed her, and her motherly instincts were seldom wrong.

Hours had passed and A'shai hadn't returned, which gave Liberty time to become familiar with her new surroundings. She made herself at home and as she nosily went from room to room, she found herself becoming slightly jealous of how easy A'shai's life had been during the years they were separated. *He has no idea how lucky he is,* she thought as she pulled out a photo album and made herself comfortable at the kitchen table. Just as she was about to flip it open she heard the front door open. Happy that A'shai had finally come back, she rushed into the living room.

"Hey, it took you long enough. Where did you . . . ?" Liberty stopped mid-sentence when she realized that it wasn't A'shai.

"You must be the girl that has stolen my son's heart away from me," Willow said as she looked Liberty up and down.

Liberty's mouth fell open to respond but she was at a loss for words.

Willow smiled slightly because she could see that Liberty was slightly intimidated to be in her presence. "You can start with your name sweetheart," she said.

"Liberty," she finally spoke. "My name is Liberty."

Willow paused for a moment as she realized that she had heard the name before. "A'shai used to talk about you all the time when he first came to live with us. You're the famous Liberty. He used to call you his wife," Willow said with a chuckle. "He's right: you are a very pretty girl."

Liberty blushed slightly. "Thank you," she replied.

"I'm Willow," his mother said.

Willow noticed the photo album in Liberty's hand, and Liberty handed it over, feeling intrusive. "I was just looking at your family."

Willow stared at Liberty, slightly taken aback by her features. "You're from Sierra Leone as well?" she asked.

Liberty nodded.

"You're a long way from home," Willow stated.

"I don't even remember where home is. It feels like I never had one," Liberty whispered to herself.

Willow's heart immediately went out to Liberty. "I cannot imagine the things that your eyes have seen."

Liberty teared up a bit, and she quickly began to wipe the tears away as she turned around in shame. "I'm sorry."

Willow smiled sympathetically as she reached out and grabbed Liberty's hand. "You have nothing to be sorry for. Come on. Let me catch you up on my son."

The two ladies sat down at the kitchen table and flipped through the large photo album as Willow told Liberty the story of A'shai's upbringing. She explained each photograph, allowing Liberty to share in A'shai's rejuvenated past.

"You gave him such a good life," Liberty commented.

"We tried to. He was and will always be our world," Willow replied.

"Mine too," Liberty answered as she looked Willow in the eye.

Willow was usually a jealous woman who liked to have the love of her son and husband to herself, but Liberty's devotion to her son was admirable. They had spent more time apart than they had together, but fate had still brought them back to one another. Willow could tell from the starry gaze in Liberty's eyes that she was genuine. *She loves him,* Willow thought. As much as she didn't want to like Liberty she couldn't help but see what A'shai had raved about when he was younger. Her spirit was so gentle, and although she was rough around the edges from years of being misused and abused, Willow could see through the stained glass to the beautiful soul that lay within Liberty.

"I didn't mean for things to get so out of hand," Liberty said. "I wasn't trying to come into Shai's life and ruin everything that he's worked so hard for. He was lucky. He got out of the system. He broke free. But me? I'm trapped. I sold my soul to the devil a long time ago. I barely remember where I came from. The only time I remember love is when I think of Shai. I think that's why he means so much to me. He's always taken my pain away."

Willow fell hard for Liberty and liked her in that very moment. The only thing that a mother could want for her son is for him to find a woman who sincerely loves him. A'shai had found that woman and although their circumstance was unconventional, Willow was a firm believer in happy endings. She was rooting for them, and she now fully understood why A'shai had chosen to remain loyal to Liberty despite Baron's wishes.

"You know the two of you being together has started a war? Samad . . ."

Liberty cringed at the mere mention of his name.

"You're afraid of him?" Willow noticed picking up on the way that Liberty's body tensed up.

"He was going to kill me. He was crazy over me . . . over anything that he thought was his. He treated me like I was a possession," Liberty said with emotion.

"No man should have that much power over you, Liberty . . . not even my son. The moment you start to feel like an object is the moment you leave out the door. You have to know your own self-worth. Coming from where you come from, I know that's easier said than done . . . but you don't belong to anyone anymore sweetheart. The past doesn't define your future. Be the woman that GOD designed you to be. Trust me, with beauty like yours HE didn't make you simply to decorate some man's arm. You're special . . . that's why Samad wanted you for himself. He saw it . . . A'shai has always seen it. Now that I've met you, I can see it. Now all you have to do is open your eyes," Willow schooled as she touched Liberty's chin and gave her a smile. "You take good care of my son. He is putting himself at risk by being with you. I know him, and he wouldn't do that for just anyone. You be good to him."

"Always," Liberty replied.

A'shai stood in the living room listening to their conversation. He had noticed his mother's car as soon as he pulled up and had rushed into the house expecting to interrupt a confrontation between the two most important women in his life. He already knew how she had found him. Nico was the only person who knew where to find him. A'shai was pleasantly surprised to find his two ladies getting to know one another. He could tell from the tone of Willow's voice that she was smitten with Liberty, and it pleased him to know that she supported him. He knew that Liberty had a checkered past and that by being with her, he was adopting her problems with Samad but it was all worth it to him. He would lay any man down in order to protect her. He had no problem rocking a nigga to sleep, and if Samad wanted to go night night A'shai would gladly oblige him. As he stood in the doorway he thought that he was looking at the two most beautiful women in the world. He cleared his throat to announce his presence and interrupted their bonding moment.

They turned around, and Willow stood to her feet to embrace him. "I'm glad you're okay, Shai. I was worried about you. Things are going to get very bad," Willow stated.

"I can handle any beef that comes my way. You don't have to lose no sleep, ma," he stated surely as he kissed her cheek. "What you doing driving all this way? It's bad out there. I know your little Benz was sliding all over the road."

"It was hell getting up here but a woman does what she has to do to protect her family. You didn't answer my calls. I needed to come and see with my own eyes that you were okay. Samad isn't to be underestimated, A'shai," Willow warned as she took his face between her hands and kissed his forehead.

He nodded his head, choosing not to respond with words. *That bitch ass nigga got mu'fuckas thinking he don't bleed,* he thought as he clenched his jaw.

"You're not superman, boy. You may be a grown man, but you'll always be my baby boy. You took his woman. That's a grudge that doesn't die. Just promise me you will be careful," she said.

"I promise, ma. You don't have to worry about Samad," he assured. Willow hugged him, and A'shai held her tightly as he winked his eye at Liberty, who was still seated at the table. "I love you," he mouthed.

She smiled and blew him an air kiss.

"I'm going to get out of here. I know your father is wondering where I am," Willow stated. "I just couldn't resist driving up here to check on you."

"You can't drive back home tonight. Your car won't make it down the block in that snow," A'shai argued. "Call pop and tell him you'll be home tomorrow."

Willow shook her head and replied, "No, I need to get back. You have really ruffled your father's feathers. I need to be there for him right now. Maybe I can convince him to give the two of you a chance. I know once he meets Liberty he would approve."

A'shai went into his pocket to retrieve his car keys. "You can take my car. It'll get you through the snow better," A'shai said.

"Walk an old woman out?" Willow asked.

"If there was an old woman in the room I surely would," he replied smoothly, flattering Willow. She was in her late 40s and far from being an old head. She still had it and they both knew it, but it felt good to hear her son say it. Liberty stood to hug Willow.

"Thank you for accepting me," Liberty whispered in her ear.

Willow hugged her tightly and Liberty could feel the sincerity radiating from the kind woman.

"I'll see you soon. You remember what I said, beautiful girl," Willow complimented.

Liberty went to the window as A'shai walked his mother to the car. He opened her door for her and said, "Tell pops I'm sorry. This is something that I have to do."

"I know Shai and now that I've met her, I understand why. I believe in love and that girl in that house is your soul mate, Shai. She looks at you the way that I look at Baron. She's good for you. She softens you. You be a good man to her, and you both stay safe. If you need anything just call my cell phone. I will never turn my back on you, Shai. You have made my life so much better over the years. I know you have a pretty young thing in your life now, but don't you forget about your old lady," Willow said with misty eyes. She shivered slightly as her tears hit the cold wind, and she pulled the mink shawl she wore tighter around her neck.

"Never," A'shai said as he kissed her cheek and pulled her coat tighter around her. "Get out of this cold weather, ma. Call me when you make it home just to let me know you made it. I'll answer."

He hit the top of the hood once she was inside and turned to walk away. As he stepped onto the porch he heard her blow her horn. He turned and saw her smiling face as she gave him a wave. He waved back and then remembered that the duffel bag full of money was in his backseat. He held up one finger to signal for her to wait and just as he took a step toward the car, he watched her turn over the ignition . . .

BOOM!

A'shai was thrown to the ground as his car exploded before his very eyes, sending burning $100 bills flying into the sky along with a cloud of black smoke. "Nooo!!!!" he shouted as he scrambled to get to his feet, crawling and slipping through the snow covered ground towards the blaze. Liberty ran from the house and grabbed A'shai, but he threw her off him as he went to rescue Willow.

"Noo!" he cried as he bent over and punched at the snow as the fiery steel burned slowly in front of him, crackling sinisterly as if it were taunting A'shai. He knew that Willow was dead. There was no way she could have survived. He knew that this was the work of Samad and that the bomb had been intended for him. He stood and stormed over to Liberty. He gripped her by her arm and pulled her into the house.

"Oww, Shai, you're hurting me," she cried as her tears mixed with the snot that ran from her nose. She was frantic and felt extremely guilty because she knew that Willow had just died because of her.

"What's his number?" A'shai asked as he picked up the house phone. "Dial it!"

Liberty dialed Samad's digits and as soon as A'shai heard Samad's voice he spazzed.

"I'mma dead you, you bitch ass nigga. You don't know how I get down, but I'mma teach you, homeboy. On my dead mother, I'm going to make you wish you never crossed me," A'shai shouted before hanging up the phone. He picked up the entire base and ripped it out of the wall as he tossed it across the room. A'shai didn't normally lose his cool, but this was a blow that was so unexpected he reacted without thinking. His legs gave up on him, and A'shai collapsed onto the couch as he buried his head in his hands while sobbing.

Liberty knelt before him and pulled him into her arms as she stroked his head soothingly.

"I'm so sorry A'shai," Liberty whispered. She was the sole reason his world was being turned inside out. He was too good of a man to ever admit it, but they both knew it was an unspoken truth. "I'm sorry."

SIXTEEN

"I WANT THE MUTHAFUCKA'S HEAD ON A fucking platter by nightfall! I'm burying my WIFE today! If he isn't in the dirt before this day ends, I'mma make the fucking streets bleed!" Baron shouted to his henchmen as he stood in his conference room. It had been years since he had warred with a nigga. He had gained too much respect in the streets for any of the young gunners to ever test him, but Samad had no reservations. He had brought conflict to Baron's homefront and had taken the one person in his life that had been irreplaceable. "Get the fuck out," he whispered as he stood at the head of the rectangular table and placed both hands on the surface. He hung his head solemnly as his men left him alone. The range of emotions that filled his chest made it hard for him to breathe, and he loosened his neck tie to open his airways. It had been exactly one week since he had gotten the worst news of his life, and he had yet to shed a tear. He was too full of rage to allow his sadness to set in. He had the rest of his life to mourn; right now he just wanted vengeance. A knock at the door caused him to look up as he watched Nico walk into the room.

Nico didn't say a word. He was too full of guilt. He was the one who had put the call into Samad, giving him A'shai's whereabouts. Nico had always been jealous of A'shai. Ever since Baron and Willow had brought A'shai home, he had stolen Nico's shine. Nico was tired of being behind A'shai. He wasn't family . . . the same blood didn't course through their veins. When Nico saw an opportunity to get rid of A'shai, he took it. He had no idea that his beloved aunt would get caught up in the cross hairs. *I tried to stop her from going. If she would have just waited like I told her to none of this would have happened. A'shai's bitch ass would be a distant memory.*

"You heard from Shai?" Nico asked.

Baron shook his head, not wanting to speak about his son at the moment. Although he knew that A'shai wasn't directly to blame for Willow's death, he wasn't innocent either. *I can't believe I'm putting her to rest today. She is the love of my life. What am I going to do without you?* Baron thought. He cleared his throat as Nico put a firm hand on his shoulder and said, "We have to get going, Unc."

Baron squared his shoulders, composed himself, and fixed his tie before walking out of the room. Even at his weakest state, he still radiated strength. His long stride was unflinching. The average eye could not sense the turmoil he was going through but those who knew him best could see that the light inside of him had been snuffed out. Willow had been his reason for everything. Without her, he was nothing. He would live out the rest of his days reliving their times together and seeking revenge. Killing Samad would not be enough because it wasn't a fair trade. Willow's life was ten times more valuable than Baron's enemy so an eye for an eye wouldn't do. Baron wanted to annihilate Samad's entire existence and wipe him completely off the map. Baron walked into his foyer and shook hands with one of his workers. The man was dressed exactly like Baron and was the same skin color as his boss. Baron handed him a nice-sized wad of hundred dollar bills and nodded at him as the man was escorted out of his home with a bodyguard who was holding an umbrella up to conceal his face. At first glance the man looked just like Baron. He was a decoy for prying eyes just in case Samad had people watching him. Baron waited until the decoy had pulled away in the limo before he and Nico went to the five-car garage and entered his bulletproof black Infiniti truck. Nico pulled open the rear door for Baron and then got into the driver's seat to escort his uncle to the funeral.

Bitter resentment filled Baron as he stepped out of the car. He touched his hip to make sure his pistol was in place and then discreetly scanned his surroundings. It was a private ceremony so any unfamiliar face would be considered an enemy, but all Baron saw were loved ones around him. As he ascended the church steps he noticed that his hired guns were in place and ready. Anyone who wanted to show up unexpectedly wouldn't get past the front door. He had made sure to send Willow home in style. No expense had been spared. White calla lilies had been her favorite flower and they filled the church's altar, surrounding her casket like an angel's halo. The 14-karat-gold casket sparkled up front. He couldn't believe that he was about to say his goodbyes. Inside he was broken, but outwardly he remained intact. There was nothing that Willow loved more about him than his strength and he knew that she would want him to stand tall in her final moments on earth. As he stood over the closed casket he bowed his head in silent mourning. The fire had completely singed her skin, not allowing for an open casket ceremony. He would never see her face again, but it didn't matter. It was etched in his memory like the name of lovers drawn in wet cement. Nico tugged at his suit jacket to get his attention and Baron turned on his heels sharply in discontent as he stared a hole through him.

"Don't disrespect my final moments with my wife!" he barked.

Nico took two steps back, his eyes wide as he stammered, "It's . . . I was just . . ."

"Whatever it is, it can wait," Baron said lowering his voice.

"It's Shai. He's here," Nico stated.

Baron walked briskly towards the church's entrance. Part of him needed to lay eyes on his son. They were all each other had now that Willow was gone, but the obstinate side of him wanted to place blame on A'shai's shoulders for what had happened. At that moment Baron wanted nothing more than to embrace his boy and share his grief with the only other man who understood. A'shai knew what the world had lost. They were the only two who truly felt the blow.

A'shai got out of Willow's car wearing a double breasted Versace suit, all black with a slim tie. For the past week, he and Liberty had hidden out in a downtown hotel. He had gone over the last moments of his mother's life repeatedly, wishing that he had never volunteered his car to her. Her death weighed heavily on him and although he knew that he needed to skip town, he would never forgive himself if he left without paying his final respects. As he walked up the church stairs none of Baron's soldiers would look him in the face. He went to enter the building and was stopped by one of Baron's block lieutenants.

A'shai looked down at the hand that was touching him and frowned up as he slapped the hand from his chest. "You must want to lose that hand my man," A'shai stated calmly as he gripped the man's wrist at his pressure point, causing him pain.

"Yo, you can't come in here Shai," another one of Baron's workers stated.

"Fuck you mean I can't come in here?!" he questioned. "That's my mother!"

"We're just following orders," the worker said solemnly, not really wanting to be involved in the family conflict. He gently nudged A'shai, trying to get him to leave, which only further enraged A'shai.

A'shai reached inside his waistline and gripped the handle of his pistol, ready to pop off. He didn't remove it, but was just waiting for things to get out of control.

"You can move aside or I can lay you down in this mu'fucka. Either way I'm coming inside that church," A'shai stated.

At that moment, Baron appeared.

"I've got it from here," Baron said as he stepped directly in the entrance to the church. As father and son stood face-to-face they both could sense the extreme hurt in the other. Baron wanted to reach out and embrace A'shai but instead he cleared his throat. "You can't be here. You're not welcome, A'shai. I told you what would happen over that girl . . . now look where we are . . . what it's led to," Baron stated.

"What you mean I can't be here, Baron?" A'shai said, calling his father by his name for the first time in years. "That's my mother in there, fam! You think I wanted this fa' her?"

A'shai had so many emotions pulsing through him but the one he recognized the most was rage. He needed his father right now, but Baron was showing him shade . . . shunning him and A'shai took it personally.

Whatever small piece of his heart that Baron had left was being broken as he denied A'shai entry. It was taking everything in him to stay firm in his decision. Pig-headed, Baron refused to move aside as he shook his head and repeated, "You can't be here. You have to leave, son." Baron turned to one of his goons. "See him to his car."

A'shai's nostrils flared as he backed away from the church while nodding his head. By denying him access to Willow's funeral, Baron had just ripped his heart from his chest. A'shai could barely breathe as he grit his teeth while retreating. He pointed at Baron, stabbing his finger through the air. "Fuck you, Baron. We're through. You hear me. You tell my mother I love her . . . but you . . . you no longer have a son," he said vehemently as he turned to walk away. No one moved to escort A'shai to his car. They knew firsthand how A'shai's temper could flare, and no one wanted to see him. This was between Baron and A'shai; no one else dared to intervene. Baron noticed how his men respected A'shai. They were all fearful of him and secretly Baron was proud but he refused to speak up. His relationship with A'shai had run its course. A'shai was a grown man now, and it was time for them to part. Baron's eyes misted slightly as he watched A'shai get in his car and drive away. He felt in his bones that this would be the last time he would ever see his son and it hurt. Baron gathered himself quickly not wanting to wear his heart on his sleeve. He refocused on the task at hand and prepared himself to bury the greatest woman he had ever had the pleasure to meet.

Baron paced the same back and forth pattern in his home office for two hours as he awaited the phone call. He had just watched helplessly as men put dirt over his wife's casket, and he was full of wrath. He wasted no time when it came to putting in work. He already had shooters on the ground in L.A. watching Samad's home. They had been tracking his every step all week and had learned his routine. Baron was determined to have Samad in a six-foot hole before 12 A.M. Baron's home was full of guests, but he was in no mood to socialize. Everyone was respectful and gave him their condolences, but there was only one thing on Baron's mind.

Murder

Baron couldn't focus on anything but executing Samad. He only wished that he was there to pull the trigger himself. He went to the mini-bar and poured himself a glass of his finest cognac before taking a seat behind the desk. He took a large gulp and closed his eyes as it burned his throat on the way down. It was funny how quickly life had changed. Things had gone awry in the blink of an eye. He pulled off his neck tie and threw it across the room as he turned to look out of the large floor-to-ceiling windows. His estate was immaculate and vast, but now that he had no one to share it with all he felt was lonely. It was a painful reminder of better times. *I'm getting too old for this,* he thought, knowing that it was time for him to bow out gracefully. After handling Samad he was through. Without A'shai he had no one to will his empire to. All that he had built over the years would be divided and nitpicked by the vultures until there was nothing left. Years of living the champagne life had come to an ugly end. He sipped his drink and watched his phone, waiting impatiently, torturously, for his peoples to call. He was tempted to check in on them but there was no need. They were well-trained and obedient young killers. They would get the job done. All he had to do was let them play their positions and within the hour balance would be restored to the winning team. His doorbell rang, and he winced because he could feel the headache coming on. There were too many people around him. He wanted to clear the house but he felt that they deserved to be there. They were celebrating Willow's life. How could he turn them away? He arose from his seat, taking the cordless phone with him as he went to answer the front door.

"We have a flower delivery for Baron Montgomery," a young white boy said, while holding a black vase with white lilies spilling out of it. Baron stepped to the side and held out his arm to welcome the boy inside. "I have twenty more arrangements in the van."

Baron couldn't believe the amount of love that Willow was receiving. The church had been full of flowers and now his home was being invaded with them as well. It showed how much people really would miss his wife. She was a good woman, and the entire hood loved her. They were really showing out for her, and it didn't go unnoticed by Baron. The people loved him and were sorry for his loss. Once all of the arrangements were inside, Baron tipped the delivery boy and then closed the door.

The ringing of the phone in his hand made Baron pause mid-step as he hurried back to his office to find some solace.

"Is it taken care of?" he asked without saying hello.

"If you're asking if your little hit squad murdered me, the answer is no."

Baron clenched his jaw when he heard Samad's voice.

"Now you've got three more funerals to pay for," Samad said. "I hope you enjoy the flowers. It's just a little token from me to send my most genuine condolences," he stated. "Say hello to my friends when they get there."

Before Baron could respond the line went dead and the sound of yelling alarmed him, causing his attention to shift to the sounds coming from his living room.

"Detroit Police Department! Everyone on the ground now!"

Baron immediately speed dialed his attorney and said, "Meet me downtown as soon as possible." He hung up just as the task force came into his office with their guns drawn.

"What the fuck is this? You disrespectful mu'fuckas come into my home on the day I bury my wife?" he asked the lead detective. Baron wondered why he hadn't been tipped off about this little intrusion. As many cops as he had on his payroll, there was no way he should have been taken by surprise. "I'm going to have your job for this," he said calmly.

"Oh yeah, Mr. Mafioso?" the white detective shot back sarcastically. "You are gonna get me fired? You're connected, huh?"

"Like the interstate," Baron spat.

"Well, we have a warrant to search the premises." The detective shoved the papers directly in Baron's face, but Baron was not intimidated. He had nothing to hide. He never kept any work inside his home. That was the number one rule. Never shit where you eat. A smug smile crossed his exhausted face as he stood toe-to-toe with the detective.

"Be my guest," Baron said. He was so confident that the police wouldn't find anything that it wasn't even a worry in the back of his mind. His home was clean, and he felt slighted as he thought of how Detroit's finest were intruding and disrespecting Willow's memory.

Baron followed the police into his family room and watched as they went straight for the flower arrangements that had just been delivered. They cracked the black vases and Baron's heart collapsed when he saw them begin to pull kilos of cocaine from the inside. There were twenty vases in all and each one contained a separate key, wrapped in clear plastic. Samad had set him up and as Baron held up his hands in surrender, the detective forced him to his knees.

In disbelief Baron shook his head as the entire thing seemed to play out before him in slow motion. His guests looked at him with sympathy and shock as they watched him be handcuffed and read his rights. *Fuck. How did I let him catch me like this?* Baron asked himself. He knew that his head hadn't been in the right place. Willow's murder had him distracted and after all of his years of flawless hustling, this is what it had come to. Because he was caught red-handed with twenty bricks inside his home, he was done. They were about to cook him and Baron couldn't do anything but chuckle slightly to himself at the irony of it all. Samad had set him up good, and Baron knew that with the raw uncut cocaine Samad had access to that he was in for the fight of his life. Years of flying under the radar had just gone straight out the window. Baron felt the cut of the handcuffs as they dug into his wrists and he realized that he could be going away for a very long time. As he took the walk of shame to the police car, he held his head high. He looked at each one of his workers in the eye as he was led out. He had never bowed down to anyone and had enjoyed the fruits of his street labor. He had lived high off the fast life and had risked it all for the sake of the American dream. Now because of Samad he had taken the plunge from grace, but he would take his fall like a man.

Just as he had ridden the wave to the top, he would ride it to the bottom because it was all a part of the game. He had hoped to be one of the lucky ones and come out unscathed, but the loss of a loved one had been the tragic event that started the downward cycle. Now he was facing the loss of his freedom, an inevitable opponent that every kingpin must contend with.

SEVENTEEN

AS SOON AS A'SHAI WALKED INTO THE hotel room, Liberty could read the defeat all over his face.

"Are you okay?" Liberty asked as she sat up in the bed and got on her knees. A'shai sighed, not in the mood to talk about what happened. Seeing her waiting anxiously for him was like a band-aid to his ego. He was bleeding on the inside, and Liberty was what he needed to forget about the day's events. Her long hair cascaded over one shoulder as the white plush hotel robe hung off the other shoulder. Her golden skin glistened.

A'shai had entertained his share of women, but none of them could hold a candle to Liberty. He remembered how he had been enthralled by her when his father had kidnapped her from her village. At first sight Liberty had effortlessly stolen his heart.

"Come here," she summoned as she beckoned him with her finger. Since reuniting, A'shai hadn't touched Liberty . . . not in the way that he wanted to. There was no doubt in his mind that he was attracted to her. Liberty's body curved like a coke bottle . . . hips wide . . . waist narrow . . . and face as pretty as an evening sunset; she had to be the 8th wonder of the world. He went to her, sitting on the edge of the bed as he bent over solemnly. She crawled over to him and kissed the back of his neck, awakening his loins as her lips tickled his skin. His dick jumped and began to grow in his pants, but he removed her hands as he fought off the temptation. A'shai had two reasons for not wanting to sleep with Liberty. He didn't want to take advantage of her the way that every other man in her life had done. He wished that his other reason was as noble, but it was purely selfish. He was uncomfortable with her promiscuous past. Just thinking of another nigga inside of her had him heated. He wasn't mad at Liberty directly, but the situation in general was just fucked up. Too many men knew what she felt like . . . what she smelled like . . . what she tasted like and although A'shai was not superficial he couldn't deny the fact that it bothered him.

"Why don't you want me?" she whispered as she leaned back. A'shai turned towards her and saw the sting of rejection in her eyes.

"I want you, ma. I want you more than I've wanted anything in this life . . . but I can't help but think . . ."

"That I was a whore? That I slept with men for money? I can't change who I am," she stated sharply as she stood up and crossed her arms.

"I'm not asking you to," A'shai replied as he looked up at her. He pulled her over to him, and she stood between his legs. "I'm a man . . . a jealous man when it comes to you."

"You don't have anything to be jealous of Shai. I've had sex with men . . . men who hurt me . . . who forced me . . . who hit me. I have never wanted to have sex with anyone in my life. I did what I had to do to stay alive. You can't fault me for that. I hated every minute of it but I learned to become a great actress," Liberty admitted as her voice cracked from emotion. "Even with you. The only reason I even threw myself at you was because I feel guilty . . . like I owe you something! I'm the reason that your mom is dead! I owe you everything for taking me away from that life but I have nothing. Shai, I have nothing to offer you! Sex is all I know. It's all I have."

Hearing Liberty's words broke A'shai in pieces. She was lost and it was up to him to help her find herself. He pulled her down on the bed as he wrapped his arms around her. All of a sudden the men she had been with didn't matter. He held her as she cried on his shoulder.

"Get it out, ma. Let it all out. Because after tonight we are both leaving everything behind us," he whispered. "It's you and me, Liberty. Fuck the world."

Liberty's body tingled and a moan escaped her lips as she spread her legs open. She thought that she was dreaming and that the sensation pulsing through her body was coming from her own fingertips until she glanced down between her thighs. All she saw was A'shai's eyes as he looked up at her while licking her clit slowly.

"What are you doing?" she asked as she tried to sit up.

"Shhh," he whispered as he put his hand in the middle of

her chest and gently laid her back, all without ever stopping the rhythm of his tongue. Liberty closed her eyes as he worked her over and although she was tense at first, the more he satisfied her, the more relaxed her legs became. It wasn't long before she was grinding into his tongue. She could hardly contain herself. The act of sex had always felt dirty to her, but with A'shai it felt right.

"Ooh stop," she moaned as she felt her clit become tender as blood caused her labia to swell. "Shai . . . Shai," she called out. Shai smiled as he felt her ankles interlock behind his head, and her body began to shudder. He maneuvered himself over her, his swollen flesh pressed against her stomach.

"Me and you," he whispered in her ear as he entered her.

"Fuck the world," she answered, repeating the motto he had taught her earlier.

"You want me to stop?" he asked as he pulled back so that he could see her face. "I want this to be your choice. I don't want you pretending with me. I would never hurt you."

Liberty hesitated as she waited for the empty feeling that always preceded sex to fill her in this moment. If any doubt did exist, she couldn't recognize it. She was blinded by the intense devotion and attraction she felt for A'shai. "I want to," she whispered, and as he entered her she gasped in fulfillment. Nothing had ever felt so good. A'shai worked her middle passionately, digging her back out as he grooved to an inaudible beat. The only sound that could be heard was their erratic breathing, and the familiar sound of skin slapping skin. There was no need for theatrics. They were both too into it to sing each other's praises. Liberty matched A'shai's intensity as she thrust her hips at him, literally throwing the pussy at him. A'shai received it gently, stroking slowly . . . deeply, as he kissed her lips and rocked in and out of her womb. Her tight walls almost inhaled his manhood, sucking him into her warm insides and tickling his loins. She fit him like a tight glove as she flexed her muscles to contract around him. She felt so good that A'shai could barely stop himself from busting too early. Liberty soaked the sheets beneath her as her eyes rolled in the back of her head. She came up on her elbows and whispered, "Lay down, Shai. Let me please you." In all her years of being a professional no man had ever worked her over this good. She just wanted to reciprocate and show A'shai how much she loved him. This moment had been years in the making. Frustration, attraction, deprivation, and adulation all contributed to this explosive moment. Even when they didn't realize they needed one another, subconsciously they had always yearned to be together.

As she mounted A'shai, he palmed her breasts, making circular motions on her perky mounds while rubbing her hard nipples. Just the sight of her naked body atop of his made his dick brick. The tip of his penis swelled as pre-cum oozed out of it. He grabbed himself and stroked gently as she lowered her head between his legs. Without any reservations she took him into her mouth and replaced his hands with her own. She moved them up and down around his shaft while making his shaft disappear and reappear. It was a lovely sight to A'shai and his toes began to curl as she adjusted the tightness of her mouth while running her tongue up and down the veins in his pole. He inhaled and reached down to pull her up. In one smooth motion he placed her on top of him. Without losing their rhythm, she rode him. Neither of them wanted the moment to end, but as Liberty began to moan A'shai could feel himself losing his cool.

"Shai," she called out in a complete euphoric state. The sound of his name falling off her lips took him over the top, and he released his seed inside of her. Liberty collapsed on top of him, her ruffled hair falling in her face. He swept it to the side so that he could see her face clearly and he noticed that her eyes looked different . . . less worried, as though he had lifted a burden off her soul.

"I love you," he said.

"I love you too," she replied. She stood to her feet while smiling mischievously.

"Where you going?" he asked.

"To take a shower," she said. "But I'm not doing it alone. I don't want to do anything without you ever again." She reached down and grabbed his hand to pull him to his feet.

A'shai followed her into the bathroom where they resumed their sex session well into the night, making up for lost time.

As daylight crept through the hotel blinds A'shai realized that he had not been to sleep. His mind was racing and he felt extreme stress, despite the beautiful night that he and Liberty had shared the night before. As he listened to her steady breathing he felt the same responsibility for her that he had felt when they had run away from home as kids. It was up to him to lead her to a better life and this time he was determined not to drop the ball. She had no clue, but his pockets were dwindling. All of his money had gone up in smoke in the car explosion and all he had left was the paper in his pocket. He eased out of the bed, moving Liberty off his chest before climbing out of bed. He went into the pocket of his suit jacket to retrieve the small knot of bills. He flipped through it quickly, but when he discovered the total he knew that he may as well have been broke: $3,000 wouldn't get them very far . . . not when they were running from a man whose resources were limitless. A'shai couldn't even purchase any decent fire power for that amount. *Fuck am I going to do?* he thought. *I've got to come up on some paper.*

His thoughts were interrupted by the sound of his cell phone ringing. He reached in his slacks and retrieved it. He recognized the name instantly. If Baron had taught him anything, it was to always have your attorney on speed-dial and as the call came up he answered it.

"Don Clarkston," A'shai stated.

"A'shai, good morning. I'm sorry to call you so early, but it is very important. It's Baron," Clarkston said. "He was arrested last night. He was arraigned this morning. He asked me to call you. I need a $50,000 retainer to render services to him, and he says that you are the only one who knows where his money is."

"Arrested?" A'shai exclaimed, stirring Liberty from her

sleep. He knew that it was uncharacteristic for Baron to be caught slipping. "How did this happen?"

"Apparently, Baron was caught with large quantities of cocaine in his home," Clarkston replied.

A'shai shook his head in disbelief. He knew his father would never bring his business home. "What's his bail?" A'shai asked, instantly reverting back to his loyal duties as Baron's son and next in command.

"Your father is considered a flight risk. Bail was denied," Clarkston said. "Time is of the essence, A'shai. The sooner you can get me that retainer the better."

A'shai hung up the phone and turned around to find Liberty staring at him.

"What's going on? What's wrong?" she asked.

"Get dressed, ma, we have to go," he stated.

A'shai pulled up to his parents' home and parked his car in the circular driveway, directly in front of the door.

"Stay here. I'll be in and out," he instructed as he kissed her cheek and rushed into the house. He went to the basement and into the cellar where Baron kept his money secure in a safe. He located the large wine rack that hid the industrial wall safe. He pulled down one bottle and pressed the button that was hidden behind it. The entire rack slid to the side, revealing Baron's hidden treasure. A'shai quickly put the combination in and rubbed his hands together as he prepared to unload the riches. He froze in disbelief when the door popped open and he witnessed the inside of the bare safe. It had been wiped out. The only thing that remained was a single handgun . . . his father's signature .38. Every dollar that had once filled the space was gone. *This can't be right . . . fuck is all the money?*

Liberty sat in the car antsy as she waited for her man to return. *Where is he? What is taking him so long?* she thought as she looked around nervously, feeling like a sitting duck. She noticed a black Acura pull up to the house, sitting curbside. Liberty tried to peer inside the windows at the driver, but the dark tint hindered her vision.

A bad vibe filled her as she whispered, "Come on, Shai, . . . hurry up." Her worried eyes were locked on the open door of Baron's home.

The sound of squealing tires caused her to focus her attention on the car, but before she could even process what was going on the black Acura rammed into the side of the Benz.

"Ahh!" Liberty screamed, terrified as she ducked down as the driver-side window burst from the impact. The car backed up and rammed into the side of A'shai's ride again. Everything was happening so fast that Liberty didn't know what to do. She climbed into the driver's seat and attempted to throw the car in drive, but before she could even put her foot on the pedal, the Acura drove into her once again. Liberty felt the metal crunch into her side as she screamed out in pure fear. She mashed the car horn, trying to get A'shai's attention without letting up.

BEEEPPP!!!

As she watched the Acura back up once more, panic

filled her. Wide-eyed, she stared at the car as its engine revved. She struggled to put the car in drive but the way that A'shai was parked she had nowhere to go. She closed her eyes and waited for the impact as the car burned rubber before her.

A'shai heard the horn sound off and he grabbed the gun out of the safe before he shot up the stairs. He raced outside, knowing that the way Liberty was laying on the horn could only mean one thing . . . she was in trouble. When he saw the Acura ram into the side of his car he chambered the first round of the .38, knowing that Baron kept it loaded, and then removed his own gun off his waist. He clicked it off safety in one swift motion and started spraying. The semi-automatic spit specks of gold fire as he aimed at the car while walking towards it. Fed up, he didn't hesitate. He had a marksman's aim and was trying to eliminate whoever was behind the wheel. He knew that Samad was gunning for him, and A'shai felt no remorse as he tried to send someone's child back to them in a box. Bullets riddled the car until finally the driver reversed all the way to the street. A'shai didn't stop shooting until the car pulled away. He ran and snatched open the driver-side door. He wrapped his arms around a shaken Liberty.

"You're okay . . . I'm here. I've got you," he assured as he kissed her repeatedly. "Are you hurt?"

"No . . . no, I'm okay," she answered, her voice shaking as she slid back into the passenger seat.

A'shai knew that Samad had his killers after them. A man

of Samad's power didn't take insolence without retaliation. A'shai had given Samad the ultimate sign of disrespect . . . he had snatched his bitch, and A'shai knew that the conflict was only just beginning. Samad was a man with limitless means. Whoever he wanted touched would be touched, and A'shai knew that the threat was real. Things would have been so much easier had he had his father backing him, but A'shai knew that this was not Baron's fight. He had his own troubles at the moment, and A'shai was too proud to admit that he needed help.

"We have to switch cars. Come on," he said. Liberty was shaking like a leaf in the wind as she climbed out and followed him back into the house. A'shai went straight to the attached garage, revealing three luxury cars. He grabbed the spare key to Baron's Lexus coupe and then pulled off.

"We have to get out of here, Shai. I know Samad. He's not going to stop, and the longer we stick around here the greater chance we have to get caught," Liberty said, her voice still trembling. He could tell that she was shaken up.

"I know, ma . . . I know. I just have to handle a few things first," he said, not wanting to tell her that he was broke. He had been depending on Baron's stash. He knew that there had been close to $1 million in that safe and after paying Baron's bail he was going to take a portion to get them safely out of town . . . but his plans had been spoiled.

"Handle what, Shai? Let's just go . . . please," she pleaded.

"We won't get very far with no money," he said.

Liberty paused and looked at him in disbelief. "What you mean no money? I thought . . ."

"Every dollar I had was in a duffel bag in the back of my whip when it blew up, and my pop's safe was empty," A'shai said in frustration.

"Who else had the combination?" Liberty asked.

A'shai paused as a light bulb went off in his head. "Nobody! The only people who can access that safe is me and my Pop's . . ." A'shai suddenly remembered that he had given Nico the combo. "Fuck!" he shouted. "Nico took that paper."

A'shai knew what he needed to do. He wanted to go to the county jail to visit Baron and inform him of what was going on but he couldn't. Samad wasn't an amateur, and A'shai knew that if he showed up to visit his father that Samad's shooter would be there waiting for him. He wasn't about to walk into a trap. A'shai had to find Nico and get that money. His life depended on it.

EIGHTEEN

PUSSY WAS THE ONE THING THAT COULD make the sharpest hustler dull and as Nico sat in the strip club making it rain on his favorite dancers, he was the epitome of stupidity. He was lax because he knew that Baron was powerless from where he was sitting, and A'shai was on the run. The way he saw it, there would be no consequences for his actions. Contributing to Willow's death had been a mistake, but hitting Baron's safe had been a lovely caper. He had no intention of sticking his uncle until the police arrested Baron. The opportunity had presented itself and Nico was too greedy to let his loyalty override the temptation to come up. He was in the clear, and because he was family he knew that Baron would never suspect him. Being an intricate part of Baron's operation, Nico wasn't new to money, but he was a virgin when it came to prestige and power. He wanted respect in the streets and as the dollar bills danced in the air around him he felt it for the first time. What he didn't realize was that the half-naked chicks in the club didn't respect him. In their eyes he was a trick. They could tell he was an easy mark because he was too flamboyant. He was eager to flaunt his cash and in many ways the ladies around him were on top of their hustles more than he would ever be. He sat back as he watched the girl on stage as she shook her derrière while he reveled in his newfound status. He had been asking for more responsibility for a long time, but Baron had dismissed him. *I'm his fucking blood nephew, and he made me second behind Shai. That's the only person he saw. Shai wasn't running the trap by himself, but he took all the credit. Well now I'm taking what's due to me,* Nico thought as he hit the shot of Patron and relaxed in the plush booth. He felt his manhood brick as he watched one the dancers put her thing down on stage. She pulled her thong to the side revealing the prettiest pussy lips he had ever seen, and she bent over, grabbing her ankles as she made her ass cheeks give a round of applause. There was nothing like a bad bitch on a pole to stroke his ego. He knew that he should be lying low and keeping his newfound wealth a secret but splurging in the club made him feel good. As Nico popped bottles of Rose in the club, he and his new crew of young gunners lived it up. He had assembled a few shooters and some new block lieutenants, forming his own squad. What Nico craved was an empire, but he was merely copying what he had seen while working underneath his uncle. The men who had worked for Baron had pledged their allegiance out of loyalty and love. The only larcenous snake that had been around Baron was Nico, everyone else was family. Nico's organization was newborn. They were wild, reckless, and out for self. They were only 'yes' men because Nico was the new money man. They respected the money . . . not the man and the thought of being loyal to anyone other than themselves was a joke. But as Nico balled out, he was blind to it all. He felt like the new king and couldn't wait to take the game by storm.

"That bitch badder than a mu'fucka," he commented as he watched the dancer work the pole as if it were a fine art. She had to have a degree in seduction because she was making Nico feel like he was the only man in the room.

Nico's eyes were low from the effects of the champagne. He was feeling good and a night cap with the beauty in front of him would set the night off. As one of the waitresses passed his booth he put a $50 bill in the air and waved it arrogantly to gain her attention.

"Can I get you something?" she asked.

"Yeah . . . her," Nico replied as his eyes never left the stage and he nodded towards the dancer shaking her assets to the new Drake beat, grinding slowly. She was mesmerizing Nico with her slim waist and round ass. Her curves were killing him, and his dick was so hard that he had to adjust his hard-on in his jeans to conceal it. "Tell her I pay nice. I want a private dance."

"New girls don't do dances, but I can hook you up," the girl stated flirtatiously as she tried to steal the other dancer's one-on-one.

"Maybe next time, ma. I want her," Nico commented.

The girl rolled her eyes and sucked her teeth as she took

the $50 tip from his hand before leaving to go deliver the message. He had a couple stacks in his pocket and had a goldmine in the trunk of his car. So if the girl was for sale then he could afford to buy her, and he was ready for a fun night of mind-blowing sex.

A'shai sat in the shadows of the strip club as he watched Nico out of the corner of his eye. He admired the stripper on the pole, wanting to appear to be just another patron. The black Armani Exchange hoodie and NY fitted cap he wore concealed his identity. He nursed a drink as he scoffed at his idiot cousin while rubbing the scar on the side of his face. *This nigga is making this shit too easy,* A'shai thought. Nico had not been hard to find. A'shai knew that Nico lived in the strip clubs and wouldn't be able to resist flashing his new paper for the hood to see. As he watched carefully he noticed the bulge on Nico's hip. He then noted the four flunkies that Nico was surrounded by. He was sure that they were all strapped. *They must'a paid the bouncer to get in here with the strap,* A'shai said to himself as he felt his own steel in the front of his hoodie. As Nico flirted with the girl, A'shai watched intensely, peering at the couple and slowly rubbing his scarred face as Nico's hands slid up the dancer's thighs. *I can't wait to clap this clown ass nigga,* he thought. Nico and the girl stood to go to a private room. There was only one way in and one way out so Nico would have nowhere to run. Once A'shai had sat back to analyze the situation, he realized that Nico had always been a snake in the grass. What Baron had been willing to dismiss as incompetence, A'shai saw as sedition. Nico had sparked a chain of events that Shai could never pardon. *I don't know why I didn't see it before. Nico was the only person who knew I was up north . . . that's how Samad was able to find me. That bomb would've never been underneath my car,* A'shai thought angrily. Because of Nico a woman that A'shai loved had been murdered. Outwardly, A'shai appeared calm but inside he was fuming. Many people had taken A'shai's controlled demeanor as his weakness, but it was simply the calm before the storm. He didn't talk bad or make scenes . . . he put in work. There wasn't a need to talk about his actions. Talking too much was a quick way to get caught up on the wrong side of the law. As he saw Nico's back disappear into the backroom he slid his hand inside the front pocket of his hoodie and clicked his gun off safety. He stood to locate Big Ray, the club's owner. Big Ray was a close affiliate of Baron's . . . in fact Baron had put up some paper a few years ago to help Big Ray keep his establishment open after running into some financial issue with the IRS. Big Ray owed Baron a favor and helping A'shai set this trap was a part of the deal. Unbeknownst to Nico, he was flossing Baron's cash in an establishment that Baron in fact owned a percentage of.

"I can't believe that boy. Baron's raised him as his own and this is the way he repays him," Big Ray stated.

"Don't worry about it," A'shai stated. "All I need for you to do is keep his goons occupied. Show em' a good time." A'shai winked his eye as Big Ray looked over to the table where Nico's new entourage was partying.

"I'll show em' a real good time. I've got the perfect

distraction," Big Ray stated. He pulled one of his best girls to the side and sent her, along with four other ladies, over to their table with a bottle of premium vodka. Big Ray nodded his head, and A'shai slid him his last $2,000 then patted the older man on the back.

"I'll handle the rest," A'shai said.

Big Ray nodded, admiring A'shai's actions. He had been present at Willow's funeral and had been one of many who had witnessed A'shai be turned away at the door.

"You're a good son, Shai . . . Baron knows that. Willow did too," Big Ray said.

A'shai nodded his head and walked towards the private room where Nico was being entertained. It was show time, and A'shai was about to send one of the devil's minions right back down to hell.

Nico's hands rested on the girl's ass as she danced between his legs. He groped and grabbed at her curvaceous frame.

He pulled out a thick rubber band knot and placed it on his thigh. "I got it to spend, ma . . . now earn your keep," he said daringly, knowing that just weeks earlier he was the most humble nigga in the club. Before he had robbed Baron he would have never had the nerve to behave so piggishly, but he was smelling himself.

"My time is valuable, but from the looks of it you can afford it," the girl replied as she began to unbutton his jeans before sliding the zipper down slowly. She licked her red stained lips and positioned herself between his legs as he revealed his manhood to her.

He was comfortable and had a pocket full of rubbers. He waited for her to get it popping and he massaged himself as he watched her walk across the room. When he saw her step into a pair of jeans he frowned.

"Yo. What's up, baby? What you doing?" he asked.

"Setting you up," she replied.

"What bitch?!" he shouted, caught off guard. A set up was the last thing that he had expected when he had entered the soundproof, private lap dance room. He started to lunge towards her but was halted instantly when he saw her pointing his own gun at him. Her hand shook slightly, revealing her nervousness, but Nico knew that all it took was the slightest tug on his hair trigger to send lead flying his way.

"Sit your ass back down," she instructed as she walked over to the door and unlocked it. Moments later A'shai walked into the room. He kissed Liberty on the lips and tapped her behind slightly.

"Finish getting dressed, ma," he said. "Did he touch you?" he asked, slightly vexed that Nico had even gotten a chance to see Liberty's body. *Don't matter. The nigga won't be seeing nothing in a minute. As soon as I get that paper I'm rocking his ass to sleep,* A'shai thought.

"Damn, fam," A'shai said sarcastically as he looked at naked ass Nico in disgust. "You got your little dick all out, making it rain . . . you doing it real big, huh?" He took a glance at Nico's manhood as it went soft. "Or should I say little."

Nico kicked himself for not recognizing Liberty. The

last time he had seen her he hadn't been paying attention to her face and because of that she was able to lure him without arousing suspicion. Liberty finished dressing, and A'shai nodded towards the door. "Wait for me in the car, ma," he said.

Liberty put Nico's gun inside of her handbag before walking out onto the crowded club floor. A'shai stared menacingly at Nico. His pistol wasn't even drawn, and he could already see the intimidation in Nico's eyes.

"What is all this about, fam? You coming up in here like this . . . going through all of this to catch me by surprise. What's going on?" Nico asked playing dumb.

"Where's the money?" A'shai asked.

Nico's eyes shot behind A'shai as he hoped that his crew would come in and save him.

"If you're looking for the clowns you came in here with you can stop. A few of my lady friends are taking care of them," A'shai said as he rubbed his hands together. "Where's my father's money? You're the only other person who knew the combo."

Nico knew that there was no use denying it, but his mind spun as he tried to think of a way out of the situation. "That's what this is all about?" Nico asked. "Unc's paper? I wasn't going to steal it, fam. You got it all wrong. I was trying to make sure the FEDS didn't take it. After Unc got arrested, I went into the safe. I thought I was looking out. I moved the money so that the FEDS didn't get to it first," Nico explained, lying through his teeth.

"Why all the shady shit then, fam? Why didn't you just

say that?" A'shai stated as he kicked Nico's clothes over to him. "Put your shit back on, duke. You straight slipping out here. If I had been another nigga, you would be slumped."

"I know cuz . . . I'm tripping. That shit with Baron got me kinda fucked up. You get the head, the body will fall, nah mean?" Nico asked. "I thought we were all next. I'm up in here trying to get my mind off things." Nico quickly put his clothes back on, and A'shai palmed his own pistol inside the hoodie. His finger was already on the trigger just in case Nico tried to jump stupid.

A'shai shook his head and wrapped one arm around Nico's shoulder as he patted him sympathetically. He was putting on a naïve show befriending Nico, when he really wanted to splatter his brains all over the floor. Not wanting to create a scene inside of the establishment, A'shai played nice and lured Nico outside, making him think that all was forgiven. "You got to move smarter, fam. You had me worried . . . thinking you had pulled grimy. I go to check the safe, and it's empty . . . you know how that can look," A'shai schooled as he led him towards the exit and into the parking lot.

The only light that illuminated the parking lot was the overhead street lamp. Although the lot was full of vehicles, no one loitered outside. *No witnesses,* A'shai thought, the murderous part of him coming out.

"I need you to take me to that paper. Pops need it for the lawyers," A'shai stated as he walked behind Nico.

There was no way that Nico was coming up off that money and thoughts of killing A'shai filled his mind.

"Of course. I've got it in the trunk," Nico said. A'shai shook his head in disgust at Nico's carelessness. He was surprised that his bone-headed antics hadn't led the police to them a long time ago. A'shai knew niggas that would tie up a bitch and her kid for that type of paper and here Nico was riding around with it in an unsecure trunk.

Sweat formed on Nico's brow as he hit the alarm and popped the release on his trunk. He reached into the trunk where the bag lay and reached right beside it to grab the chrome .9mm that rested beside it.

"You still keep that nine in your trunk?" A'shai asked letting Nico know that he was two steps ahead of him.

"I..uh..yeah why what's good?" Nico asked.

"I'mma need that too," A'shai stated simply. Nico knew that if he tried to come up shooting A'shai would blow his brains off. He had the drop on him and at that moment all Nico could do was concede. He came up out the trunk and handed A'shai the bag of money, then dropped the gun inside.

Nico held out his hand, and A'shai embraced him, pulling him into his chest to show love. "Sleep tight, you bitch ass nigga," A'shai whispered as he squeezed his trigger.

POP! POP! POP!

Nico's body crumpled instantly to the concrete and Liberty immediately pulled up beside A'shai. He hopped into the car and she pulled off smoothly, disappearing from sight before anyone even came out the door to witness their departure.

NINETEEN

LIBERTY AND A'SHAI DISCREETLY RUSHED INTO THEIR hotel room, and A'shai tossed the duffel bag full of money on the bed. "Look in there," he stated.

Liberty unzipped the bag, and her mouth fell open as she looked at all of the street money that it contained. "How much is this?" she asked.

"I don't know . . . start counting," he said with a smile.

Liberty dumped the money out on the bed and then tossed two handfuls into the air. It floated down around her and she laughed giddily in disbelief. "I didn't know you were getting it like this," she said.

"There's a lot about me you don't know," A'shai replied as he joined her on the bed. "But I'mma teach you. I'mma share everything with you . . . always. Before you get too excited, that's not ours."

Liberty stopped flipping through the bills and looked up at A'shai in confusion.

"I've got to give some paper to my father's lawyer. I'll put the rest of the money in the streets. I need to re-up and flip this so that we can be straight. Baron will never know. In the end he'll be paid back, and we'll have enough money to be straight for awhile."

A'shai dropped the money off to Baron's lawyer and picked up on the details of his father's case. Things weren't looking well for Baron, but Clarkston assured him that money could buy any judge in the state if the price was right.

A'shai left Clarkston with a quarter million dollars, more than enough to handle Baron's case, and he kept the rest so that he could hit the streets with it.

"Please let Baron know that the rest of his money will be waiting for him in an off-shore account. I would like to visit him . . . let him know to be expecting me sometime in the near future," A'shai stated before leaving the office.

A'shai hit the streets as a one man army going hard to ensure that he could provide for Liberty. They had to keep low to avoid Samad so Liberty was confined to a different hotel room night after night. She was trapped there because it was unsafe to leave, but being trapped with A'shai was like heaven to her. Although he kept long hours in the street, the few hours they were together they used to become reacquainted. They fell in love all over again, and although they were in hiding, for the first time Liberty felt content. Cramped inside old hotel rooms, she had never been so free.

A'shai quickly found a new connect out of Miami and purchased so many kilos that he had to hire two drivers to bring them up to Detroit in separate U-haul trucks. He wasn't fucking around. Nothing about his situation was a game. He was hustling for the love of a woman . . . the love of his life. He refused to lose Liberty, and he was determined to provide a better life for her, the life that she deserved, the life that GOD had designed her to lead. MURDERVILLE had never been her destiny. A'shai had personally misguided her down that ruthless path, and it was the one regret that he had in life. She didn't deserve the suffering that she had been through, and he would turn cold in his grave before he allowed her to return to Samad. A'shai spent a lot of time in the streets, hustling from the bottom up in order to move the bricks that he had purchased. He barely slept because he was working so hard. He had invested Baron's money without his knowledge, and he wanted to put every dime back before Baron ever realized it was missing.

Some people know how to cook, some people are good at math, and others are experts at science or English . . . A'shai was good at hustling. He hit the pavement hard and took no prisoners as he continued to reign over Baron's empire, making sure to put up interest for his father so that there would be no ill feelings. He was grinding so hard that it felt as if he had a nine-to-five, but in his mind it was all worth it because when he went to lay his body down each night it was always beside Liberty. What he was doing couldn't be explained using reason. A usually logical A'shai was acting strictly off emotion, and it felt right.

A'shai entered the hotel room that had become their hideout and temporary home. He had Chinese food in his hands and expected his girl to greet him with open arms as she did every night, but she was nowhere in sight.

"Lib, I'm back baby girl. Where you at?" he asked. "I got your favorite from the Chinese spot."

He sat the food down on the small round table and began to remove the dishes from the bag.

"Hey Liberty!" he called as he went to knock on the bathroom door. He knocked lightly. "Yo, ma!" he said. He frowned at her silence and entered the room. When he saw her lying on her side in the middle of the floor, A'shai's heart sank. *Samad*, he thought as he rushed to her. "No, baby girl no . . . not now. I'm almost done. I'm doing this for you, ma . . ." he mumbled as he checked her body, trying to find the bullet hole that had ended her life. He pulled her into his arms and put his fingers to her neck. The racing pulse that he felt startled him slightly and his hands shook as he realized that she was alive.

"Liberty! Lib . . . wake up," he said as he patted her face urgently and lifted her up from the floor. He burst out of the bathroom door into the room, knocking over the nightstand as he frantically carried her over to the bed. "Wake up . . . Liberty," he whispered in her ear as he rubbed her hair. It was as if she was waking up from a deep sleep, and her eyes began to flutter wildly as she came to.

"What happened? Who did this to you?" he asked as he hugged her tightly, bringing her to his chest as relief flooded over him.

"Shai?" she whispered, confused as her brow creased and she reached out to touch his chest.

"Don't do that to me, ma. I thought I lost you," he whispered. He held her as if he would never see her again. His worst fear felt as if it were so close to coming true. "Who hurt you? What happened?"

"I was dizzy . . . I've been exhausted all day. I was lying in bed and I couldn't get up . . . my body . . . it was just so tired. I couldn't even force myself out of bed to order room service. The last thing I remember is stumbling to the bathroom. I must have fainted or something," she explained.

A'shai exhaled and kissed her lips. "I'm sorry, ma. I had you here all day by yourself. I've got to take better care of you," he said guiltily.

"You do take care of me, Shai. I know that you're in the streets for me. You're doing all of this so we can be together. I'm a big girl. I can handle it. I guess I was just hungry and tired," she dismissed.

"Then let's get you something to eat," he said as he retrieved the food and brought it to her.

As Liberty dug into the food, A'shai walked over to the hotel closet and counted the remaining bricks he still had to move. He was running through product quickly and as he took the duffel bag of money he had recouped that night he added it to his stash. It had only been a month and already he had earned Baron's money back. The remaining bricks he was sitting on were his to flip as he pleased. All of that profit was coming straight to him. Once his paper was proper he already had plans to move to one of Detroit's low-key, affluent, suburbs and establish a quiet, comfortable life for the two of them. He was leaving the streets alone for good.

As A'shai bumped his hustle up a couple notches Liberty seemed to withdraw into her own world. She lay around all day and slept all night. A'shai thought that she was falling into a deep depression but no matter what he said she couldn't shake the sudden lethargy that was taking over her. He did not have time to babysit, however. Moving as quickly as he was doing was reckless and he had to concentrate on not getting caught. It took two months for him to move the entire product and afterwards he was $2,000,000 richer. With Baron paid back and his future in the form of rubber banded $5K stacks, A'shai felt like a new man. He wasn't equipped to go to war with Samad, but with his newfound and hard-earned wealth he was more than capable of escaping him. He was about to put on a magic act and disappear. He had already reached out to a realtor who had found him a beautiful and massive estate in a quiet neighborhood outside of the city. If he moved smart, Samad would never catch up to them.

A'shai drove his car down the freeway, being sure to do the speed limit as he made his way to Liberty. He couldn't wait to tell her that he was out and to share his world with her. As he neared the hotel he reached in the backseat and gathered the five bouquets of roses he had purchased. He grabbed his duffel bag and the flowers and exited the car before rushing inside. He hoped that the news would pull Liberty out of the funk that she had fallen into. Living out of different hotels for weeks at a time had not been easy, but he knew that it was especially hard for her. She was never allowed to leave, unless she was accompanied by A'shai.

Since he was in the streets so frequently, she was forced to stay inside. He fully understood how her happiness had been jeopardized. But now that was all over, A'shai was ready to spoil her.

He rushed into the hotel room and picked her up off the bed. Her eyes were low and exhaustion plagued her as she rested her head on his strong chest.

"Stop Shai . . . you're making me dizzier than I already am," she whispered.

"I'm out, ma . . . I'm done. We have enough money to blow this bitch and to go somewhere safe," he whispered in her ear as he nibbled on it gently, causing electric sparks to awaken her clit.

"I love you Shai. Thank you for doing all of this . . . for saving me," she whispered as she put her soft hand against his cheek while staring him in the eyes. "What would I do without you?"

"You won't ever have to be without me," he replied. He scooped her off her feet and carried her in his arms towards the bed. Their lips danced sensually as they enjoyed a deep kiss. "I love you ma. I want you forever. Marry me."

Liberty's eyes widened and she pulled away from him so that she could stare him in the face. "What?" She was sure that she had heard him wrong. Although she knew that they loved each other, she never thought that he would ever make her his wife. The notion never even crossed her mind. While their love was deep, fate was always tearing them apart.

A'shai placed her on the bed. "I'm so tired," she gasped

as she looked up at him. A'shai chuckled as he hovered over her. "That's all you got to say Lib? You gonna make me work for it huh?" A'shai climbed out of bed and Liberty followed him.

"Wait, Shai, I . . ."

Before she could finish her sentence A'shai reached into his duffle bag and removed a small ring box. "Let me do this right," he said. "I love you, ma. Marry me. Be my wife," he said as he got down on one knee.

Liberty nodded her head, speechless. She was so full of emotion that it poured out of her as her eyes misted.

"Yeah?" A'shai asked.

"Yeah," Liberty confirmed. A'shai took her hand and placed the ring on her finger, then kissed it. He planted kisses on all five fingers, on the back of her wrists, on her stomach . . . moving south until he discovered her womanhood. Liberty gasped when she felt his warm tongue lap over her stiffened clitoris. He parted her lips and sucked gently while she moaned softly, her legs giving out slightly. He was making her weaker with every lick.

"Ooh, daddy," she whispered. "I need it."

"Me too, ma," he replied as stood to his feet and devoured her. A'shai pinned her against the wall and unzipped his True Religion jeans. His dick was hard, and he unloosened the belt on her robe as he rubbed the head against her thigh. He kissed her, sucking her lips into his mouth and entering her simultaneously as he stroked her gently. He ravished her, taking her to heights so drastic that she felt like she was flying. A'shai's sex was incredible, and he catered to every part of her body, expressing his love through his lust as he worked her over slowly . . . gently.

She threw her pussy back at him feverishly as she felt her orgasm building. She grinded and moaned as the head of his dick tapped on her spot.

"Ooohh, I'm cumming," Liberty moaned. "Ooh, Shai . . . I'm . . . I'm . . ."

Suddenly Liberty couldn't catch her breath as she gasped desperately for air and hit A'shai on the shoulder to alert him that something was wrong. Caught up in the rapture A'shai thought that she was into the moment until he felt her go limp in his arms. He pulled out of her, and his world crashed to his feet.

"Liberty!" he shouted as he put her down on the bed and put his ear by her face to check if she was breathing. He felt her heart beat and noticed that it was beating extremely slow, as if it would stop at any moment. *She needs help. Something's wrong,* he thought as he stood and frantically stepped into his jeans. He tied the robe tightly around her naked body and then in a panic rushed her to the hospital, praying to a power greater than himself that everything would be okay.

A'shai held Liberty's hand as she sat with oxygen tubes pumping fresh air into her nose.

"You feel better?" he asked her.

She nodded as a doctor stepped into the room.

"I'm Dr. Simmons," the man introduced.

"I'm A'shai. Liberty is my fiancé," A'shai spoke up. "What can you tell us? Is she going to be okay?"

"Liberty, you have a bad heart. She has a heart disease called cardiomyopathy. The fatigue and dizzy spells . . . even the fainting is all attributed to this," Dr. Simmons replied.

"What?" Liberty asked as tears filled her eyes. "Am I going to die?"

"That I cannot say. You have an unhealthy heart. It needs to be replaced," Dr. Simmons said.

A'shai didn't even hear the rest of the doctor's response as he blanked out. Rage filled him as he thought of everything that he had been through to be with Liberty . . . now she was sick. As hard as they had fought to be together . . . fate was tearing them apart. The grim reaper had been their ultimate enemy, and there was no running from this problem.

A'shai stormed out of the room as the unfairness sent him over the edge. He pounded on the hallway walls and slumped to the floor as he cried tears of sadness. He was resentful and his hurt outmeasured any misfortune that he had ever experienced.

Liberty gave A'shai a half smile when he finally returned to her side. She held out her hand and gripped his tightly as he sat down on the edge of her bed.

"How do you feel?" he asked.

"How do you feel?" she replied as she rubbed his knuckle with her finger.

"My heart is gone, ma. Hearing that doctor tell you that hurt my soul," he answered as he buried his head in her neck while she stroked his head lovingly. Liberty shed tears of pain, knowing what the end result would inevitably be.

"No one can have perfection, Shai. You and me . . . we're too good together. This is our flaw. My sickness . . . is the issue for our relationship. This is our imperfect love, but it's the greatest love I've ever felt. If this is what I have to go through in order to be your girl then I accept that. Just love me, Shai . . . that's all I can ask for," she said.

"I'mma do that forever," he replied. "I bought you a house."

"A house, huh? My very own house?" she asked with a smile. She hadn't had a place to call home since her childhood.

"All yours baby girl," he replied. "It'll be safe, and we can be together without having to look over our shoulders every second of the day. It's just waiting for us. I'm sending you there as soon as you get released from here."

Liberty's smile faded as she sat up in the bed. "Sending me? You're not coming?" she asked.

"Yeah I'm coming . . . of course I'm coming ma. I just have to do one more thing . . . I have to be here for Baron through his trial. After they render his judgment, I'll join you," he replied.

"I want to be wherever you are, A'shai. So I'm staying, and when you're ready we will run away together."

TWENTY

A'SHAI TOOK A DEEP BREATH AS HE stood outside of the police department. He prepared to go see Baron, hoping that he could smooth things over. The guilt of that horrible night haunted A'shai, and he knew what Willow would have wanted. He had to get back in good graces with his father Baron for his mother. A'shai entered the precinct and stood in line as people waited to see their locked-up loved ones. He went through the motions and finally got to the conference room where the visiting booths were set up with thick glass separating the visitors and inmates. He walked to the booth where his father sat waiting. As soon as he locked eyes with Baron, Baron's facial expression changed. He expected to see his lawyer, not the person who was responsible for his current awful situation. A'shai sat down and picked up the phone to communicate. Baron didn't move at first. He just stared at A'shai trying to find something in his heart to give him kind eyes and forgive his son. However, he couldn't.

He took a deep breath and reluctantly picked up the phone. "Why are you here?" he asked coldly.

"I'm here . . . because I love you. I'm here . . . because I am your son," A'shai said as his voice began to crack and his eyes started to water. The visions of the car being blown up and his mother smiling while in the car invaded his mind. A'shai closed his eyes trying to shake off the thoughts, but they still remained. The deep regret was killing him inside-out.

"You are not my son. You murdered the only woman that ever loved me . . . the only woman who ever loved you. You took her away from me!" Baron yelled into the phone as his bottom lip began to quiver. His eyes were bloodshot red from the sleepless nights and his aching heart. A'shai just stared into the eyes of a broken man, and he didn't know how to respond. The pain in Baron's eyes was imbedded deeply and A'shai could feel the hatred screaming from Baron's soul.

"I'm sorry. I didn't know," A'shai said as he thought about what his father had just said. Did he sacrifice his mother for Liberty? Was he wrong for following his heart? He asked himself hard questions and came up with no answers.

"I never want to see you! I'm done," Baron said through his clenched teeth as tears slid down his face as he rejected his son.

"I'm always going to be loyal to you . . . even if you hate me. I'm sorry. I'm so sorry," A'shai said as he watched as his father stood up and slammed the phone on the hook. He left A'shai behind, sitting with the phone in his hand. A'shai slammed the phone in frustration and stormed out. His life was falling apart, but he still vowed to get things right with Baron. It didn't matter if it took years to reconcile their relationship. He would visit him as often as he could until Baron was ready to forgive him.

It was the day of trial and Baron rode in the back of the police van handcuffed. He was being transported to the courthouse so that he could stand before a jury. He wore a gray Armani suit that his lawyer had provided for him and the thought of his reality hit him. His lawyer had explained to him that they would take a plea for ten years to avoid a potential life sentence. Baron hated to wave a white flag, but the hard evidence was basically a nail in the coffin. They couldn't take the risk, so Baron's inevitable prison term was about to begin. Baron thought about A'shai everyday but he always ended up with a bad taste in his mouth. He would forever be bitter and it was out of his hands at that point. Baron silently prayed, hoping that his wife was in a good place. *I love you Willow,* he thought, but his brief conversation with his wife was interrupted by a violent jerk. Baron's body was hurled to the back of the van and the sound of screeching tires was followed by a crash. The airbag in the front seats exploded in the cops' faces causing them to be temporarily disoriented. Baron yelled as glass shattered everywhere and the sound of the van's horn blared.

Two Hummer trucks sandwiched the police van. They were being ambushed. One of the Hummer's back doors flew open and three masked men sat in the hatch of the truck and pointed automatic assault rifles at the driver and passenger cops. They let bullets rain before the cops could even pull their guns out. Meanwhile, Baron was in the back of the van covering up, not knowing what was going on. "Fuck!" he grimaced, knowing that the assault was intended for him.

The masked men jumped out of the Hummer and ran around to the back of the van with guns drawn. One man had a shotgun, which he used to blow off the lock on the back door. The door flew open and they quickly grabbed Baron and pulled him out of the back of the van. They hurried him into their trailing car and sped off. The whole fiasco was started and finished within thirty seconds. They were skilled professionals that flawlessly executed the plan. Baron was now a high-stakes fugitive and he had no idea what had just happened. Guns were on him and he tried to piece together what was happening. *Did Shai send someone to bust me out?* he thought.

Baron had been taken by surprise, and he asked the masked man what was going on, but he got no answer. The truck sped into an empty parking lot and Baron was swiftly forced out after which they jumped into another tinted vehicle. Everyone, even the driver, hopped into the new car. One of the masked men then grabbed a can of gasoline from the back of the Hummer and began to pour it all on the car they had just exited.

"Hurry up!" one of the men yelled as he left the door open for the man to jump in when he finished. The masked man threw the can on the ground and jumped into the truck with the others. The truck pulled off and the man reached out of the window and fired the assault rifle at the old getaway car. The sound of a loud explosion erupted and the Hummer went up in flames. They sped off, jumping on the freeway and escaping smoothly.

Baron remained silent as he was taken a few miles down the road and the truck pulled into a empty parking ramp. A limo awaited them. Baron had already figured out who was behind the current fiasco. *Samad,* he thought to himself as he grinded his teeth and sat in between the two gunmen.

The truck pulled about thirty feet from the limo, and the masked man opened the door.

"Get out," the masked man said to Baron. Baron slid out of the car and saw that someone was stepping out the back of the limo. He saw the fancy shoe step onto the concrete and just as he thought . . . it was Samad.

"I never meant to harm your wife," Samad said first as he slowly began to walk towards Baron. His goons got out of the cars and began to circle Baron, all with guns out.

"Why did you do this?" Baron asked, not wanting to talk about his wife. He only wanted to figure out Samad's angle. *Why did he bust him out? What was his motive?* Baron wanted to know.

"I want to know where the girl is. Enough bloodshed has been spilled. I just want to get the girl back. Give A'shai up," Samad said as he opened his arms and shook his head as if the problem was simple and without conflict.

"Fuck outta here," Baron said after he sucked his teeth,

blowing Samad's request off. Although he was at odds with A'shai, he would not break the code.

"I can't understand how you are so loyal to a hoodlum that had plans to kill you. He was plotting against you since day one," he lied. Samad was trying to turn Baron against A'shai and get the information that he needed to find Liberty. Samad's jealous streak was a mile long and he was determined to find Liberty and kill her for crossing him. His ego, on top of his bitterness, made him a heat seeking missile hell-bent on revenge.

"That's a lie!" Baron yelled as he scowled and spit flew out of his mouth.

"No! That is the truth. He told me where you lived, and how to get you set up. How do you think I got the address? Huh? He wanted you out of the picture so he could take over. He was impatient. He didn't want to wait for you to retire. Now I'm giving you a chance to double-cross him because he stole something from me. I want revenge," Samad lied, leaving out the fact that Nico was his inside source. Baron took in Samad's words, and they were like daggers to his heart as he tried not to believe what Samad was saying.

"You're full of shit. You killed my wife and if you let me live . . . ," Baron began to shoot his threats as he stared at the man that stood before him.

"Am I? Think about it. How did I get your address? How did I know about your secret cabin up north? He planned on taking you out of the picture. That was before he laid eyes on Liberty. That's when the plans changed," Samad said trying to mind-fuck Baron . . . and it was working. Under different circumstances, Baron wouldn't be as susceptible to manipulation. But with Baron's mind in disarray and sorrow clouding his judgment, Samad's story began to seem like it made sense.

"Fuck you!" Baron said as he dropped his head and hoped that what Samad was saying wasn't true.

"Fuck me? No fuck that rat who betrayed you. Look where he is. He is lying up with a woman while you are on trial for your life. You can't blame me . . . I didn't break the rules, your boy did!" Samad yelled as he pointed his finger at Baron. "If he cared so much, why didn't he break you out? I did this for you! I got a deal for you. You help me set him up, and I will send you on a helicopter anywhere you want to go. It's all up to you," Samad said as he placed the deal of a lifetime on Baron's plate. There was no doubt in Baron's mind that Samad's offer was more of a demand than a question. Baron knew that if he denied Samad that he would be shot down right then and there. He then began to feel the grief and hatred towards A'shai for putting Willow in harm's way. Baron dropped his head and thought about his decision.

TWENTY-ONE

A'SHAI RUSHED OUT OF THE COURTROOM AND held the phone to his ear tightly as Baron spoke to him on the other end. Liberty hurriedly trailed behind him as she exited the courtroom. She wore oversized shades and a conservative black dress as she eavesdropped trying to figure out what was wrong. She knew it was an important call because of A'shai's instant change in behavior before he rushed to leave.

"I need you to come and get me quick. I'm at the old trap spot off Woodward Ave. I just escaped, and I need your help," Baron said.

"Don't move. I'm on my way," A'shai answered as he flipped the phone down. He was waiting at the courthouse for Baron's trial to start and got a call from him while in the pews. Baron had informed him about the breakout and failed to mention that Samad was behind the escape. A'shai quickly flipped down the phone and whispered back to Liberty, "We have to go now. I don't have time to drop you off so you are going to have to go with me," he said as they headed out. Liberty tried to keep up with him as they made their way to their car. She didn't want to ask any questions, so she followed A'shai, trusting that he would take care of her.

A'shai sped down the freeway trying to get to his father on Woodward Avenue. He pushed his car 100 miles per hour down the highway trying to cut his travel time in half. Word was already on the street that the infamous Baron Montgomery had escaped from custody. Baron had the streets on fire, and every cop in the city was now looking for the drug pin escapee.

The radio blasted through A'shai's speakers and the news alert came over the airwaves. A'shai and Liberty listened as the reporter called Baron armed and dangerous and a threat. The authorities encouraged civilians to not approach him and call authorities if seen. The entire city was up in arms and they were painting the picture of a villain on Baron's name.

"Fuck that," A'shai mumbled as he pushed the button on his radio, turning the newscast off. He was focused on getting his father out of the city and eventually out of the country. He sped off the exit towards the trap spot where Baron was hiding out.

A'shai pulled up to the house and threw the car in park.

"Come on," he said to Liberty as he hopped out. He wanted to keep her by his side while he figured out the plan. A'shai went to the back door and saw that it was kicked in, obviously by Baron. He walked in and saw his father sitting on the couch. "Pops, are you okay?" A'shai asked as he motioned towards him. A'shai never saw it coming. Goons were waiting for him and before he knew it, he heard Liberty scream. Before he could even react he felt a blow to the head, and then everything went black.

Baron sat in a beach house in Costa Maya, Mexico. He had taken Willow to the expensive paradise many times before. He had made love to her on that very beach, and it pained him that he would never share that experience with her again. He would never be able to kiss her forehead or slow dance with her to a smooth jazz tune. Baron looked out of the window of the small beach house and watched as the sun began to rise. He retrieved funds out of his offshore accounts and then fled to the beach house that was under an assumed name. He was glad that his wife had convinced him to buy the home before her passing. Now it had become his greatest asset. He would reside there in peace under an assumed name.

It had been a week since he had given A'shai up and the guilt was eating away at him. He sipped cognac and contemplated suicide daily. He was at rock bottom. It was as if he was losing his mind. He looked at a picture of Willow, A'shai, and himself that was taken a year after they had taken him in and they all were as happy as could be. They had taken it while vacationing on that same island. There was a time when Baron could have made different choices which would have changed the outcome of what had happened, but he chose to grind harder instead. Getting deeper and deeper and eventually leading A'shai into the same lifestyle.

Baron wished he could rewind the time. He would have quit the drug game a long time ago. He would have put his family first and thought about how his profession could and eventually would put them in harm's way. He understood that A'shai could have been molded to be anything other than what he was. A'shai, under the right direction, should have been a Wall Street banker. Baron had created a monster, and it eventually came back to haunt him.

Why didn't I show him another way? I failed my family, Baron thought as he downed the ninth glass of liquor. The thought of betraying A'shai ate at his soul and he knew that he had made the wrong choice. Baron walked over to his untraceable cell phone and quickly dialed up an old friend. He had to try to right his wrongs because the guilt was going to eventually kill him. He knew that he had to call in some professionals to do the job, he called the most efficient and ruthless crew he knew . . . he called the Murder Mamas.

A'shai groggily began to wake up. He had a pounding headache, blood dripped from his mouth and his body was full of purple and black bruises. His entire body ached as he had been beaten within inches of death. His hands were tied above him, and his body slowly twisted in the air. He saw that Liberty was tied to a chair and turned facing him. Samad circled him with a crowbar in hand. A'shai had been beaten by Samad for days, and Liberty watched as they both were tied up. A'shai was the closest to death than he had ever been.

"You are finally up. I have been waiting on you," Samad said as he began to roll up his sleeves so that Liberty could watch him beat A'shai once again. Over the past few days A'shai had been tied up and beaten badly out of pure revenge. He never thought that Baron would be the one to set him up. He walked right into a trap and he never saw it coming. Samad wanted to give A'shai a slow death while Liberty watched. He also planned on murdering Liberty after he killed A'shai. Samad just wanted the lovers to hurt a bit longer before he ended their lives. Samad began to walk around the beaten warrior, and he called him every nasty name in the book as he spit on A'shai and totally disrespected him.

Just as he was about to strike A'shai again, he heard the sound of the glass shattering and two girls burst through the door with their guns drawn. Before Samad could even react bullets were sent through his chest, dropping him instantly. Liberty squirmed as the bullets whizzed by her and she saw two slender figures get into gunplay with Samad and his goons. By the end of the gunfight, when the flying bullets finally stopped, the two masked shooters stood alive. One of the masked men walked over to A'shai and pointed the gun near the top of his heart. They shot and the bullets pierced the rope holding A'shai and he fell to the floor. The gunmen then pulled off their masks, exposing silky long hair and two very different but equally beautiful faces. A'shai realized they were a part of the Murder Mamas, a special hit team that Baron occasionally told stories about. A'shai had always dismissed the tales as myths, but as they stood before him he realized that these women were legends in the street game. That's when A'shai knew that Baron had sent the Murder Mamas to his and Liberty's rescue. She handed A'shai the gun and looked over at Samad. "Me saved de honors for you," one of the women said in a heavy island accent. A'shai struggled to get to his feet and hobbled. However, he managed to stand straight up and grab the gun from the lady. He then put a bullet through Samad's left eye, rocking him to sleep. He dropped the gun and collapsed after he asserted all of his energy to hold himself up. He breathed heavily as he grimaced from his wounds. He hobbled over to Liberty and unleashed her from the tight ropes. She collapsed into his arms. The war with Samad was finally over. A'shai and Liberty could now finally have each other without any hurdles or complaints. Their lives had come full circle, and their fate brought them back together. Despite all of the odds that had worked against them, their love had seen them through.

As A'shai and Liberty were escorted to an awaiting vehicle they clung to one another. "You know that house I told you about," he whispered as he held her body up, even though he felt as if he would collapse at any moment.

She nodded weakly.

"It's time . . . we're going to live there for the rest of our lives . . . happy. Only now we don't have to hide. I love you, Liberty, and wherever you go, I'll follow. Nothing will keep me from you ever again. I'm sorry for everything," he whispered.

"Don't be sorry, A'shai Montgomery. You saved my life."

TWENTY-TWO

BACK TO PRESENT DAY

LIBERTY SMILED AS SHE LISTENED TO A'SHAI tell her the end of their journey. It was supposed to be a happy ending. Neither of them expected her health to fade before their very eyes. They had heard the doctor's diagnosis but in the short time of two years she had lost a little bit of energy every day. Now she had none left and there was nothing left to do. Her time was coming to an end. The passionate few years she had spent with A'shai felt like a lifetime, and she was grateful to feel that type of love before dying. She remembered the day she found out that she had a failing heart. All of the signs had been there long before any doctor had confirmed the condition. She had lived a harsh life, and it took a toll on her heart. The doctors said that it was a genetic glitch, but A'shai somehow believed that if he would have protected her better she wouldn't have had a shortened life. She had experienced so much heartbreak in her time, and it had weakened her. Since the day they met, their time together had been on a constant countdown. A'shai saw that she didn't have much longer. It was evident in her eyes. They were not the same and he could tell that Liberty wouldn't make it through the night. A'shai leaned down to kiss his love and ran his fingers through her hair gently while grief flowed down his face. He had spent the last seven hours telling her their life's story. He had nursed his drink and let his words flow, all the while knowing what the ultimate unchanging end would be. His heart ached because he knew that it would be his last time telling her that story.

"I'm cold, babe," Liberty whispered as she closed her eyes. A'shai couldn't help himself and even though he tried to fight his emotions, not wanting to appear weak . . . tears slowly fell and dripped off his trembling lip. He knew that his love was fading away into GOD's glorious light.

"I'm cold too, baby," A'shai said as he downed the last of his drink and lay next to Liberty while holding her tightly. He knew that the Black Tea that he had sipped while he told Liberty their story was slowly killing him. He wanted to die with her. Nothing had separated them since their escape, and he vowed that nothing ever would. They would be together forever on the other side. "I love you," he whispered as he felt himself becoming drowsy as a weak sensation took over him.

"I love you more," she whispered as she struggled to keep her eyes open. She was on the edge and was about to slip off. He felt his heartbeat slowing down, and he managed to release a small smile along with a final tear of joy.

They were about to die together. It was a beautiful death.

They would both finally be free as birds with none of the ills that the world had to offer. None of their past burdens weighed them down . . . not MURDERVILLE, not Sierra Leone or the Rebellion, not even the harsh hand that the streets had dealt them. They transcended all of the pain as their bodies failed them. They lay in each other's arms, and they both closed their eyes as they embraced, wanting to hold onto one another forever.

EPILOGUE

"TELL ME WHERE THE MONEY AT BITCH!" the goon said as he circled the girl who sat bound to the wooden chair. The beauty just sat there and cried in agony; the ropes were tied so tightly that they stopped her blood circulation. The masked goon grew frustrated and struck her across the temple with the butt of his gun, splitting her flesh open. The blood trickled down her face as she remained silent, but cringed in pain. "Tell me! Where does Po keep the money?!" he screamed as he ripped the ski-mask off his head, tired of waiting for a response. He knew that the money was somewhere in the house because he had been following her drug dealing boyfriend for two weeks and witnessed him enter the house with his street money, only to exit empty-handed. He knew that the stash was inside the house somewhere. The woman just cried in pain and never answered the intruder's questions, only frustrating him to the brink of rage.

"Yo, if you don't tell me where the stash at . . . I'm going to blow your brains all over your pretty little wall," the goon said as he pointed the gun at the young woman's head. He waited for a response, only to get nothing from her except the constant crying. The goon knew that he didn't have a lot of time, and he had already searched the house from top to bottom and came up with nothing. He slapped the girl out of anger, taking her silence as disrespect. He put his gun in his waist and hostilely wrapped his hands around the girl's neck and squeezed with all his might. He watched as her face turned blush red and she squirmed but there wasn't much she could do because of the ropes restraining her limbs. The goon thought about how she had blatantly ignored all of his questions, and he wanted to see her die. In his twisted mind, it would be payback for her undermining his authority. He continued to squeeze her throat until the squirming stopped and her eyes stared into space, gazing at nothing. She was dead.

The goon loosened his grip, letting her chin fall into her chest. He breathed heavily and stepped back looking at the woman's lifeless body. He then took one more look around the room and noticed a plaque on the wall. It was a high school diploma that read: Michigan School for the Deaf, with the name Scarlett Jones under it. That's when it began to make sense to the goon. *She couldn't answer my questions . . . because she was deaf. She didn't even hear me,* he thought as he was overwhelmed with guilt. He quickly fled from the house empty-handed leaving the twenty-two-year-old beauty asleep forever.

*   *   *

James "Po" Taylor drove down the highway and yawned as he glanced down at the clock on his dashboard. He hated that he was coming home so late but it was for a good reason. He had picked up all the money he was owed in the streets. He finally had enough paper saved to buy the house he had promised his long-time girlfriend, Scarlett. He was deeply in love with her and had known her since she was a child. Although she was deaf, they had no problem communicating because Po had learned sign language years ago. He smiled as he thought about her beautiful face. He knew that he could finally give her what she deserved and that was a beautiful house and a way out of the ghetto. Po pulled into their driveway and grabbed the duffle bag full of money.

Po entered the house and reached for the light switch. He flicked it on and off repeatedly and smiled. He expected Scarlett to come from the den where she usually watched television until he came home. He saw the flickering of the television coming from the den and heard the news being telecast. *She must have fallen asleep,* he thought to himself as he began to take off his coat. He hung it up and reached into his pocket for the ring that he had bought her earlier that day. He couldn't wait until the morning to tell her that they were moving and decided to wake her up. Little did he know, Scarlett would never wake up.

He walked into the den and noticed that she wasn't in there. He then went upstairs and his heart dropped when he noticed the way the house was torn up. It was as if a tornado ran through it. The bed was flipped over, and the drawers were pulled out and emptied onto the floor. "Scarlett!" Po yelled as he frantically rushed to the other room. As he burst into the room, he saw the love of his life bound to a chair. "No!" he yelled as he raced to her and dropped to his knees in front of her. He began to loosen the ropes to release her, and tears began to fall as he noticed she wasn't moving. Her lips were dark purple, a far cry from the blush red they usually were. "Please GOD, no. Please!" he pleaded as he released her from the ropes and she fell into his arms. He rocked back and forth with his love in his arms. Tears flowed as he begged GOD to somehow make Scarlett wake up. He looked down at her and rubbed his hand over her face to close her eyelids. He then knew that she was gone forever.

The suns beams crept through the blinds and shined on A'shai and Liberty's faces as they lay next to each other. The sound of the hospital-issued pager rang out, and it began to vibrate making it dance across the nightstand. The sound woke a sleeping Liberty. She opened her eyes and couldn't believe her ears. It was the sound that they had been waiting on for an entire year. Liberty's body felt so weak. She could barely lift her head, but she managed to smile as joy overcame her.

"Shai. Shai baby wake up. We have a heart," she whispered faintly as she rubbed Shai's cheek with the back of her hand. "Shai?" she called again, noticing that his skin was cold to the touch. "Baby, wake up," she called as she managed to prop herself up. She nudged him with all the might that she had, but he didn't move. She didn't know at that point, but all along she had thought he was having a glass of cognac when in actuality he had been sipping on an old Creole drink called Black Tea. He had slowly ingested it as he told her the story of their lives, wanting to die with his soul mate. A'shai had been dying before her eyes and she didn't even know it. His "special drink" was a slow death and showed his commitment to his love for her. If she couldn't live then he no longer wanted to, so he chose to die with her so they could forever be together.

Liberty continued to shake A'shai but it was to no avail. A'shai Montgomery was no more. She noticed that he wasn't breathing, and it all hit her like a ton of bricks. She mustered all her strength and grabbed the phone to call 9-1-1.

"Nine-one-one. What is your emergency?" the operator asked.

"Somebody please help. A'shai isn't breathing. Oh GOD . . . he's not breathing!" Liberty said, not even caring about her own health or the heart pager. Her time was also ticking and if she didn't get to the hospital she would also die, but at that point she didn't care. She was ready to meet him on the other side.

Tears began to run down her face as the harsh reality set in. She collapsed on his chest on the brink of her own demise.

Liberty saw a bright white light and she smiled knowing that she was about to meet A'shai and they could finally be happy together. No more pain and no more of life's ills. She was ready to go to the after-life. She saw a little boy standing in front of the bright light. As she looked closer she saw it was A'shai as a young boy. He smiled from ear to ear and called her name.

"Liberty," he said in a playful tone. "Liberty," he repeated as he reached out his hand for her. Liberty knew that she was approaching death and rather than being scared . . . she was happy. She began to walk towards him but for some reason she could not get any closer.

"Liberty," the paramedic called as he stood over her.

"No," Liberty whispered as she slowly shook her head. "No . . . Let me go with him." The paramedics scurried to save her life, something that Liberty did not want. Liberty tried to tell the paramedic to let her die, but she was too weak to get another word out. An oxygen mask was placed over her mouth as she tried to mouth to them that she didn't want to be saved. She overheard the other paramedic talking.

"What happened to the guy that was there with her?" The second paramedic asked who stayed in the car while the other two went to retrieve Liberty.

"He was D.O.A. We had to call in the coroner."

ONE MONTH LATER

Po stood over the grave of his lost love and gently placed a bouquet of flowers on the grave. Po rubbed his hand across her tombstone and bowed his head as he prayed, asking GOD to take care of his woman. Guilt overwhelmed him as he thought about how he had put Scarlett in harm's way.

A single tear streamed down his cheek as he knelt down and shook his head. "Whoever did this to you . . . they are going to pay. I promise. You . . ." his voice began to crack. "You didn't deserve this baby," he continued. Po stood up and began to walk to his car. He felt his phone vibrate on his hip. He looked at the caller ID and noticed that it was his right hand man, Rocko.

"Hello," he said as he placed the phone to his ear.

"Yo, I know where the kid at that ran in your spot," Rocko said with the hostility showing in his voice.

"Word?" Po asked as he clenched his jaw and his heart began to speed up. Po had been waiting on a break for two weeks, and his man had finally found one. Po had put fifty thousand on the goon's head, and it had paid off quickly. The streets had spoken.

"Yep. I'm in front of the kid's mother's house right now. Niggas is saying that he skipped town because he knew that you would be looking for him."

"So, let's bring him back into town. You already know how we going to do that, right?" Po said as he felt his trigger finger begin to itch.

"Say no more," Rocko said just before he hung up the phone. Without saying it, Po had just ordered the goon's mother to be killed and he would find out the logistics later. He had to return to the hospital and pick up Scarlett's belongings and sign a few papers since he was her only family. Scarlett's parents were killed in a car crash, so Po was all she had. He also had to sign off on the donor papers. Scarlett always expressed that she would be an organ donor when she died and Po had kept her wishes. As fate may have it, someone with the same rare blood type as Scarlett had needed her heart. The organ was immediately removed from her chest cavity moments after she was pronounced dead. It was one of the hardest decisions Po had to make but he knew that Scarlett would have wanted it that way. For some strange reason, something in the gut of Po's belly wanted to know where her heart went. He wanted to know where the love of his life's special heart had ended up. Nevertheless, he would never know. It was against the hospital policies so all he could do was wonder.

Liberty walked into the hospital to see the surgeon who performed the heart transplant. She had been released from the hospital only a month prior and was instructed to return on that day to get a check-up. Although she had a new heart, it was still broken. It would forever be empty, and A'shai was the only man that could fill the space. She felt the soreness of the stitches that rested on the left side of her chest and it would always be a constant reminder of the reason A'shai committed suicide. *If only he had waited . . . then we would be together right now,* she thought. She kept replaying the night that he drank the Black Tea that had eventually sealed his fate. Her life was like a blur for the past couple of weeks. Burying A'shai, going back into the home that they once shared, and living alone. She felt like her life would never be normal again. A'shai had enough money stashed away so money wasn't a problem. She had a nice home and every material thing that she wanted but none of it mattered without her knight in shining armor. Liberty went to get checked by the doctor and after getting her prescription she was on her way back out. She headed out the door, and it seemed like time slowed down and everything began to happen in slow motion. She saw a young man coming towards her in a black hoodie and then a tinted truck slowed down behind him. The only thing she saw was the back window roll down, and it felt like her heart dropped to her stomach. The sinister face of Samad appeared. He had been looking for Liberty for years and had finally caught up with her. It was as if she had seen a ghost. A'shai's bullets hadn't been enough to take his life. Since that day, Samad sought out revenge and vowed to kill A'shai and Liberty. He sat in the back seat and looked at her with pure hatred and crazed intentions.

Liberty saw another masked man stick his body out of the window while holding an AK-47 assault rifle. She froze in fear, her mouth dropped and her legs began to shake. She could see the goon point the gun directly at her and she braced herself, preparing for her death. Her life flashed before her eyes and she dropped her purse and waited for the gunshot that would end it all . . .

TO BE CONTINUED

For more information on the authors,
giveaways and new releases check out

Twitter: Ashley and JaQuavis
Facebook: The Writers Block~ Ashley & JaQuavis Books